Venus Preserved

THE SECRET BOOKS OF VENUS
BOOK IV

VENUS PRESERVED

TANITH LEE

(Il Libro dell' Angelo)

THE OVERLOOK PRESS
WOODSTOCK & NEW YORK

First published in the United States in 2003 by
The Overlook Press, Peter Mayer Publishers, Inc.
Woodstock & New York

WOODSTOCK:
One Overlook Drive
Woodstock, NY 12498
www.overlookpress.com
[for individual orders, bulk and special sales, contact our Woodstock office]

NEW YORK:
141 Wooster Street
New York, NY 10012

♾ The paper used in this book meets the requirements for paper
permanence as described in the ANSI Z39.48-1992 standard.

Library of Congress Cataloging-in-Publication Data

Lee, Tanith.
Venus preserved / Tanith Lee.
p. cm. — (The secret books of Venus ; bk.4)
1. Venice (Italy)—Fiction. 2. Genetic engineering—Fiction.
3. Murder victims—Fiction. 4. Resurrection—Fiction.
5. Gladiators—Fiction. 6. Composers—Fiction. I. Title
PR6062.E4163V46 2003   823'.914—dc21   2003054850

Book design and type formatting by Bernard Schleifer
Manufactured in the United States of America
FIRST EDITION
ISBN 1-58567-474-5
1 3 5 7 9 8 6 4 2

Did the fallen angels remember their time
in the house of their father, God, with shamed
nostalgia? Had they been happy then?
                              —*Faces Under Water*
                   (*The Secret Books of Venus*, Book I)

Crying *What I do is me: for that I came.*
                              —GERARD MANLEY HOPKINS

Contents

AUTHOR'S NOTE

In this parallel, and future, Italy, some names are still spelled phonetically. But an *e* at the end of an Italian name is always sounded, (as *ay* to rhyme with *day*.)

The Latin in this book is of three kinds: (1) Classical, i.e., the type employed in ancient Rome and her provinces, (2) Medieval or renaissance, or (3) of a freestanding, *parallel* kind. (For the first two categories, I remain indebted beyond thanks to Barbara Levick, of St. Hilda's College, Oxford.)

A glossary that may assist with other, "futuristic" terms can be found at the back of the book.

The connection between the last Julio-Claudian Emperor and the Beast of Revelation, (as mentioned in Part Three, Chapter 12) is also of interest in our world. The analysis of the fateful number 666 can be found in many historical or theosophic works, or books of numerology.

Lastly, the speech which informs parts of the novel, and which is fully quoted on the final page, is of course from William Shakespeare's *The Tempest*.

PROLOGUE

DEATH IN STAGNA MARIS

"Kill him! Give him death!"

She lifted her head and looked all around at them, the shouting, screaming thousands. She raised her hand again, asking for him, for mercy. Knowing it would never come.

And "Kill him! *Death! Iron death!*" they shrieked back. The young woman turned and looked now at the single human figure there with her in the sanded pit.

He was lying on his side, on one elbow, like a citizen at table, but *he* was the feast for the screaming horde. An Ethiopian, his skin like a smooth black grape, marred only by the cuts of her sword. In her ignorance, two years before, she had been astonished, fighting her first black gladiator, that he bled red, as she did, and the rest. What had she expected? Purple, she thought, like the sweet blood of grapes.

"They won't have it," she said. She remembered his name. Phaetho. But it was a Greek-Latin name, of course; anyway, the name he had been given here, or in some other Romanized place. He only blinked his great angry arrogant eyes at her. "I'm sorry," she said. "Do you want to pray to your gods before I do it?"

Above, around, the crowd, baying now, but the noise falling off a little. They knew how she was. Because they liked her, they allowed her these eccentricities.

But he would not answer. Just as he had refused to fight at first—not from cowardice, obviously—from disgust, the very thing that showed on his face now. She had made him fight, forced him to with her assaults, stinging him like a bee. (The sticklers had not intervened, leaving all this to her.) He was young and strong and had been well trained, she knew. He could have given a good fight before she brought him down. Then the crowd might have taken to him, and spared him. But they had not liked his hanging back, and *her* they thought they loved—if not enough to let her be merciful. So it was hopeless.

Nor could she waste any more of their time. The noise was getting up again, with an ugly note in it.

"I must do it now. Turn your head, and it will make it easier and more quick." His lip curled, and he did as she said. She raised her sword. The arena terraces roared. This was the lonely moment. "Forgive me," she said.

Then he spoke. "Never. I'll meet you in Hell."

She had heard all that before. She brought the sword down and killed him cleanly in the seconds before he felt the cold beyond his pride.

And then, of course, they erupted from their seats, and now it was her name they bellowed. "Jula Victrix! Jula Flammifer!"

Not till she was walking away did she notice her own blood trailing thick across the sand.

PART ONE
Thin Air

1

WHAT WAS ON THE COAST was the body, not the soul. The buildings looked pleasing enough, classical even, washed in faded rose-browns and creamy vanillas. But they were mostly given over to administration. Inside, behind the stucco and the birdcage balconies and the windows like fretted pastry, were sheer glass, plasticore, and the half-heard thrum of CXs.

Besides, the traffic on the sea and in the canals ruined any effect. Power-boats and raz'scafos churned and spooned the serpentine water.

And when you came down to the subvenerine station, all illusion was dashed to bits.

It was a modern marina. The jetty wasn't even fifty years old and erected to deal with Jet Skis and other contemporary surface-water vehicles. Not even fishing-craft, not any more. The actual building was a rigid white maw, like the mouth of a glacial Hades, and arched above with dark blue glass, and fluted fins that belonged, perhaps, on the moon. (Or on the planet Venus. Maybe that was the joke.)

You went down in the air-conditioned elevator, to Visitor Control. Which was like those things always were.

There were no viewing windows.

Some Russans in iridescent shades were complaining

about this, a smiling hostess explaining that they must wait, the views would come.

The Amerian who (Picaro recalled) had sat beside him on the plane, remarked, "Like waiting for Santa on Christmas Eve." Picaro glanced at him. "And if the kids ain't good, he won't arrive, right?"

Picaro smiled. It was the smile he kept for decent people passing through his life. A nice smile, but far off.

The Amerian, whose name was Flayd, said, "I guess you and I read the literature beforehand."

Picaro nodded. Then they reached the check-in. It was quick for Picaro, longer for Flayd, an archaeologist, who had come laden with hand-held equipment. He was soon left behind.

Having been read for weapons and illegal substances, Picaro watched his hand scan under the blue tracer. It looked as it always did at such times.

"Professional musician."

"Yes." (He was seldom recognized.)

"Purpose of visit."

"To live here."

"Here it is on screen now. PB Status. Congratulations. You have your apartment details? That's fine, Sin Picaro. Pass through."

The corridor, which ran down to the subvenerine's hull, had a moving floor, and sang, via its CX system, to a small guitar.

A steward saw him aboard.

Two minutes later, a puffing Flayd, a large man garnished with long auburn hair, shouldered his bags through the hull entry.

Apparently embarrassed, he took the last seat, beside Picaro.

"We gotta stop meeting like this."

But now Picaro gave no response at all.

Then the safety arms moved around them all, and the little complimentary drinks rose from the plasleather, in their plasticrystal shakers. There came the rumble of the ship's internal motors.

Flayd downed his drink. "Here we go." (He frowned, Picaro could see it, reflected in the window, glaring at Picaro's unresponsiveness.) "Hang on to your dreads, man. Hang on to your bloody heart." Belligerently Flayd added, "You're about to fall in love."

THE WATER WAS SHRILL blue beyond the lock, from the sub-sea lights of the port. Fish scattered like diamonds and drew a little tweeting from the passengers. But the lights drained away behind the vessel. Like nocturnal animals, the subvenerines needed no illumination to find their way.

Now the travelers, shut in their bubble, stole through a darkness thick as primeval night. And then the cabin lights also went down. And those who hadn't "read the literature" on what to expect let out some anxious squeaks, which needed the stewards' soft voices, here and there, to calm them.

The lamps went down so you could see.

And then they went *out*.

And you *saw*.

"Jesu! Maria!"

Only one man shouted; a few of the other passengers laughed, amazed, conspiratorial, knowing why someone always did shout.

The Amerian, who had come this way before, was silent now.

Picaro stared out through the optecx window-port, across the blood-dark sea.

The water, *there*, caught by the day-radiance of Venus's Viorno-Votte, was the color of the iris of a peacock's feather.

But the pupil of the feather's eye was made of glowing silver, and in it rested the City of Venus, as if in a star's heart beneath the ocean.

Even from this distance it was possible to pick out the threaded jewelry of spires and domes, arcades like filigree, the sheen of a blue air ice-floated with soft pearls of cloud . . .

"The Primo Suvio!" cried a woman. "Look—look— Do you see?"

As if they had become one, the entity in the subvenerine whispered, murmured, called back to her "Yes, yes, we see—that white cupola—"

The cloud-capp'd towers, the gorgeous palaces, the solemn temples . . .

In the light of Venus now, the sea was parting for them, making way.

The fish that fountained before them were rainbow opals. There were flotillas of weed strung with sequins of luminescence. And hardly anyone saw them, eyes fixed only on the City, under its inverted goblet of Venusian glass.

PICARO SAW VENUS under water, meshed in his own reflection caught on the window. Some glim of light, and proximity, had made his image linger there, when Flayd's had mostly melted from view.

Curious, the transparent globe with the City shining in it, set there in the black of Picaro's skin, and his black-and-white plaited hair streaming away from it— and all the while the City took more of him, more of his face, and then his body, replacing them with its gleaming self. Until he was gone, and only the City remained. Eclipsed, he watched as the burning dome came nearer and more near, and towered up, a cliff of glass. He too studied the buildings, and the sky, inside. Then closed his eyes against them.

"We will now ascend into the entry port. There will be some adjustment of light and minor sensation of displacement. This is normal and will quickly pass."

Consoled by the mechanical voice, the passengers now had no fear. And as the levers raised them, their cries of delight became orgasmic.

Dark changed wholly to light. (Picaro's eyes opened of themselves.) The vessel had broken through a surface of apparently prevailing sea—and into shining Venus day. They were now inside the dome. Positioned directly before them on the water was a vast church, sudden, and from another time. Not of course the Primo, but one of the thousand churches of Venus, exquisite, golden. Its marble façade had the bloom of a white rose. Windows of excrutiatingly beautiful color threw shards of cobalt and wine, and a tower poised above, with a silver clock clung round by winged girls, whose damp-induced verdigris had been also lovingly restored. Maria Maka Selena, which had already lain drowned under the lagoons long before the sea swallowed so much more of the City, beamed in her risen glory upon astounded pilgrims.

"What do you think?"

Flayd again, seeming unable to restrain himself.

What did Picaro think? "It's wonderful."

"You don't sound convinced."

"Why else," said Picaro reasonably, "could I be here?"

"Sky looks real, doesn't it?" asked Flayd. "That takes some doing. Perfect atmosphere, guaranteed safe for human consumption, and kept entirely clean, to protect the buildings. Not one speck of pollution can survive. Gets sucked straight out. You know about the Viorno-Votte."

And Picaro must speak again. "Of course."

"Venus has a twenty-seven hour diurnal cycle. Twenty-seven hours and thirty seconds, to be exact. Look. No sun, you see? Don't need any sun, the light is *behind* the sky. But they fix a sunset—and a dawn—and they put in a moon and stars for nighttime. Well, you can't have Venus without the moon."

Still far off, a backdrop to the glamour of the church, the dream of Venus hung across the water. While naturally, already you forgot that any water here was not quite water. That the *true* water lay *outside* now, beyond the magna-optecx of the dome-walls, and beyond the pale sapphire of the sky that was not a sky.

Presided over by the ancient church, the subvener-ine had sprung from the green lagoon. There was only one lagoon now, separating the City, not from ocean, but from the dome-sides. Would Flayd tell him this, too?

They had docked against the island where the church stood. Little boats were already waiting. The seat-arms had let go. Everywhere, the buzz and flurry of excited exits. Flayd rose to his feet—quite a distance. "Nice to meet you. Enjoy your stay."

Picaro waited until most of them were off, until he too got up, and left the last of the real world—for the Fantasy.

PALAZZO SHAACHEN STOOD by the Canale Alchimia. It had been named for Shaachen's abilities. Although in eighteenth century Venus, the palace hadn't stood on such a canal at all, nor among these other palazzos that were now its close companions.

This was how all the City had become, after its submergence by an encroaching sea, its rescue and refurbishment under the protective dome.

The records were also a little muddled. Picaro had guessed this, said nothing, as probably no one did who was lucky enough to be awarded PBS—Proven Bloodline Status, which meant you could "inherit" an apartment in the City, since your ancestors had formerly lived there.

Picaro's PB wasn't so old. It dated to 1700 or thereabouts. But it was sufficient. The fact that he had been housed in the rebuilding of a palace reckoned to be that of the alchemist Dianus Shaachen, was only a slight mismatch. It seemed Picaro's true ancestors, who were not related to Shaachen, had yet roomed in his palazzo for two or three years. They were now known only by the names Furian and Eurydiche, but they were strange enough, both of them. He had been a rich man who had perversely chosen poverty. She was a young woman whose facial muscles did not move, making of her a lovely icon—the condition then called Stone Face.

A wanderer, (there was no modern traffic allowed in-dome) with its guiding wanderlier, brought Picaro to the Alchemy Canal. The wanderlier sang during the journey. He had a very good voice. Picaro, driven crazy by the triteness of this touch, kept silent.

Arrived, the boat was tied to a mooring pole decorated with the figure of Neptunus, the antique god of the sea, once one of the Custodians of the City. The wanderlier, unlike the boatmen of former times, assisted Picaro with his luggage.

"A fine palazzo." They idled on the strip of terrace

above the water-stairs. "Do you know which are your windows, sin?"

"No."

"Do you want my boat later?"

"Maybe," said Picaro.

"I will come back, signore," said the wanderlier, giving him now the full address rather than its contemporary abbreviation. "Show you the sights."

"Maybe," said Picaro again.

Two young women stepped into view, passing through the slender space between the Shaachen Palazzo and its right-hand neighbor, a building leaden green as a swan. Emerging on the half-meter-wide terrace, they stood there, looking at Picaro. They wore replica dresses, dated from 1890, perhaps. They whispered. One smiled directly at the musician.

"They seem to know you, sin."

Indeed they did seem to.

Picaro took hold of the luggage and hauled it through the palazzo door, which had opened, also recognizing his identity. He heard the door shut behind him after a moment, closing him away from the boatman and the possible autograph hunters.

The house vestibule was cool, dark-tiled, with brown-spotted walls that looked as if they had survived at least five centuries, but were doubtless (mostly) much, much younger. A stone staircase swerved upward. He wondered if the palace had really always looked like this. Perhaps not. And yet much of its brickwork, wood, and plastering had been rewoven here, these tiles had belonged to it, either in this area or another. And the windows, with their iron bars, had conceivably always looked out on a canal, though never this one, with its dirtless glycerin water.

A small soft light had come on in one wall. A small soft voice, like a woman's, called to Picaro gently that he was welcome. A panel then opened under the light, a function of the house's hidden CXs, and drew the bags and the crate away to their destination by a concealed route.

Yet, when he had gone up a few steps, and glanced back, the wall was only a spotted-brown expanse, centuries old, and the water-glimmer through the windows flickered timeless on the tiles.

He passed no one in the corridors. Gaining his personal door, he reached into his sleeve pocket for the required key. Had he ever used a key on a door in his *life*, before this moment? Picaro thought he had not. But he was thirty. Others here wouldn't find keys so peculiar. It worked, anyway, as well as CX.

And beyond the second door was the apartment.

It resembled precisely the disced recx he had been sent. It was also utterly different. Here the sunlight and the shade were not merely virtual. There was a smell of things too, of the various materials, and faint dampness (fake?) he had detected in the rest of the palace, of newness and great age, weirdly commingled. Of emptiness.

A ripe red terracotta floor. A window, there, with amber glass bottles and glasses like jade, and a magenta stained-glass jewel. An unlit lamp hung from a hook in the ceiling, round as a latticed moon, oriental and from long ago, reconstructed, durable, and charming.

He walked from room to room. Each was vacant but for its occasional enhancing detail: a narrow, carved black wood cupboard in a corner, with a skull—very real and *not* real, re-created—on its top. A red embroidered rug, fresh and new and old *once*, and no doubt from fabled Candisi. Such things.

Already invisibly deposited in place, the luggage balanced against one of the walls, which themselves had a color like dark honey and glowed in slots of light.

In the last room of the seven, a long window gave on a balcony. Walking into this room, Picaro halted. Outside, perched on the balcony's outer ledge, and clinging one-handed to the ornamental iron, like a mad, wild human bird, was one of the girls from below.

Picaro undid the ancient bolt mechanism of the window. He went out on the balcony, and the girl regarded him with bright eyes. How had she got up here? Perhaps the other one, still standing on the terrace by the canal, helped hoist her aloft—awkward enough in their tight-waisted, swirling dresses.

"What are you doing?" he said.

The girl below had a somber skin and looked sullenly up at him. This one was pale, with a storm cloud of dark hair.

"I love your music," she said, "Magpie."

"Thank you."

"I have all your decx, every one. And a music file of the notation. Everything you've composed, everything you've played and sung. I love you," she added.

"Thank you," he said again.

He wondered how to get rid of her. He hadn't expected this, of all things, not here.

"I'm Cora," she said. She jerked her head at the girl left on the terrace, "She is India."

"What nice names. But I think you ought to get down." Even as he said it, his heart sinking, thinking of having to escort her into, before out of, the rooms.

But Cora said, "Please, your autograph."

"All right."

He went over to just within a meter of her, no closer.

24

He set the wristecx swiftly, and waited, and she pointed to the bodice of her dress. "Here." The wristecx fired a tiny flick of compressed energy. Together he and she watched the miniscule spangle form on the cloth, above her breast. "Does it," she said, "speak in your voice? What does it say? Does it play music?"

"My voice. It will say, *Picaro to Cora*, and then it'll play you three bars of the Africarium."

"I love the Africarium."

"Good. Now—"

"Don't trouble," said Cora, the mad, wild, wingless bird, and winglessly she flew off the balcony, so his sunken heart leapt into his throat instead. But a second later she had landed, without a hitch, flawless, back on the terrace in the arms of her unfaltering friend. Both girls then turned adjacent cartwheels, revealing their modern briefs and white lace stockings. Acrobats? He laughed despite himself, despite everything. And then they laughed too and ran away, back through the alley by the green palazzo. They had been young; neither, he guessed, more than nineteen.

They were cute enough. He hoped they wouldn't return.

PICARO, THE MAGPIE, sat on the floor, in the hot, sweet stillness of Viorno-Votte afternoon.

Sometimes he drank water from a tall emerald flagon. He watched unsunned sunlight make patterns.

She had had a harpsichord here, he knew that, Eurydiche, but that was then. No harpsichord now, not even a recx harpsichord. Instead the Africara stood, pot-bellied, horned, and brown-black as a bull, against the wall. Sometimes the rich clear light seemed to flutter its strings, as if bees went over them. Illusion.

How noiseless the palazzo was, each apartment CX-insulated. But outside the open window there had been intermittent footfalls, notes of other laughter, music, shouts even at one point, some dispute along the Canale Alchimia. An hour changed, then another, and bells rang from all the churches as they had rung from these churches always, before the sea came in.

Then the wristecx rang like a tinier non-bell. Angry a moment, Picaro took it off and shut it in the carved cupboard under the skull. Let the skull keep it quiet.

No matter how you obscured your tracks, in this present world, people could always find you. Even here, where a private wristecx, ruled by the City's machines, was not supposed to be capable, of relaying incoming calls, unless you applied for an override.

The call signal was silenced.

He stretched out his body full-length and slept, head pillowed only on the many braids of his hair.

"WHO THE FUCK is this?"

"Flayd—it's Flayd. We met on the plane."

"Yes. What do you want?"

Pointless to ask how Flayd had found the call number. And no wish to ask why he had kept on signaling until the skull cupboard rattled.

"I'm at the University Building," said Flayd. "Come and have a drink with me."

"No. Pleasure meeting you and good-bye. Chi'ciao, Sin Flayd. Don't use this signal again."

Outside, sourceless sunset now spilled over the canal and the coppery roofs and the palazzos. On a slight rise, a church flashed a gold spire. The sky became sand pink and geranium red.

And then a wanderer being poled along the canal was stopping, the male passenger scrambling out and up the watersteps, a tumble of muscle and weight and hair the color of the roofs.

As had the autograph hunters, Flayd the archaeologist now stood below the balcony, beady eyes upon it.

"Don't lose your cool," cautioned Flayd. "I have to talk to you."

"Is this a sexual proposition?"

"Christ, no." Flayd grinned suddenly. "Sorry to disappoint." Then his face fell heavily. "Come down, or do I come up."

"Tell me what you want?"

"That'd be telling the whole block, wouldn't it. Come down then, I'll wait. We can go visit Phiarello's—Victorian ice cream—I have to talk about something. I mean it, Magpie."

"Don't call me that."

"It's your professional name."

A terrible rage, evil and sentient of itself, took Picaro's face. He felt it do so, felt it remake him, and turned to Flayd in obscuration the profile that had once been described by Magpie admirers as "chiseled by a sculptor from black coal." Picaro thought about that, until he became only one more re-created carving. Then he glanced down at Flayd, bulky, immovable, still staring.

"Goodnight," said Picaro. He shut the Amerian, and Venus, out behind the shatterproof glass of Shaachen's window.

2

THAT NIGHT, UNDER THE CURSE of the dead Ethiopian warrior, Jula had considered her first memories. They were very spare.

Houses built of packed earth and branches—huts, a Roman would say—woodsmoke and half dark, the shadows of trees in mist. And that was all. No recollection survived of the destruction of this place, the crying and blood. Nothing either of how she, presumably with other infants, was taken away.

She thought next of the Ethiopian, *his* homeland. (That was while they were sewing her up under the arena, the gut thread pulling like the biting of ants.) What had his homeland been? Lush, with a river of crocodile green—or some desert?

It was a while before the surgeon had finished with the long gash in her left arm, the wound below her ribs—the Ethiopian had just missed her intestines. Yes, in the end Phaetho had fought well—few others had, in recent years, come so close. But the crowd had not seen his skill or valor, because he had delayed at the start, and by the finish they hated him.

When she went up into the ending afternoon, the last matches in the arena were over, the horns silent, the crowds dispersed, the corpses carted away. The victors,

with their palm leaves, or—as she had been—crowned
with laurel from the precincts of Apollo, were taking up
their evening lives.

Tonight she would not be going back to the school
to sleep. Her owner would be showing her off, with some
of his other successes. In the arena baths she had become
clean and scented, been skilfully shaved of all bodily
hairs but for the hair on her head; this, kept short and
waxed to spikes when she fought, freshly hennaed. Jula
Flammifer they called her, Fiery Jula, for her combats
and her hair. But in reality she was a blonde from the
backlands of Gallia. None of her was really quite her own
belonging. She was a slave. Even her forename came
from that of her owner, Marcus Libinius Julus, though
she had been titled by him, in recognition of her worth,
as his daughter would have been, if he had ever had a
legal one.

In the tradition of what she was, a gladiatrix, off-
stage as it were, she still wore the garb of a man, a rich
actor's clothes, of course without the town toga, or ring
of citizenship.

Four bodyguards attended her, also gladiators, now
freed. They never spoke to her, nor she to them. Their
instructions had always already been given.

There was a litter. She got into it and the curtains
fell, and the bearers began to run, her escort trotting to
keep pace.

Her thoughts were slow and obstinate tonight. They
kept going back to the man she had killed.

In Rome, generally, women were not matched with
men. But here in the provinces, it was different. She was
a secutor, a *pursuer*, and she was paired always with men.
In Rome too, she had heard, women fighters were sometimes mocked, or brought on for a laugh, like the clowns

who entertained the crowd between the serious matches. But there were famous women fighters in Rome, too. One of these was the Emperor Narmo's favorite.

Jula started. She had half fallen asleep on the cushions, lulled by the throp-throp of running feet. The fight with Phaetho, the loss of blood, had wearied her. But it would be a long evening, Julus's dinner starting late and going on probably until the sixth hour. She parted the curtains and looked out. The Via Gracula, a fine road closely paved with mathematically cut and placed stones, ran from the stadium to the town gates. It passed through woodland at first, cleared back a hundred paces on both sides, and here and there a marble tomb stood, catching, as the woods did, the slanting westering light. Behind, the other way, lay the sea, dark blue in its readiness for evening.

Julus's villa reclined just off the Graculan Way, where the woods mantled rising land.

A pillar marked the entry to her master's estate. From here a track ran up the slope, wide enough to take two chariots, and lined with the same stone pines that clustered around the stadium.

The sun was very low now, red and flashing like a tarnished sword between each tree.

They passed the little temple to Temidis, goddess of prosperity-through-chance. The escorting gladiators sang out to Temidis some raucous salute of their own, in their secret jargon.

Beyond the temple the land leveled, and over the brow of the hill, the villa gardens appeared below, basking in sunfall among olive orchards and vineyards. The villa itself, long and scarlet roofed, showed vivid lights. The guests would already have arrived.

A waft of music blew up the hill.

Jula left the litter. It was Julus's wish that she approach on foot, with only two of her escort.

As they stood a moment, one of the men swore softly. Across the deepening upper sky, a shooting star traced like a runner's torch, high over Stagna Maris. The Romans were made uneasy by such stars. The Christiani would say, however, such a falling flame was something to do with angels . . .

This Jula knew. But she thought the fallen star marked the Ethiopian's death. Maybe he had been royal in his own land. Perhaps his own gods, that he did not deign to pray to before the mob, had honored him instead.

He had left an impression on Jula. She had made an offering for him at the altar of Judging Fate, in the stadium precinct. There was nothing else she could do. He would not even be given burial rites, for he had lost his first fight. With the bodyguard swaggering behind her, she strode down the track towards the lamplit villa, and the wine and feasting of her glamorous, victorious slavery.

3

ELEVEN MINUTES AFTER PICARO had shut the balcony window, fists hammered heavily on the reinforced wood of the apartment door. He knew who it was. He did not respond. The hammering of the fists stopped.

Presently Flayd called through the door.

His voice was muffled somewhat by the noise-conditioning, but that was mainly in the walls; the door necessarily would let sounds through.

"Picaro—listen—this is serious—" on and on.

Picaro flung open the door.

In the dimming of the daylight, unlit, he confronted Flayd who burned there in the corridor like the last of sunset.

"*What?*"

Flayd shook his head and raised one hand in a pacific gesture. "Sorry. But let me borrow your wristecx, will you."

"Why?"

"I need to call the mainland."

"Use your own wristecx, on your wrist."

"She don't work, Picaro."

"Then find a public CX—"

"Just—just let me try and make this call."

Picaro relaxed. He was bored with the rage, it now

seemed meaningless. He let it go, snapped off the wristecx and held it out to Flayd, no longer caring very much
what he did with it.

As Picaro walked off across the dark red floor, Flayd
stepped into the apartment and shut the outer door.
Then he activated the call reflex. Leaning on a wall,
Flayd tried for some while to make a call with the wristecx. (He must otherwise be agile with CX—he'd fixed
the one on the palace's main door and got in.)

Picaro watched, sitting now on a table in one corner
of the wide vestibule, drinking water from the emerald
flagon.

Eventually Flayd left off tapping combinations.

"Yours is the same as the rest. You can't call out. Did
you know that?"

"No."

"Only in-dome calls either way. Nothing to or from
anywhere else." Flayd heaved a sigh. "Same with the
three public CX I tried. All of them I guess."

Picaro said, "So what."

"So, this is new, Picaro. Last month, *yesterday*, anyone could call out-dome if they wanted. And now none
of us can."

Picaro raised his head. Lazily he said, again, "So what."

"I gotta talk to you," said Flayd. "The rest of them—
shit, I can't. But let's get out of here first."

"There is a conspiracy," said Picaro flatly, "and the
CXs are wired to pick up what we say."

"Yeah, I know. To people like me there is always
some conspiracy. Come out," said Flayd. "Let me tell you
about this one."

"Why would I want to know?"

Flayd said, "Why the hell wouldn't you?"

Picaro shrugged.

Flayd opened the door again. "Last chance."

Picaro sat on the table. Then slowly he got up. For a moment, he saw it in Flayd's eyes, the Amerian thought he had finally gone too far, and Picaro might leap suddenly for his throat like a cat. Flayd could handle himself, so much was obvious. But Picaro was the unknown quantity.

When Picaro did not attack him, Flayd moved off along the corridor. By the time they reached the stone stair, they walked side by side, and Flayd was saying, "I took your call number from the coder at the University. It registers everyone in the City. Like the archives. You should see those. Room after room. Everything, dating back to tribal times here."

Outside, the wanderer Flayd had brought waited on the water. Evening stars were threading in chains across the long lingering of fake sunset.

Phiarello's lay to one side of the Primo Square. In the dusk, outdoor tables under candy-striped umbrellas surrounded the restaurant, full of tourists and locals, who had come to drink alcohol and coffee, and eat dinner, or the strawberry or damson or mint ice cream.

The Primo's lunar dome floated above the square as the goldwork of its walls faded. The great Angel Tower lifted its russet arm to the sky-that-wasn't. Even this basilica had gone under the sea, before the rescue operations began. Parts of the building, both inside and out, like so much here, were architectural recxs, and parts exact reconstructs in the original materials. But you would never know. It was as real, composite and eternal as any human thing felt itself to be, in the beginning.

Pigeons and doves flew back and forth to their

roosts. They were, mostly, living birds—only some of the more exotic species of Venus-creatures were mechanical recxs. And the dome had fooled the pigeons and the doves. They thought the sun had set now, and it was time for bed.

Everyone was fooled. They strolled across the square arm in arm, or took off in wanderers, heading for the Bridge of Lies—which had lost its true legend of torture victims who lied to stay alive, and gained a romantic legend instead of the lies that lovers told. They stared, the people, up at the hardening stars, and waited to swoon at the moon.

At the square's margin, the water of the laguna, seldom now called Fulvia, shone phosphorescent and darkly green. Fulvia was the last and only lagoon. The others had passed away, returned into the outer, upper sea, which now, invisible, surrounded all this, beside, below, above.

Flayd had ordered antipasto and grappa.

Once they'd stepped into the boat, even after they'd reached the square, he had talked only generally, pointing out churches and palaces and canals. He was a mine of information. Picaro scarcely listened to him.

Now the drinks and food arrived. Flayd started to pick about through his olives and coils of ham and prawns, fastidious as a greedy stork.

Picaro tasted the grappa. Bitter and perfumed, different in this place. He waited.

Flayd said, "We're fine out here. Probably. I guess it won't matter anyhow. No one can do a damn thing. They've sealed us in and cut communications. And pretty soon some of these innocents are going to realize that, and the questions'll start. Of course they're letting out anyone with prior arrangements due to leave today. Last subvenerine out the locks at midnight. After that, anyone in here stays put."

Picaro ate an olive. He said, "If that's true, why?"

"Because something they've been trying to do down here has finally gotten done. They're all over it. But until they know what happens next, nobody leaves to spread the word. And no one phones home either. It's our—what did they say to me?—our *privilege* to be in on the act."

Picaro looked outward at the water. The slender wanderers plied to and fro. A weightless ship with sails moved further out, at the limit of the horizon. The moon was rising on the lagoon. Others saw it too. Look, look, the moon, the moon, on the lagoon, the lagoon.

It resembled precisely the world's moon upstairs. Better, maybe. But then it was younger and more new.

"So do you want to know what they've done?" asked Flayd. "God, you're one helluva non-curious guy."

"Tell me first why you want to tell me."

"I need to *talk* to someone, pal. I really do. They sprung this on me. I didn't know, and this afternoon, soon as I dropped by, they called me in that office and, Well, Flayd, what do you think of *this*? And I goddamn don't know what I think of it. My mother was a Hindic Buddhist. Christ knows what she'd say."

Picaro laughed.

Despite his apparent anxiety, Flayd grinned, seeming delighted to cause a response.

"Why should it matter to a Hindic Buddhist?"

"It could matter to anyone thinks there's more to life than—life."

Picaro said nothing. He drained his glass and poured another.

Flayd was eating prawns and ham neatly and ferociously.

Across the square, Picaro spotted the two autograph girls from earlier, Cora and India, strolling like others arm in arm. Tonight they wore replica renaissance dresses with high waists, respectively crimson and sage.

Flayd wiped his lips on the napkin. He stared morosely at his empty plate.

"Worry gives me an appetite. Let's take soup, pasta. What they're doing is bringing back from the dead."

Again—Picaro—silent.

Flayd said, exasperated again, "Damn it. I'm not giving you all the truth here. You are involved."

"I thought everybody was . . . according to you."

"More than that. Much more. You're on the list."

"List."

"PRS."

"Which is?"

"Possible Related Bloodline."

Picaro shifted slightly. "Possibly related to what?"

"The dead I spoke of just now."

"And *they* are?"

"There are two of them," said Flayd. He waved up a human waiter dressed in Victorian tailcoat. Flayd ordered again several dishes. When the waiter had gone, Flayd said, expressionlessly, "There's a chance one of these . . . one of these dead, these *people* they've been working on—may have been your ancestor, I mean the guy who was your ancestor here. Both of *them*, you see, lived here, but in different times. In fact, there's a difference between them of around seventeen centuries."

"I know about my ancestors here."

"I've seen your data. It ain't who you think. Maybe."

The moon was now a big white lantern in the purple dusk. Stars were everywhere else, thick as daisies on a field of dusk purple moss. Too many stars. There had never been so many in reality over these Mediterranean shores.

Soon another hour would strike, and the Primo's brass horses go trotting around the spire.

Picaro said, "So tell me."

"You mean I have *interested* you?"

"It'll pass the time."

"Until *what* for Christ's sakes?"

"Oh, that would be betraying a family secret."

Another bottle of grappa came, and Seccopesca, and a bottle of Geneste, all with separate glasses. They were in for a heavy night, if Picaro stayed. Otherwise Flayd was in for it all by himself.

Across the square, now prettily lamplit in the mode of the mid 1800s, Picaro could see India and Cora drifting through the Primo Suvio's carven portico.

Flayd was like a woman, Picaro thought, strong and dominant and impatient, compensatingly over-tactful, blurting. As with a woman then, Picaro felt himself relent.

"My ancestral line. They were called Furiano and Eurydiche. His name is a pseudonym only."

"Yeah, I know that. I know their names. She had a child. She also had a condition known as Stone Face—Strael's Palsy, which in many medical circles is still reckoned to be impossible, unless caused by hysteria."

Something moved in the back of Picaro's eyes.

That was all.

"Yes," he said.

"The condition made giving birth extra dangerous for her. She couldn't breathe through her mouth, couldn't get enough air because the frozen face muscles didn't allow it. This alchemist, Shaachen, did something to her—put her in a trance, used drugs, it's hazy—and performed a Caesarian section. He got the kid out alive and kept *her* alive. Tied her tubes to stop it happening again, sewed her up good as new."

"Yes, I've read that."

"Only it seems Furian may not have been the child's father."

Picaro nodded. "At this remove, hardly seems crucial."

"It *is* crucial. If it wasn't Furian it was Eurydiche's previous lover, a man who was a musician and composer —sound familiar to you? He was called Cloudio del Nero. He wrote a song back then that drove the City of Venus crazy with joy. And then he was murdered, very mysteriously, by some weird and wonderful psycho-alchemical method involving a poisoned mask. Nothing to do with Shaachen, however. Del Nero's body went into the canals at carnival time, in fall."

Picaro blinked. "And?"

"He's the first they're bringing back. They wanted to do this with real special people, that was the big idea. And with all the bones we've been archaeologically digging up, tossed around, then needing to be sorted out after the reburial laws of the early 2000s—he was DNA identified. Reburied. Accorded an ornamental tomb, one of the few remaining plots on San Fumo—the graveyard island, before it too went under the water." Flayd poured the Seccopesca into its peach-tinted Venusian glasses. "But somebody kept back—illegally—one splinter of bone. And that's all it takes. Ever heard of *E.S.*DNA? No? I won't bore you. But *that* is all it takes. So they tell me."

"To bring him back."

"*Regrow* him—*them*. It isn't cloning. I don't understand *what* they've done. I'm into the past, not all this scientific crap."

"But you're useful to them because you *are* into the past."

"Yeah. That's it."

"They want you on this—project."

"Me and a few others. God you shoulda' seen them, my *colleagues*. They were all blushing and dewy with enthusiasm. It's so *exciting*. I think the whole thing yerks. I think it won't *work*. To make a human thing over, some-one that's been dead for centuries—bring them back—bring them back out of *what*? Yes, it can't work, can it? But they say it already has."

"They give you any proof?"

Flayd shook his head. "No one's allowed to see, not yet. But all the rest of it—cutting off the call-phones, shutting up the dome—*telling* us. I mean, Picaro, who is going to make all that up?"

Two Victorian waiters, greatly laden, came and set out the dishes—pasta, *brodo di pesce*, a rose-pink lobster that hadn't ever swum in the dome lagoon—When they were alone again, the two men sat staring at their feast, as if not knowing what on earth to do with it.

"Who is the other one?" Picaro eventually asked. "You keep saying, there are two."

"A woman. That's worse."

"Because of the gender?"

"No. Because she is much older. Not in age, I mean in the centuries between. Del Nero—what's that?—a handful of hundred years ago. But she—she's first century AD."

"There was nothing much here then, was there? You said they were both from Venus."

"There was something here back then. *Rome* was here, like it was most everywhere, then. There used to be a Laguna Aquila, named for the Roman's Eagle Fort, and for the Roman town built round it. Not Venus. They called it Stagna Maris, for the sea lagoons. They had a stadium—a circus—out where the marshes and the sea moved in later. It was forests and woodland then—hence the name of the area, Silvia. All under the ocean now, washed away."

"So she was a Roman."

"A Gaul."

"You sound partisan," Picaro remarked. The drink had loosened his tongue, and his mind. He had lifted up above it, everything else, and become only a young man again, sitting at a table under a false moon, taking an interest in current affairs. Tomorrow none of this would matter. But tonight—tonight was a kind of holiday from himself.

"I'm partisan all right," said Flayd. He cracked the lobster open after all. "I can aquadive. I helped locate and excavate her tomb, in the undersea mud near the drowned circus. She was quite a find. A true rarity."

"Why?"

"She'd been one of the Ludicae—the Games Girls— a gladiatrix. A damn good one—she'd fought regularly in the local amphitheater for five years, before she died. And they buried her like royalty."

4

YOUNG GIRLS DANCED, with garlanded, whipping hair.

The guests barely looked at them, their quick feet and quivering breasts, the dark-skinned flute girl playing, and her sleepy, cunning eyes.

Later there would be a battle from *The Iliad* of the Greeks, enacted by five male dancers with genuinely sharpened blades and little bows. Probably they would incur some injuries, despite their skill.

The second course was still in progress. After the eggs, snails and lettuce, the olives and white figs, the roast hares had come in, the peacock skewered in his brazen skin, the slices of goose liver and tubs of venison and architectures of thrushes braised with honey and poppy seeds, and the silver cradles of shellfish from the Fulvia district. The sweetened wine had been replaced by a Greek wine of Karia, chilled with splintered ice from the villa's ice well, and heady with myrrh, aloes, and oil of cinnamon.

The myrtle fans of the slaves brushed off the heaviness of the evening air. Boys, chosen for their looks, poured the drink into the goblets, each of which was decorated with gold.

Aside from the dancers, and the attendant slaves, there were no women.

For the one woman seated at the end of her master's couch did not count as a woman at all.

"Oh, Julus, you miser. Lend her to me. You said you would." (This, fat Drusus, scrubbing his mouth with a napkin now as greasy as his face.)

"No, dear Drusus. I think I never did."

"But you did. For my bodyguard. She can teach the others how to fight."

They laughed.

"What does Jula Victrix say?" asked another of the guests, a bald and sweating man prone to fondling the wine boys.

Jula looked in his direction. She spoke frankly and emptily, "I am my master's property." Nothing was really expected of her here, but obedience, docility—and her own essential show. She was a tamed leopard on a chain, trained to take food at table like a human being.

The bald man chuckled now. "True. She's made the wretch richer even than he was."

The others made no comment. The gracious dining-room, with its mosaic floor and painted walls, was no place to talk crudely of money.

But then Drusus mildly offered, "Myself also, let it be said. I bet on Julus's Jula, as always, and as always I won."

"Once she lost me sesterces without number," said the bald man. He chewed some meat and said, "I never did believe in a woman gladiator. By Minerva, women weren't meant to do such things."

Julus said, "Come now, Stirius. You see they can. Besides, any legionary could tell you as much. In Gallia and Hispania the women will put up a fight like she-bears. In the Tin Isles they ride into battle in chariots. The men have to run to keep up with them."

"Harsher and more cruel than any man," agreed the other, the scholarly guest known as the Scroll.

"Are you harsh and cruel, Jula?" asked oil-greasy Drusus.

The gladiatrix looked at him with her lowered eyes, and away.

This flirtatious carping did not generally last long, though sometimes it occurred in patches. But the wine, with its mix of scent and narcotic, (diluted occasionally by water, or the effusions of roses) blurred the edges of their discourse. They would get on to other matters soon. The dancers would be pulled on to the couches, or the wine boys, if Julus allowed it.

The bellaria was being brought in and laid out on separate ivory tables, to engage the eyes of the feasters, saffron pastries, and pomegranates, cakes decorated by white flowers, and twisted sweets of honey.

A couple of Julus's male gladiators couched across from the diners. Their table, like the others, was of patterned citrus wood. They were served from the same dishes. Yet, unlike Jula, they had been kept a little apart and already shown off, their muscles and teeth admired.

The dancers finished. They glided from the central floor, over the tesserae of maenads. Stirius caught one and she sank beside him, doll-like and compliant. (Jula noted Drusus and Julus exchange a surreptitious nod. It seemed they had been betting too on which their companion would choose, boy or girl.)

That Stirius missed. Instead he had an observation. "Now *this* is a woman."

His hand detached itself from his wine cup and slipped the dancer's tunic from her shoulder, revealing most of a round young breast.

"But your gladiator woman," said Stirius, "gives no evidence of that. *Is* she a female?"

Jula had met such questions before. In the arena

her breasts were bound to steady them, and so hidden, just as her red spiked hair, once she had been seen and identified in the processional Pompa, was covered by her secutor's helmet.

Now she did nothing, but under her leveled lowered eyelids, she took in the person of Stirius.

Such faces had come before her belonging to armed adversaries. Ones usually that she found easy to kill. But this time, (obviously) not.

Her master waved his arm, indicating the messy meat dishes should be cleared to make way for the bellaria. That was all. But as slaves swarmed between the tables whisking things up, mopping over spills, Stirius lay along his couch, one hand on the dancer's waist, staring, perhaps noting that his coarse remarks, too, were being cleared from the dinner.

What did he want, the bald man who had lost money on her? So many lost money at the games. Any victory was always unlucky for some.

A third wine came with the dessert. It was a swarthy and terrible wine, meant to be much diluted, and sipped.

The scholarly Scroll had interrupted the proceedings, insisting on reading to them all a tale he had come across in one of his books.

Julus indulged him. The Scroll was wealthy and influential and, by some distant relationship through marriage, had connections to the young emperor in Rome. The tale anyway was lewd. It concerned girls who fled gods and were changed into animals, trees, or rivers, which, in each case, the god in question then still ravished.

They'll let me go soon, then I can sleep.

She had eaten little. This sort of food was not her normal fare, nor did she greatly like it. Given her always as a reward, titbit or feast were meaningless, of course.

For she had no choice but to attempt to please, to *fight* well. She had wanted to live from the first—unlike the Ethiopian, who determined not to.

I am like Playful, she thought.

Playful was the old lioness. Kept now at the town's expense, after years of her successful slaughterings of those criminals and lesser swordsmen sent against her. Playful had been "freed," was popular, and might be visited in her cage below the arena. In the Pompa, too, Playful was walked on leash, with flowers around her neck.

That then, Jula's fate? To survive and gain freedom —the ultimate reward for her inevitable struggles—to live at the whim and expense of Stagna Maris . . . in a cage?

But she would not live. No. Her expectancy of life was, at the most, seven years. The majority did not last even so long.

And they would never free her. As if they guessed that unlike Playful in this one thing, if ever set free—she would be gone, gone for ever, although she did not know to where.

But where did any man or any woman go?

We vanish, she thought. *We disappear*.

Strange thoughts. The Ethiopian had done this to her. Had he cursed her truly? And would it claim her, his curse?

Her wounds, which all night had ached and stung as if biting at her under her actor's draped gown, had been quite severe. They might have killed her, if the surgeons were not so skilled. (They hurt less now—the wine.)

So why think of this? . . . the other country . . .

Stop thinking of this.

Yes, the wine was very strong, and through the blur of it, thickening like the smoke of the lamps, the torches round the villa walls, the guests' faces, bulbous and distorted, like fish swimming in water and seen through an amber lens—

Jula heard rain falling hard against the house. Yet through the columns, in the summer courtyard, the night was still and close and silent.

Despite the open court, the air was too thin in this room. Drained by these Roman men, this master-race, it had no substance for her heavy leaden barbarian lungs to take hold of. So she did not pull at it any more, simply let it whisper in as it would.

Bald Stirius was rubbing his hands over the body of the dancer. Drusus had had the leftovers of the peacock brought back, was selecting what he would take home with him.

Fishes, swimming . . . to the sea—

Out on the floor, they were fighting *The Iliad* now. Bizarrely, with no sound at all, mouths gaping and shutting, dumb.

Though, through the rush of the sea she had mistaken for rain, she heard the Scroll mutter: "Look, Julus, she's nodded off. Look at that. She was cut about rather today, wasn't she, your prize girl?"

Julus said, along the couch behind her, a mile off, "A scratch or two. Nothing to her, I promise you."

Oh, they speak of me.

"Well, she's tired. She's asleep. What a fine profile she has! She should be copied in marble."

"She isn't asleep. Her eyes are open. Look. She's watching our mock fight. It must amuse her. She's smiling, aren't you, my gladiatrix?"

THE BOAT, THE BOAT in the dark, out on the night lagoon. That of Aquila, yes Aquila, for there was the shadow of the fort, the cresset burning high over its parapet . . .

But a coin, did she have any to pay him?—the One who poled the boat away, away, out and out, across the water to the sea.

Save it would not be sea, not now. It would be the River.

And the night sky—no, that was not sky. It was the world above, which made the roof, without a single star.

And oh, the cresset of fire was not the beacon of Aquila either, but the last bright sunset of the funeral pyre.

5

THESE OUR ACTORS, as I foretold you, were all spirits, and are melted into air, into thin air . . .

"What, sin? What did you say to me?"

"Nothing."

"I thought you said the air was thin. Let me assure you, the air is just perfect, signore. Nothing to worry over. Full CX maintained air function. The dome is one hundred percent safe at all times."

Half invisible in darkness, Picaro was lit a second by the lightning flash of his smile. The one he kept for decent people, passing through.

THE WANDERLIER WAS SINGING again. It didn't offend so much, now Picaro was drunk. To be drunk—was all that currently mattered.

At last he could really see the liquid black of the canals over which the boat glided, and the dim floating by of seemingly unanchored walls, some with lights, that glowed like the illuminations of long ago; latticed Eastern renaissance globes, oil lamps and gas lamps from the nineteenth century, candles . . . and these silvery-gold glimmerings, smashed, broken over and over by the oar-pole of the wanderlier.

It was beautiful, the City. But false as the set of a movie or a virtuality. Even if these buildings might be seen from all sides, *lived* in.

Picaro glanced at his wristecx and touched it for the time. The luminous numbers displayed for a moment the fact that it was after 4 A.M. But it wasn't, not any more, for he had omitted to instruct the wristecx to reset to the Viorno-Votte. And he had asked the wanderlier, getting into the boat, and been told, fifty minutes earlier, that it was the twenty-fifth hour. He had let the man pole him to the Rivoalto then, to watch the moon go down behind the palace of the Ducemae.

Now, in the great loom of darkness with its gilded light-lace edges, a flotilla of salt swans moved by, long necks snakelike, black in shadow. Before, gulls had flown over. Few of these creatures were actual. But they looked entirely real, and if he had been able physically to put his hand on them, they might even have convinced him that they were, for half a second.

Was that the secret? Not alone of the undersea Venus, but of everything—of the earth—of life?

Flayd had talked so much about the woman gladiator, and Picaro had forgotten it all as soon as Flayd sank his head on his arms, on the aftermath of table, and begun softly to snore. Picaro left him there, left him and his gladiatrix and all the talk of the two dead who could be brought back. Picaro informed the waiters the meal should be charged to his account. He even left the gratuity in dollari—the coins that were still used in the City, and carried the head of the goddess Venus.

It would be necessary to tip the boatman too. Indulgent, scornful, Picaro watched him, a strong man, in costume, without a care in the world.

"Sin, there is a wanderer following my boat,"

announced the wanderlier as they swung into the next turn, and above, a glistering, spectral church sailed near and then away.

"Yes," said Picaro. "Is there?"

"Look, signore."

Picaro, (indulgent, scornful) half turned.

As they swam on, another wanderer swam after them into the latest canal. Under the cats-eye lanterns along the church front, Picaro made out two women sitting back in the second boat, one in a crimson and one a sage-green gown.

"Sinnas," said the wanderlier, beaming congratulatory. Picaro shrugged.

"Can you lose them?"

"*Lose* them, signore? Demisellas of such pulchritude—"

"Yes."

"You're unkind, sin. Very well. But remember, Venus is the City of Love—"

"No. Venus is the city of darkness."

"That too," allowed the pedantic wanderlier, guiding them suddenly away through a side channel, where the adjacent, apparently ancient buildings leaned each side close enough to finger. "That's the old name. Ve Nera—which means 'Going to meet the Dark.'"

Something—it was like the high-strung note of a violin—sounded kilometers up in Picaro's brain.

"Lose the other boat," he repeated. "Then take me to the Alchimia Canal."

HE HAD MEANT DEATH, surely, the poet-dramatist, when he wrote about the sorcerer's actors who were really spirits, and had vanished "into thin air." Picaro considered this, and with surprise, saw he was still in the boat, adrift, yet now it was quite different.

That the canals of the new restored Venus were clean, and odorless, was not quite true. They had a kind of faintly *laundered* smell.

This water smelled ripe, nearly swampy, of rotten fruit, of fish—like the polluted seas that elsewhere hugged the coasts.

And it wasn't, any more, a boat he was on. Now it was an island.

Picaro stood on an island in a great lagoon, and no lights showed, but the boat was coming toward him, over it, and he was waiting for the boat.

I'm dreaming.

He saw a woman in a long grayish robe stepping through the shallow surf, walking up on to the island. Her head was covered by a veil but he caught the pallid glitter of her eyes. She reeked of sulphur. She must be a sibyl from some cave of the Romans.

He confronted her on the path.

Behind her, the sky was thick with stars, but they were dull, not half so bright as her eyes.

She said, "You will meet your death at thirty." And paused.

Picaro said, "I know. You told me this before. I was sixteen and it was in another place. You weren't as you are tonight."

But remorseless, the sibyl added, "You will die under water. Though not from drowning."

"I know," he said again.

And effortlessly woke. And in the met darkness, said once more, "I know."

6

PICARO RAISED HIS LONG-FINGERED, calloused hand, and held it up to block out the flickering light of the CX words, which seemed engraved across the window. But they were fading anyway now, mechanically aware they had been seen.

A weather alert. Weather was controled indome, as in many places elsewhere above. Only here, *weather* was really superfluous, unneeded—employed for amusement, as the "literature" had said. Some days there were high seas in the lagoon and the canals foamed and—not tidal, but appearing to be—the waters flooded over by a handful of atmospheric centimeters, quite unreminiscent of the floods of long ago. Other days there were dramatic clouds, and downpours, which helped sluice the buildings. Nothing rough lasted long. The storm today was to take a full three hours, a (safe) spectacle that people would go out on their balconies, out to the hilly Equus Gardens and up the Torre dell' Angelo of the Primo, to admire.

Behind the blackness of his hand, the letters vanished. Only the pane of perfect daylight remained.

Picaro lay staring a moment, *seeing* his hand, as children and mystics sometimes did, a representative of his body—familiar but abruptly alien. Was it his? Was this body lying supine on the sheet—also his? Debatable.

The pain behind his eyes though, that decidedly *was* his.

He hadn't drunk like that, not for seven months. How quickly you forgot.

Feeling peeled and toxic, he left the bed, and walked into the apartment's lavish and anachronistic bathroom.

When he came back, the window was still clear. It was now the wristecx that was twittering from the outer rooms.

Flayd? Maybe not. Flayd's state should be worse than Picaro's . . .

Picaro went and stood on the terracotta floor, looking at the squeaking wristecx. Which didn't give up.

"Yes."

"Sin Picaro, we have your call number from the University Coder. We wonder if you would be so kind as to visit us, at your convenience, in an hour's time."

"That isn't convenient."

"Very well. Two hours."

"Why?" he said. (How many times had he asked that yesterday? It was becoming the Eternal Question.) He touched the wristecx to get the caller's code and identity. It was indome—but now these were the only calls possible, according to Flayd. The locale was a building on the Blessed Maria Canal, behind the Primo. The University itself? The caller was a fussily titled S'in Chossi, of the UAS—University Auxillary Staff.

"We will of course explain fully. We can expect you then, Sin Picaro?"

"Not until I know what you want."

"It's routine administration, I regret, sin."

"I never heard of it."

"In your case, sin."

"Why my case?"

"Your PBS."

"That's been cleared," said Picaro. His heart was suddenly knocking loudly against his aching brain. "Before and when I arrived."

"No, no, sin. The PBS is fine. But there's a connection we wish to verify."

The voice was nearly mechanical. They so often were. And like a machine, which these lesser bureaucrats had been trained, presumably, to mimic—in order the better to reassure and coerce—you couldn't get much out of them, only what they were programmed to let you have—it was useless to try.

But—bloodline—*connection*? Then Flayd had been quite right?

Picaro said softly, clearly, "My ancestors are Furiano and Eurydiche. That's all I have. Minor citizens during the early eighteenth century."

"I regret, sin, we can't deal with this via your call facility. You'll understand, we need to speak to you in person."

"No."

Regardless, the "machine" said, "That's fine, sin. We will send a boat for you at 12 VV."

"Perhaps I won't be around." Picaro cut the signal.

(HE STOOD IN FRONT OF the recx mirror, ornately gilt-framed and spotted as if with age.

Those ancestors, whoever they'd been—Furian,

Cloudio—they sure as hell had not looked like him. White guys. African-Italian Picaro, like one third of the present population of Europe—just as one third of Africa was European.

The black eyes looked back at him. The long white braids in the long black dreads, stared too. For live shows, he had worn black and white. He had known the story of the magpie since he was six, and his father had received the first notification of PBS, with its attached bookdisc. Picaro remembered how his father, puzzled, turned them over— "What am I supposed to do with this? What they want?" There was not, in those days, any invite to anyone to visit Venus in her preservation jar. She was still being rebuilt, and all tourism was strictly limited.

The magpie, though, caught Picaro's imagination. It had belonged to the alchemist Shaachen. It could tell the time to the minute, and could write in ink, with its black beak. But what had the magpie been to Furian and Eurydiche? That the little bookdisc didn't tell.

"Bird of the Virgo Maria," said Picaro's father, as they sat out on the high hot roof above that other city, the city where Picaro was born. They were drinking iced melon tea, and below the traffic roared and plunged in dust and smoke, like a drove of demonic cattle. It was always worse after 5 P.M.—17 hours. The period when the last traffic for the day was allowed to run, before the nighttime prohibition on anything but emergency vehicles, which came on at 19—7 P.M. And everyone wanted to get somewhere.

Picaro, thinking back to his father's voice, heard it still above that driven rumble from the streets.

"But the magpie could *write*?"

"Says so here." And then the man's still face, turning towards him. "But you can't have one, son. They wouldn't allow it. Magpie's a wild bird."

And there had been a dream he had, the child then, of seven magpies flying, black-white-black—like something from a picture by Escher. But by now the actual image of the dream was gone, the memory remained only as words. And even the face of Picaro's father had faded, returning solely in abrupt, surprising dazzles of recollection. He had been dead nearly sixteen years.)

PERHAPS HE WOULDN'T BE around, but when the UAS boat came, he was standing by the watersteps, by the green iron Neptune.

Not a wanderer. A stouter, Victorian boat, with a canopy to keep off the sunless heat of the sky. An official, also in Victorian dress, (a Victorian clerk) welcomed him aboard: Chossi.

"A short trip. We are permitted to use engines, you understand."

They took off fairly rapidly, leaving a curling wake in the shiny, thick-clean water.

"There, do you see? The roofs of Santa Lala—and just there—"

"What's this about?"

"Routine at this stage, sin. Nothing to worry you."

Another man ran the boat, steering it through the canals and out into the sky-flamed sheet of the lagoon.

A funeral cortège was crossing the water, a tourist display only, for there was no longer any Isle of the Dead. The black angels and black, horse-headed prows eased between sparkling plates of lagoon and air, and mourners from the fifteen and 1600s posed in their black and gold. From windows and terraces and other boats, came the tiny soft blinks of a hundred camerecxi.

There was attractive merchant shipping along the

quays to either side of the Primo Square, tall sails the color of tortoiseshell or iced Campari.

The Victorian boat, chugging now in keeping with its pretend-antiquity, waddled in the opposite direction and into the narrow Blessed Maria Canal. The University had not first been built quite where it was today. But it looked enough of a fixture. Gray stone levels, carven pilasters, and windows with bottle-glassed, myopic panes. They drew in under a leaning, fringed acacia whose fronds almost touched the water. Chossi took Picaro in under an arch roped with ghost-blue wisteria, up carefully cracked steps, and into a long, low-ceilinged corridor.

The shadows here by day—lacking a directional sun to cast them—were curiously luminous, even inside.

Like the boat, bottom heavy, Chossi waddled before Picaro.

The room had gilding.

The man in the chair was dressed later than his clerk—from 1906, perhaps, something like that. You did not often see so recent an era represented now.

He rose and held out his manicured hand to grasp Picaro's. "Please sit, Sin Picaro."

Picaro, sitting.

"I believe, Sin Picaro, you know why you're here."

"Do I?"

"I believe, Sin Picaro, Sin Flayd let fall something about a scientific venture which has gone on here, over the past two years."

"Did he?"

"Let's not be too playful," said the 1906 man. He smiled to reassure he was still Picaro's friend.

"Then don't," said Picaro.

"It isn't," the man said, "as Sin Flayd feared, that

CX vigilance was in operation during your conversations. But it was quite obvious he would tell you. He's done nothing wrong. Flayd is always suspicious . . . Nothing can upset what has been achieved. Simply, perhaps, he's saved us all a little time. But only that, of course, if you will concede you know."

"I forget. I was pissed out of my skull."

"Very well." The 1906 man shrugged. He had a long sallow face.

Using its thin mouth, the long face told Picaro quickly and deftly much of what Flayd had already told him last night. At least, the things to do with the one, (the *dead* one) named Cloudio del Nero.

"We do think he, not the man Furiano, is your true bloodline antecedent. Of course, the genetic comparatives aren't quite conclusive. At a distance of centuries they rarely are, despite the propaganda. But even so. There are close similarities—the female ancestress remains the same, however, Eurydiche. I hope you're not offended by this change in circumstance."

"Furian wasn't supposed to be my father."

"Naturally not. But some people do take these matters very earnestly. Now, we have a great favor to ask of you, Sin Picaro. A great favor which will also be, for you, a great favor bestowed on you, and, I trust, an exciting, astonishing event."

THERE WAS AN ELEVATOR. It was Victorian, but not in its mechanism. They descended into the subsurface warren beneath the University. And so came to another room.

The room was full of sunlight, and the sunlight appeared as entirely real as it did above in the City, and was equally false.

This man sat in a carved chair, before a window that looked out on eighteenth-century palaces lining a long canal—a virtuality without recx. But a virtuality so superlative that breezes blew up from it. And they smelled, if only faintly, of an earlier time, fetid with summer water.

He wore, this man, pale, elegant silk clothes fashionable among the rich in 1701. There were rings on his fingers.

He had long, dark hair. His eyes were dark, and his face pale. Sitting so stilly, it was all—he, the room, the view—a painting.

Then he turned his head and saw them, and he rose graciously to his feet—and he smiled the smile. That was, he smiled as Picaro did, for the decent, irrelevant strangers who passed like shadows through his life.

"Signorissimo del Nero," said the 1906 man, bowing, "may I present to you Signore Picaro, the musician?"

As PROMISED, THE STORM began at 15 VV.

Picaro watched it, from a terrace in the Equus Gardens.

He was surrounded by tourists.

"Ooh!" they shrieked, as the show intensified.

Pink sudden flutters of light spasmed through the cloud banks, slender forks slit the dark masses of a cumulus that resembled the smoke from volcanoes. Then the sky went white. A laser-web of fires surged from the horizon's hem to the treed summits of the park, and beyond. Every tower and dome of Venus became a cutout of bleached paper. A rogue silver bolt hit the apex of the Primo's Angel Tower. Though harmless, it did not look it. Then the thunder bellowed, and the angry roaring of the park lions was silenced. A wind blew, smelling of ozone and electricity.

Everywhere people stood, watching.

Beside Picaro, Cora, holding fast to his arm, gazed in bacchic ecstasy at the sky.

He had found the two young women—or they had found him—as he entered the Gardens. They were today in eighteenth-century garb, (he seemed the only one in Venus in contemporary clothes) their dark hair powdered, and each wearing, though it was not either of the carnival times, sequinned half-masks. Picaro had looked at them, and when they turned toward him, held out his hands to both.

India did not speak. Cora did not say much. India was not demonstrative. Cora snuggled close, and never moved further away than the length of their arms.

He had not meant to annex them, but they were always there.

As he too watched the storm display, and the Gardens rocked as if to the wildest music and drums, he would not think about the man he had met in the subsurface room.

In any case, Picaro had not been given very long with him. The dialogue had been stilted, guided by the UAS personnel—the 1906 man and two others—who had taken Picaro down.

It hadn't been an interesting conversation, either. Or productive. Or—only once. Picaro had said little. And the man—del Nero—also little. He spoke with the accent of a previous time, and in somehow different phrases, but any accomplished actor who had studied del Nero's century could surely have managed that. Perhaps Cloudio del Nero then, was as much a fake as all the rest of it. And if he *was* real, he was of course rebuilt, like the City, and not as he had been. Not the same.

For God's sake—what did he think, behind that gracious and polished veneer? How did he think he was here? That there had been some mistake—he'd merely been unconscious a moment from drowning (they said he had died partly, too, of that) and then come to his senses and now was healthy, and well—

Or, if he understood—if they had told him a *quarter* of it, they had not made clear to Picaro—did del Nero grasp that he had *died*? Had been *dead*?

Probably, back then, he had believed in God, and resurrection through Christ. So where did Cloudio believe this was—*Heaven*?

The storm edifices of the sky gave way, and lightning billows pulsated. The audience up here, everywhere, screamed in terror and thrill.

Were their lives otherwise so devoid of such things that it needed *this* to wake them up?

And Cloudio—how, *how* had they woken *him*?

Picaro hadn't asked them anything.

He had thought, anyway, they would lie.

Cora clung to him. He turned and kissed her, and she opened like a flower. But elusive India never looked away from the sky, and in her stone-cool profile was the masked face of the ancient Indra.

They walked through the dry tempest, down the Gardens, past statues of other gods, by the lion groves, where the beasts prowled snarling among the trees, their manes bristling.

On the canal the wanderlier poled Picaro and the women through the shatterings of dark light, the whole world exploding. He didn't sing, this wanderlier, seeing Picaro and Cora were occupied with each other, and India scholastically with the storm.

At the Palazzo Shaachen, in the apartment with the

colored bottles and the skull, (the windows flashing green, black, lilac) Picaro spread Cora out on the low bed and fucked her. The galvanics of the afternoon made her insatiable and him tireless. She became the only woman on earth, and then every woman—almost—he had ever had. He did not care what he was for her. He gave her pleasure to please himself.

Outside, India, who evidently did not want him in this way, and perhaps not Cora either, sat listening to his music on various decx. She had said that was what she was there for. To please himself too, he let her.

It wasn't the first occasion he had indulged in sex to the background score of his own compositions. But sometimes India sang, he heard her behind the thunder, and the pounding in his head, her dark voice mingling with Cora's soprano moans and cries.

"Cora e 'Caro," Cora said. "'Caro, Cora . . . "

"I too," said Cloudio del Nero, "have tried my hand at a little composition. The City was kind to them, these slight pieces. A song or two." (He had been the son of a ducca.)

"You're too modest, signorissimo," said the 1906 man. "One song of yours was all the rage."

"Once," said del Nero. "But perhaps Signore Picaro will tell me something of his own work."

"I don't talk about my music," Picaro said. He added, coldly, "Signorissimo."

"Ah." Del Nero nodded. He stayed chivalrous and bland. "Then I respect your reticence."

And then, the one question Picaro had asked. He asked it effortlessly, as if he were a fool.

"Do you think of her, now you're back?"

That was how he put it—"her," and "now you're back?" Deliberately obtuse before the obscenity of it, whether fake or actual, this situation, of one of the dead *returned*.

But del Nero had himself asked politely, "*Her*, Signore Picaro?"

"Eurydiche."

The UAS men didn't stir. Yet the silence lasted.

Then del Nero had done something strange (if anything could be reckoned separately strange in such an environment). He had looked intently into Picaro's eyes. That was, he looked in a frank, quite unguarded way.

But, in those eyes, in that instant, Picaro had seen —had seen a terrible unspeakable thing, had seen—that there, in the eyes of the reliving dead, was to be glimpsed *the place he had come from*—death itself, Nihil, nothing—a *gap*—it was unreadable, not to be comprehended, yet *there. It was there.*

And in that moment of horror more horrible than fear, the aristocrat had said gently to him, "But I understand, signore, the lady named Eurydiche is gone."

PART TWO

The Return from Sleep

1

SHE HEARD HER MOTHER'S VOICE, which called her by another name. There was the dish of a flower, pink, speckled with a darker color. But then the flower, and the name, and the voice, were gone.

A sliding like stones and fine shale down the face of a cliff, shapes, noises, scents and images, an old man's face with closed eyes—a horse running—a man bent to an anvil in a gush of sparks—night on a town and the pine-tree sound of the sea.

Then she heard, instead of all that, the tibia horns mooing from the arena.

She had been dreaming. Yes, she had dreamed she had died. Was that an omen for her fight today? It might be. It might always be. Or it might mean nothing, except that the food yesterday evening, at her master's house, had been too rich and plentiful.

Strange, however, that she should be fighting today, when she had already fought yesterday. Normally she was not put out to fight more than two or three times a month, and even the enthusiastic crowd, lauding her as the best of her kind, did not demand more.

Jula stood up. The hot rectangular room in the sub-arena was packed with other combatants. Many saluted her. But there were always a couple who would mock, though it was unlucky, and someone—as always—cuffed them.

At the end of the up-sloping stone passage, she stood waiting behind the doors. Through the splits and slats of them she saw the afternoon gold of the stadium, and her ears were filled by the shrieks of the crowd—"He has it! He's taken it—Kill! Kill!"

She had never questioned any of it, since to question was not helpful. Yet now she felt a sudden strong antipathy to the multitude. She had never wanted to delight them, only to survive—and they—disgusted her.

The tibias groaned again, and she put all ideas of disgust from her mind. She thought of the first teachers, in Julus's school: "Empty your mind like your night pot. Rinse it with clean water. Then, and then only, pick up your sword and go to work."

Out there, the fight finished. One gladiator, a popular swordsman, had slaughtered his opponent, who was being carried off. The winner stalked around the length of the arena, showered with small gifts from the stands. Victory palm branch in hand, he strode away. The sand was being refreshed. Jula waited, tense, her mind rinsed clean.

The doors opened.

Never had the stadium seemed so huge. Modeled after the colossal Flavian amphitheater in Rome, this provincial miniature could still seat many thousands. Light struck down on it from a white summer sky, save for the patrician areas of the seats, the places of the priestesses and the higher military, which were shaded by extended, dark blue awnings.

The gladiatrix walked on to the sand, and the crowd boomed. It chanted the pun which pleased it so—*Jugula Jula! Jula jugula!*—kill, Jula, kill.

Jula raised her arm in salute, turning to all the terraces. As if she honored them. Was happy to be there.

She thought, *I could be another. How would they know, now?*

For though she walked bare-faced like the others in the Pompa before the afternoon bouts, now she was helmeted in the secutor's helm they called the "Fishhead," that closed off the entire skull and left only the round eyeholes to the front, and the tiny slits above the ears. It was *her* helmet certainly, bronze, skinned over with silver. But until she undid it at the end of the match, to reveal her face and her red hair flattened by its pressure and her sweat, they could not know.

Of course, she was a woman, they could always see that. Her breasts were firmly bound by leather straps, ornamented, like her belt, with beaded snakes. The greave on her left leg was Jula's, light bronze, marked with a figure of Minerva. Her arms were encircled by Jula's leather and bronze protection. The shield, painted scarlet, had as its central boss the face of Venus, goddess of love—but paramour of the war god Mars: Jula's shield. And her feet were bare. Perhaps the connoisseurs sitting in the nearer seats could even recognize her feet, the left one with its narrow purple scar.

So, she was Jula enough for them.

Her opponent was coming out from the other set of fighter's doors. Today it was to be the Neptuni Retiarius—Neptune's Fisherman.

She, a secutor, did not always fight a retiarius. In Rome it was more a custom than here. But today . . .

Curious, this man, barefaced and bareheaded, armed only with light greaves, armlet, net, and trident, (deceptively almost naked—it was the net that was so deadly) this man seemed to her familiar—not by mere sight, for he was from another school (Talio's?) but as if she had fought him before. And as if—she had *killed him* then.

Jula, behind the round fish eyeholes of her silver helmet mask, blinked. For a moment the arena swam. Then it was steady again.

The sticklers had positioned themselves, hitching up their robes to leave their legs free for running interventions or goadings with their sharp sticks—traditional, for nothing like that would be needed when Jula fought.

The boards had been held up, too, for the most distant seats, mostly unneeded, naming Jula in large letters, Jula who was famous, and the retiarius of Neptune who might come to be.

These things seemed to take too long, as if the world had unaccountably slowed its pace.

Jula stepped forward, and through the yowling of the crowd, the throb of blood, *inside* the helmet heard the voice of a man say intimately, quietly—something in an unknown tongue.

But she had emptied and cleansed her mind.

Nothing could get in. She was now only a machine.

Jula broke into a run. Despite her plating, she was agile, fast.

She glimpsed the retiarius had not expected this from her so immediately. Whatever else, *he* did not know *her*.

She slammed against him with the edge of her shield, even as he struggled to let out his net, and sprang away before he could aim the trident.

The man staggered. The crowd jeered.

The last retiarius she had fought on a showy constructed bridge over the lake of seawater they had brought in to flood part of the arena. There had been a make-believe sea fight, (with genuine casualties) and the wreckage of the little ships floated there, and she had not had to kill the retiarius because he fought so well. He had earned Walking Dismissal from the arena.

The net came swirling. Jula was gone.

Before the fisher collected himself, she was back at him again, and now her short pointed sword bit in, piercing his side.

And she—*remembered* it. This.

It had happened before. The red blood, and somehow the blood should be like wine, like the blood of grapes—but the retiarius was not black. He was a tallish fair-haired Northerner.

Her father might have looked somewhat like that. So many million years before.

She emptied her mind.

The net came in, and she bounced it off shieldwise, deflected it, the iron and bronze weights of it ringing as they smote on the ground. But he had not lost his grip.

Now he was crouching.

This was too soon—because exactly at this moment it would happen—and surely they had fought a greater time—that *first* occasion—and he had almost had her once—and she him, before this—but no—

No, here he was, the blinding sun-spangled arc of the net and the black-tipped trident of the god— Fisherman and Fish.

She moved one way, and the net came over for that Jula, who was no longer there, who had become the other Jula who was *here*, again beside him, and in that instant she felt one point of the trident slide deep into her thigh, which meant *her* blood, a weakening, and she must not delay any longer. And, as she recalled, his foot was turning on her own blood in the sand, he lost balance, and was wide before her. She stabbed in just above his belt. It reminded her, as in the beginning it so often had, of stabbing into the cattle carcasses the school had provided. The thunk of the gladius passing through the density of meat, skidding on bone, splintering it, blood-spray, and a darker blood from the liver. But it was a human scream ringing against her, so near. Nearer than the blood, this screaming.

He could not live now, not after that blow. So she carved upwards through him, strong, a butcher, knowing where to go. The gladius blade found his heart and he was dead.

He lay at her feet, his net with rubies on it.

And the wheezing water organ was playing at the rim of the arena, and the horns mooing, and somehow it was dark—she was in the stone passage, and the doors had still to open, and they opened.

They opened into a light she did not know.

The crowd howled. But their noise faded. It was a murmur now, civilized and low. She could feel the gilded palm branch in her hand.

Above her was not the sky, but a vaulted ceiling, painted palest blue.

Again a man said something in her head.

Her head would not move. So she turned her eyes and found he was not there, but out by her side, leaning forward a little.

He spoke in Latin, but clumsily, with an unknown accent and inflection, and not quite the proper words. It was not like the foreign tongue he had used before, yet still entirely alien to her.

"Are you able," he said, "to say your name? Don't try to move, just try to say your name."

But she learned she was not able to do this. She was lying flat on some sort of bed, under a sky blue ceiling, in a new light, dumb and almost immobile. She could not any more feel the victory palm in her hand.

Jula was afraid. She did not yet know why she should be.

FLAYD LOOKED AWAY from the screen. As the lights came up, he rose to his feet.

The others were already upright, jabbering, exclaiming.

Oh wasn't it wonderful? It was *wonderful*.

"What do you think, Flayd?" said Leonillo.

"Yeah. Remarkable," said Flayd. He scowled and pushed back his mane of hair, which was coming loose from its tie. "But she doesn't speak and she can't move."

"Quite the contrary. That piece of film was long ago, two or three months. *Now* she can move perfectly, I assure you. And she can speak modern Italian quite well. Better, dare I venture, than you do."

"Ain't hard, buddy," snarled Flayd. "So she's bright."

"Of course. And with present day hypno-tutor techniques, and linguisticx—"

"What about her Latin? That was what she had taught her first, I guess."

"Her Latin is fascinating. Not anything you'd find in a classical text. Although, when pressed, she can speak like something out of Ovid or Pliny—she was educated up to a certain standard for her master's amusement. He liked to show her off."

The others were crowding around, goggling. Bubbling over with praise and amaze like badly corked bottles.

Leonillo smiled, a kind uncle taking the kids on a treat. His long, pale face reminded Flayd, as it had from the first, of a shelled monkeynut. The clothes, circa 1900, fit him too well. There was not a single bulge in Leonillo's below-neck shape, not a roll of fat, a muscle, a penis, or a heart.

"Now I think we should call on our protégée. I think we should see her face to face."

"Is that *possible?*"

"Yes, Flayd. Why not?"

"You've grown her back—you say you have—from tissue and bone standard to the first century A.D. She'll have no immune system ready to cope with anything we might be carrying around—"

"Come, Flayd. I know you detest science, but are we so stupid?"

"Sure I am."

"She is completely immunized against any current or potential virus. Besides which, I can assure you, the A.D. 1 immune system, in a well-nourished adult, was if anything far tougher than our present properties."

"So you've taught her language skills and pumped her full of vaccines, and she can move about and she can talk. What the hell does she say to you? Has she *asked* you anything? What for godsakes does she *think*?"

"Come and see," said Leonillo, nearly jocular.

As he went out, the others swarmed after him.

Flayd walked slowly to the rear. But after all, she— *Jula*—she was used to moronic mindless crowds.

THEY HAD BUILT HER A Roman place, there under the surface of the dome streets and canals, exactly as they'd made a suitable eighteenth-century apartment, apparently, for the other one, Cloudio. Both these bolt-holes were halfway-houses, of course. Flayd already knew they were soon to be decanted, each of them, back into the outer world.

In many ways the dome environment was fortuitous for this. And for del Nero, the *unexplained* Venus under-dome truly should not offer too great a trauma—nothing much later than 1890 obtained there. But no Roman remains were left in Venus outside the virtuality museum, which in any case stood on the mainland. For Jula Flammi-fer, culture shock par excellence it was going to be.

For now, there was a colonnade, and then a court-yard, open to an apparent summer sky. Vines grew up the walls, and myrtle in a red Samian pot.

She was exercising in the middle of the court with two youngish men in gray tunics. Her tunic was white. They were using wooden practice swords, no shields.

As the small crowd billowed out to the edges of the yard, Jula executed what was just recognizable as a flaw-less parry, lunge, riposte, moves that came from nowhere any of them had ever seen—a barbaric, classic sequence from some sixty years after the death of Christ.

She was beautiful, Flayd thought, dismayed. Not so much her face or body, as her tanned physical absolute-ness. She had the grace of an animal, a dangerous one you wouldn't turn your back on, no sir, unless you were cracked as that bloody fake Samian pot.

Another whiplike flash of the practice sword. One of the gray tunics went sprawling. The other laughed—then had to dodge as she came for him.

She didn't look as if she had been dead a long while and had only been back (walking, talking) for a month or so. Yet she looked young as the morning. The morning of the world.

Even the fools he was supposed to call colleagues had stopped gabbling.

They all stood staring at her as she sent the second guy flying on to his butt.

Session completed, she did not bother to turn, as yet. Like he'd said to himself, she was used to gawkers.

Though they had bothered about the initial architecture and some other things, clothes styles weren't designated as a difficulty. They had all come down here in their various fancy dress, ranging from Leonillo's high collar and narrow trousers, through some riotous gowns, hose, and wigs, to Flayd's conservative Victorian cravat and frock coat. She knew after all she was among non-Roman savages. But then she herself, once, had been a "savage," a child of the great forests of Gaul.

"Jula," Leonillo called.

Flayd felt himself swell with anger.

Leonillo had no rights to call her. To call her by *name. No rights.*

For Christ's sake, what had they done?

But she did turn now, and came toward them, padding barefoot, a brown lynx, through the virtuality dust.

Her hair was a deep, improbable, nearly cherry red, from the Egyptian henna they had remanufactured. She wore it short and spiked up like the punk girls of the late twentieth century.

In one ear there was a little earring. As she drew closer, Flayd could make out it was a tiny lion of gold. And he was looking at the earring to avoid her face.

Her eyes were large and clear. *Reborn* clear. Even in the past, at the age she had been, around twenty-one—which then was more like thirty-one—no eyes stayed as clear as that. Though she hadn't been able to read and so ruin them that way, there was the smoke of clay lamps and candles, of braziers, torches; the sun, the wind, the dust, the wine. But the color of these brilliant eyes, unmarked as a child's, was the weirdest pale blue-green.

Her other scars had grown back. The healing

process memorized them—only surgery and regrafting would take them away. But then, they were hers. Perhaps she wanted them, that ragged line along her arm, from the armpit almost to the elbow, that little wedge gouged out of the perfect honey of her left upper thigh, the cicatrize, amethyst like a flower, on her arching instep.

She stood and looked at her "visitors," glancing in each face, then lowering her eyes before it, respectfully.

These people were conceivably important, maybe rich—or why else were they here?—and she was only a slave.

Having glanced at them all, Flayd included, she gave a quick little half-bow, and he wanted to yell at her, tell her not to do that, not to them, to us, because we have played God with you, and if you had hold of your own destiny, that gladius in your hand would be forged iron, not wood, and you should be splitting us with it.

She looked like a boy, and for a boy she was, really, beautiful. But for a woman, she was something else. She was a lynx, a lioness, or a wolf.

Leonillo spoke then in cold flowing Latin. Flayd didn't follow a word, though he could read the language fine. But then Leonillo continued in modern Italian.

"Please greet your visitors, Jula. You're a special person. They're here to help us help you."

Jula raised her modestly lowered head once more, and oh, the utter indifference, the utter control in those seawater eyes. She had an accent. The strange rough brogue of ancient Roman Stagna Maris. And what she said:

"I greet my master's guests. I am my master's property."

INSIDE THE ROOM there was a small grim altar, and on it a winged figure with balance and axe, that Flayd believed to be Nemesis, Fate-as-Judge. She had an ugly face, neither Greek nor Roman—something older and more unkind. But the gladiators had worshipped her, and sometimes the other one, Temidis, the goddess of fame and riches through lucky chance.

Jula stood as a boy would, quite a confident youth, feet slightly apart, hands loose but not ungainly at her sides. Her head was raised, but she kept her eyes firmly on his upper lip, no higher.

She'd been a slave. No one had told her this no longer applied. But of course, it *did*, in the most perverse of ways.

When Leonillo had taken the others away, that prick Chossi caught Flayd in the passage and said, "Go back and have a talk with her. Why not. Leon says it's what you should do."

"Why's that?" Flayd had demanded.

"Always alert for conspiracy, Flayd? Leon says only you deserve to talk to her alone." But then Chossi leered. "You two match."

"What does that mean?"

"Red hair," fleered Chossi as he waddled away.

And Flayd was left, just left there, to go see her, alone, if he chose.

There would be full CX in every wall, every *brick*. He would be seen and monitored, as she would at all times. And there were a few others about, all of these ones dressed in Roman garments, carrying on the pretense of a provincial villa and a school for gladiators.

When he returned across the yard, he had stopped thinking. He stood at her doorway.

The curtain was pulled back, and she was sitting on a stool, adjusting one of her sandal straps neatly. The everyday action made his stomach lurch. Yes, for this moment it could have been 96 A.D. When he cleared his throat, she looked up, then stood.

"Don't bow," Flayd said. He spoke carefully in Italian. "Haven't they told you, you don't need to do that now. That's over."

But the clarity of her face was clear of all things, including any belief in him or what he said. And she would not meet his eyes.

Flayd said, not planning anything, "The emperor—that's Narmo, isn't it?"

"Yes," she said.

"He followed Domitianus—the last Flavian, the old man's bastard—put up by the Praetorian Guard, like Claudius, fifty odd years earlier."

She said nothing. It wasn't down to her to comment on the emperors, their succession, the doings of Rome—did she grasp how *long* ago?

"Were you ever in Rome?" Flayd asked.

"Yes."

"How long?"

"A few days. I was a child."

"Do you remember it, or have you only been told?"

She hesitated. He saw, her eyes being so clear, the thoughts swim through them before her inner shield once more came up. "I was told. Now, I think I do remember."

"How old were you then?"

"Three or four, so they said."

"Tell me about Rome. What you saw." The eyes, full on him a moment. He said to them, honestly, "I've never been there, your Rome. I'd really like to know."

She looked away and said, "There were very tall buildings. I didn't know how people could live in them, up so high. Wide streets, and narrow. And smoke. And noise. The cart bumped on the road, and I was sick.

There was a temple, high on a hill of temples. Everything there shone—marble columns, and other marble things, and the fires on the altars—but then we went down to a dark place below. The sky wasn't blue when we came up again, but amber—it was colored with evening, then the moon rose."

Flayd sat down, unthinking, on another stool in the corner, staring at her, *into* her, into her memory.

"There was a house where I was kept, with a garden in the middle. There were trees and a tame peacock. When it screamed I ran away. But I wasn't there so long. I went north with the others in the big wagon. We went by a river, the one they called Tiberinus. And then on a paved road . . ." She paused.

Flayd said softly, "The Cassian Way?"

"I don't know its name. There was open country after that, fields and woods. Olive groves. It was a long journey. I don't remember coming into the town at Aquilla. I think I was asleep."

She stood, eyes distant. Flayd collected himself, slowly. He had no suspicion this creature was not genuine. He had seen the filmic footage, and the verifications that none of that was tampered with. He had seen, like the others, enough of how she grew, behind the milky yet translucent wall of the tank. Seen her with the machines exercising her, feeding her. Seen the seconds when she woke and looked at the man beside her. Seen the panic in her eyes like torpedoes in water, and how her brain, only just awake, gripped the panic by the slack of its neck, leashing it in, because it served no purpose.

Jula had survived five years fighting in the stadium just outside the town of Stagna Maris, for the enjoyment of the soldiers at Aquilla Fort, the wealthy townspeople, and the rabble of the lower streets.

He too had a memory. It was of finding her tomb out there, in the deep green mud, all those years ago. Her victories—147 of them—were numbered proudly on it, with the remains of fine carvings of Minerva, Mars, and Venus, victory wreathes and the symbol of the Missio—the dismissal from the arena with honor, and on your feet; allowed to live even after surrender. Though she never had surrendered. The last fight, she had killed her opponent, a black warrior named Phaetho, but later she died of her wounds. (Although there had been, Leonillo had teasingly said, something else about that . . .)

In the tomb, when they water-sealed and opened it, along with the mostly burnt bones of Jula, were her jewels, her bracelets and earrings (one of which, reconstructed, she now wore) her secutor's helmet, shield and sword, and other weapons, rich garments belonging to her, priceless statuettes in gold and silver, glass cups and por-phyry lamps decorated with Mercurius-Anubis, Conductor of the Dead. The stone tablet read, JULA VIC-TRIX, FLAME-HAIRED JULA OF THE BLOOD OF FIRE. EVEN THE GODS, WHO GRANT GLORY, CANNOT HOLD BACK DEATH.

And here she was before him. *Standing* here. *Here*—and *now*.

Flayd got up again. He towered over her. The men and women of Roman times had rarely grown so very tall, and Flayd was tall for his own era.

"What do you know," he said, "about yourself? Do you know—where you've been?" It was an astounding affrontery—a fearful risk—he did not know how he could say it, yet couldn't keep it back.

But she said, very quietly, "They told me, I'd been dead."

"They *told* you. Christ, they did, they told you."

"I know it to be true," she said.

"You believed them—

"I went elsewhere," she said. "I've been gone a great time. Everything is altered now." She glanced about at the Roman room, with its painted walls, the courtyard beyond. She seemed thoughtful. "This is like no other place I recall."

Flayd grinned. He felt a fool. "They tried to make it *just* like the places you'd recall. How's it so different?"

"In every way. I can't explain. Like a copy—as a statue could be like a man—but not the man."

Flayd frowned. He swallowed and said, "You say you went elsewhere. Between then and now."

"Yes. I know that I did."

"That's the big question," he said. "*Where'd* you go?"

Jula Victrix turned her head completely, so he saw her profile, which was classical. They might have graced a Roman coin, the aquiline nose, the great eye, and intelligent forehead. Yet she had been from Gallia, a barbarian.

"I don't remember that. Only the things then, in the town, and after those—nothingness. And now, this."

Despite himself, Flayd felt some tidal surge sink through him, heavy and inert, cold as the mud had been about her grave. *Nothingness.* That then was where they all went down to, where all the dead went, all the ones you loved, or hated, where he too would follow in due season. It was what you suspected, despite the several sumptuous religions of the world, the marvels and miracles, supernatural rumors, the sweetness of the ideas. Despite even his lovely mother, Rose, with her long dark hair, who had died fearless, knowing exactly where she went, which, she believed, was to another sort of life.

The gladiatrix wasn't afraid of it either, however. She had been brought back from it, that nothingness. And anyway there was *nothing* to be afraid of—in *nothing*.

2

ON THAT DAY, WHEN HE WAS fourteen, that hot, gray winter day, he came back up to the apartment, and there she was.

He had expected to find his father. As he swung in the door, Picaro had called out the usual greeting—"Papa—I'm home—" for he still called his father that, "Papa."

And then there Papa was, by the open window that looked down on the teeming traffic (always that sound in these remembrances, that smell of Safe Ace Gasoline and geraniums). But Picaro's father was looking back into the room. At her.

The front room of the apartment was quite large, with cream-washed walls, beads and mats hung there. The neighboring cat, who visited from time to time, lay on the coolest spot of floor under the spice fern. But even the cat hadn't closed his eyes. He, like Picaro's father, looked only at her.

She filled that room. Not because she was big or fat. She was heavily built but shapely, blacker than the man, or the cat, black as Picaro. Her hair was short and tightly curled, and showed off her long smooth black neck, the angle of her jaw, which was like a carving of a princess from the east of the Africas. She had a gorgeous mouth.

But her eyes were flat and yellow, like those of some kind of animal.

As Picaro halted there, she turned and the animal irises shone at him. She said, "This is my son."

Her name was Simoon.

Picaro's father said, "Sure. He's your son. But how would you know?"

And then she turned her long neck and her yellow eyes fixed back on the grown man.

And Picaro saw that his father was afraid of her. Just as the cat was. So then Picaro too became afraid.

Later, much later, after she had gone, he said to his father, "She can't take me, can she?"

"Not legally," said Picaro's father.

"Why does she want me? She left me when I was a baby, didn't she?"

"No. Was me she left. She said you were mine, and you are. Now she's been spying, and she's seen you're not a baby any more but a human being. She's interested. She travels around. She'd take you with her—"

"I don't want to go with *her*!"

"No," his father said again. "I don't know what she wants. She be want anything. Things. Here is a bus ticket I sent for. Pack your bag and go get the bus over to your Aunt Ethella's. Don't argue. Do it. Before she comes back."

"She's a witch," whispered Picaro.

"She is. I never lied to you about that. I've seen her put *shadow* on a girl, some girl she was jealous of. That girl she gets no luck from that day on, till she goes to Simoon with all her own long hair cut off, and lays it at your mother's feet."

"Come with me," said Picaro. "Ethella will like that."

"I'll stay here," said Picaro's father. "I'll stay here and talk it through with Simoon."

The cat had slunk away out of the window. (Picaro never saw it again.) Picaro got the bus and rode across to Ethella's in the Red House District. And three weeks later, after he could never get through on the old-fashioned call-phone at the apartment, when he was going insane over that, and Ethella trying to cheer him, and saying to her man, "Get over there, you hear me, get over there and see to it—" and he saying "Not in a thousand years, baby. Not if *she* there with him—" and after this, then, the incoming call, Picaro's father telling him, "We settled it. Come home."

But when he got off the bus, went up in the lift, put his hand on the apartment door and it let him in; it was almost back to the first scene over again.

Only this time she was in the cane chair by the window, sitting there in a long, pale, cotton dress, shelling blue peas, singing to herself under her breath.

"Where is my father?"

"At the store," said Simoon.

She smiled. When she did that, he saw her mouth wasn't gorgeous, it was greedy. But he had never made a mistake about her eyes.

She cooked a meal, good food; it smelled marvelous if not as good as the things his father could make. There was a bottle of red wine on the table, and ice-cold cola for Picaro. But his father didn't come in.

"I'll go look for him," Picaro said.

All that while, he had sat by the wall, on the floor, watching her moving about, watching her glamorous giraffe's neck, the curve of her backside that would have moved him if she had been anything but his mother and an evil sorceress.

Now when he spoke, trying for ordinariness, she only said, "Fine. Your dinner will be spoiled. That's your affair." And she laughed. In one of her teeth was a blindingly green jewel, a peridot. His father had told him about that.

Picaro left the apartment. Hungry and thirsty, he hadn't wanted to take a bite or a sip of anything she had made, even touched. He ran through the hot sunless day, down to the store where his father worked, constructing lutes and sombas, sanding, polishing, twisting out the silvery strings on pegs of plastivory.

Picaro found his father, where the others had already found him. No police or medics had yet arrived, but they knew they must not move him. He was dead anyway. Just lying there, his quiet face shut, his eyes half open, not a mark on him.

So Picaro lay down by him and held his hand until the medics finally came through the deadly-ending traffic. And they had to strike Picaro to get him to let go.

An aneurysm, the autopsy established, (Ethella telling him, on the crackly line). It could happen. No prologue, no illness. Like a blow, not *on* the head but *inside* it—a breakage, and explosion of blood, and nothing visible to the layman's eye. Quick as a blink. He had not suffered.

Picaro didn't go back to the apartment, the "spoiled" supper, the expensive cola. Nor did he go back to his Aunt Ethella's. He had enough money in his pocket. He ran.

It was two more years before Simoon caught up to him.

"CAN'T YOU SLEEP, 'Caro? Let me do something to help you sleep."

Cora's silky flesh, her warm succulent mouth, wrapping about him in the dark.

After the things he had been thinking of, that other mouth, the mouth of a toad-goddess, devouring . . .

"No, Cora. Thanks. Not now."

In half-light, the flicker of canal reflections through the glass, her head lifting like a snake's.

Unresistant, she settled beside him again, and presently he heard the renewed rustle of her sleeper's breathing.

Outside the room, the music had ceased. India too must be alseep.

Picaro stayed gentle with women always. Simoon had schooled him in that, in how to see women, how to react to them, despite herself. How had she done that? Through his utter antipathy to and horror of *herself*. For she was only something *disguised* as a woman, and all the others, the real ones, elicited his gallantry, his tenderness, even in indifference, because of a kind of relief that he had met only one Simoon, and perhaps she was alone of her kind.

WHAT WOKE HIM MUCH LATER, were the vague, subtly intrusive, *external* sounds of movement and disturbance, which he had never heard before in any other part of the Palazzo Shaachen. He lay listening. There seemed to be a lot going on, furniture perhaps being automated up through the channels in the walls, and unloaded into chambers of the building. Once also a burst of shouting came outside, not from the canal but in the alleyway between this palace and the green one adjacent.

Cora was already up and in the Victorian bathroom, lying to her neck in bubbles. India was nowhere to be seen.

Picaro showered and dressed. (Cora did not speak to him, nor he to her. A sort of decorum.)

In another of the rooms he suddenly found India, drinking Masala tea, with cardamom, cinnamon, sugar, and black pepper, all of which she must have brought with her, since he had allocated only water to the recessed store cupboard. The CX point, to which she had attached the heating container, still glowed. He wasn't surprised when she next served herself a heap of spun eggs and rice.

She offered him nothing. The container dish—where had she concealed it on her person yesterday?—she simply left for the taking.

Then Cora came in and ate from the dish and drank some tea, and Picaro went to the Africara in another room, standing tuning the strings of the black-brown bull, thinking of his father tuning strings of lutes and sombas, until all at once he heard the two girls at the outer door, leaving, and the door quietly closed. Uniquely, they had gone without a single further avowal or demand.

Soon after, from below, far down in a lower apartment, he detected the faintest jangle, some keyboard instrument, and waited, again lifting his hand from the musical bull. He could turn the noise-conditioning up. He might have to, if he, or someone else, began to produce conflicting music. Or, maybe he might listen.

The instrument must have been taken manually into a room, too fragile, evidently, to travel all the way in the walls. An old instrument, then, a genuine Victorian piano, or even its ancestral harpsichord.

A harpsichord was normally the quiestest of keyboards . . .

All the other sounds had fallen still. In any case, he walked across and turned up the noise-conditioning.

Yet again, even so, (near noon) as if through layers of nothingness, Picaro momentarilly heard—or thought he did—the tuning of a keyboard far down in the brick-work of the house. And then he heard Cora's laughter, high and rippled, (like the sounds she made during sex) down where the harpsichord was, in that other room. Or only in the backrooms of his mind.

LEONILLO STOOD IN A CHURCH, gazing up at the votive paintings by the altar. They were rich in colors, and in gold leaf, delicious recxs from the 1500s, lit now by down-hanging lamps and tall night candles.

He tended to walk about by night, having nothing else to do when his duties were seen to. Of course, he was on call always. Usually, after his solitary perambulations over the bridges, through the alleys and inner streets of Venus, he returned to his bedroom at the University. He was still dressed as an upper clerk from 1906. His face was still a pallid nutshell.

The votive paintings had been offered, in their orig-inal form, the text informed one, to end a plague in Venus. How simple everything was then, Leonillo believed, God in His heaven issuing His decrees, need-ing only to intercede, or conversely let loose a thunder-bolt. It did not strike Leonillo that humanity had itself now fully taken over this role. Or that no votary on earth could stop *them*, probably, if the ecstatic energies of gods no longer prevailed.

3

"THEY CALLED IT LETHE, after the stream in the Greek and Roman hell, the stream men drank to forget, or to sleep."

It was morning now, and Flayd was across the desk, nodding. Flayd knew about Lethe. Souls due to return to earth had also drunk from the stream, to forget the spiritually constipating miseries of their previous earthly lives, and the pleasures of Hades, if there were any. Flayd wasn't sure, however, if he had ever heard of a mixture named after it.

"There was only a trace," said Leonillo. "But naturally it was analysed. That's what we think it was. So, our young woman didn't die of her fighter's wounds, as her tomb inscription tells us."

"She was poisoned."

"Almost definitely. I suppose it was in someone's interests to do it, to get at her owner, Libinius Julus, possibly, or just to assist one of the betting syndicates that existed, as you know, in every Romanized town."

Flayd thought, Yes, and it would be easy enough. House slaves or the slaves at Julus's school could always be bribed or forced. Simple to doctor some piece of food, or drop something in one particular cup.

"She'd lived too long," said Flayd bleakly, "she was too good."

"Very likely. You take it to heart, I see."

Flayd shrugged. "Sure I do. I helped dig her up."

"She's like a daughter to you? You were married once, I think, but no children . . . *Flayda* Victrix?"

Flayd pushed back his chair. He walked across the white and gilded Victorian office room, past the antique typewriting machine and the painted oil lamp, and stood glaring out at the Blessed Maria Canal.

"You think I'm an obsessive," said Flayd. "Right. I am. My work has always been real to me. And now here it is, practice fighting in a reconstruct courtyard, and reminiscing about Century Number One. What'ya expect? Is that why you've picked on me, my obsession?"

"*Picked* on you?" Leonillo raised two eyebrows up his nutshell forehead.

"For these speciality-plus privileges, walking and talking with the reborn baby."

"Something like that."

"I have other work, you know."

"Oh come. Please. More important, more *fascinating* than this?"

"Where's it leading?"

"That's what we have to see, don't we? Where it *can* lead. What we can do with it. How did she seem to you?"

Flayd said, "Rational. She remembers a lot. She remembers things she thought she'd forgotten when she was alive before," he added, ironically, scowling at Leonillo.

"That's not illogical. She's been given full access to her physical brain memory, in a way most of us never do, save under intense hypnosis."

"But anyhow, why ask me questions," said Flayd, "you watched it all, didn't you? My conversation with her, if you can call it that."

"Someone watched. What else? She is watched day and night."

"Anyhow," said Flayd, "I have some stuff to file." Once more the eyebrows. "Nothing to do with Jula. A twentieth-century burial in a backyard behind the old land-site of the Primo, when it was upstairs. A Mafia killing probably."

"Fine. When you're done, why don't you go down and see her again."

Already in the doorway Flayd checked. "You are kidding me, Leonillo."

"No, of course not. Just go to the elevator and touch in your prints, and it will take you down to the Roman Area."

"Why me? Why not the others? Or do the others all get to do it too?"

"Your colleagues have other duties. You see, Flayd, you react to her as if she is human. The others can't do that yet, if ever. And so for that reason we let them look and monitor and make notes. All of which have their uses. But you can forge for her a link with the outer environment. The here and now."

"Can't *you*?"

"*I*?" said Leonillo. He became utterly blank. The expression *clean white sheet* sprang to Flayd's mind.

"OK," said Flayd. "If I can make the time."

And Leonillo smiled, at Flayd's lying absurdity.

As he worked at the CX in his cubicle, Flayd's mind rummaged, trying to duck the flashes of recollection. But it was in vain. In the end he sat back in the plasform chair and *thought*. Of swimming through the dimness of the mud, of the lights finding the tomb. Of the heap of treasures, the mummified victory wreathes with fragments of broken gilt on them, the Anubis lamps, the rings. And the bones. Burnt on a funeral pyre but not entirely consumed, as the organic material, then, seldom was.

He thought of the rotted, splintered, scarlet shield with the face of Venus. The rusted sword.

And then he thought of the girl he had talked to, in the basement of the dome, so far down and away from anything genuine, and yet presumably taken by her for reality.

She had come back from nothing.

Maybe, given that, the rest of this was irrelevant. Finally he walked along the corridor, where UAS security glanced up and nodded, friendly. The videcx in the walls were clicking away, without a murmur, and the elevator came and he touched in, and the doors opened.

She was fighting in her gear today, greave, arm-protection, the closed helmet like a collared silver bullet.

He watched her a while from the colonnade.

Flayd could see why she had won so many fights and it had taken deadly poison to stop her.

Oddly, looking at her too, Flayd found himself wondering almost for the first time about the other one, the musician they had also brought back. He hadn't been shown to Flayd, though some of the others had seen him. Cloudio del Nero was also doing well, it seemed, in his reconstruct living space.

Had *Picaro* been taken to see him? From what had originally been said, that had seemed to be the plan. In del Nero's case, Picaro, the bloodline descendant, was to be the forging "link"?

The practice fight was over and Jula had triumphed. Flayd stood a second or so more in the fake shade of the columns. Then he turned and went away. It wasn't the manipulation by authority that bugged him—

that was always there, in anybody's life, even if unseen and ignored. No, it was simply what had been done. What it meant and might mean, in the ever-extraordinary future. But who could predict?

4

SIMOON STOOD ON the island.

She had come up out of the water, like before, except this time not even needing a boat.

She wore her own pale dress, but he knew her now. She was the sulphurous sibyl from the cave.

"You'll die," she said. "I told you that."

"You told me. I'll die."

Her eyes were sulphur-colored too.

"You will meet your death at thirty."

"You told me."

"Believe me yet?"

"Yes. I believe you. I always believed you. After you killed my father. After you came back in my life. After the other things."

"Die under water," said Simoon, "though not from drowning."

"Yes, you bitch. I *know*. Why else could I be here? Why else am I waiting here?"

"Scared?" He saw her amusement, the sibyl's.

"Are you still alive?" he asked her. "I thought I saw to that."

"Maybe I am. Somewhere."

Up in the starless sky, there was a shooting star, pale topaz fire ripping through the dark.

"No." he said, "you're nowhere. You never were anywhere. Your kind—don't exist."

HE THOUGHT THE TWO GIRLS were back, poised outside the apartment's main door. Not knocking, or making any sound, merely calling to him with their female minds, like cats waiting to be fed.

Picaro left the bed and walked through the rooms, his bare feet on the still-warm floor. He would tell them to go away. Probably.

But he wasn't awake. He knew this. No longer unconscious or dreaming, but not fully back into the living world, or his body. He felt he levitated by a few inches, in the air, despite the contact with that warm floor.

The door opened over-easily.

The man stood less than two meters away. In the darkness, his pale skin was ghostly.

"Light," Picaro said, and the CX flashed on, hard and too brilliant, illuminating the face, the figure, and clothing, of an intimately known stranger.

Picaro was now back in his body. He said, "Are you here, or is this some virtuality projection?"

Cloudio del Nero smiled his charming, long-ago smile. It wasn't, any longer, like Picaro's. "I think it is myself."

"How?"

"How? How am I here? I was brought here earlier."

"No. There was no canal traffic, no one walked by." Picaro thought of the sounds below in the palazzo, the shouts in the alley, and the sprayed notes of a harpsichord. He said again, "So how?"

"Through passages under the City," said del Nero idly. "There have always been hidden ways of that nature."

"But this isn't—" Picaro halted. He wondered how much they had told del Nero. Picaro said, "This isn't the City as you knew it."

And del Nero shrugged the primrose brocade shoulders of his exquisite coat. "The passages persist. That was the route by which I was brought here. They call this Palazzo Shaachen? I believe I have the apartment below your own."

Picaro stood there.

"May I enter your rooms?" del Nero said. "Or do I disturb you?"

"It's the middle of the night," said Picaro.

"True," the other said mildly. "The Prima Vigile was just rung from those churches which continue to effect it."

Picaro stood back. As the living phantom walked past him into the vestibule, there came the flicker of something down the hall. Oh yes, someone would be near and watching. Picaro turned his back on that, shut the door. Shut del Nero and himself into the apartment, where, as Flayd would have been quick to assert, surveillance would still be going on.

Picaro touched the wall for the lamps, which lit up softly, even the oriental globe which hung from the ceiling. Cloudio del Nero glanced at it, no more than that. Presumably they had got him accustomed to some modern innovations.

He seemed taller than Picaro remembered. His eyes had a curious film across them, a type of luminous sheen—or it was a trick of the darkness and unreal light. Picaro had anyway been glad of the film. He hadn't forgotten what he had seen inside those eyes on the last occasion—that vacant abyss of Nothingness.

Strolling, glancing about him, del Nero had reached the room with the long window and the balcony. He went to this, and stood looking out. Maybe everything looked—as it was intended to—exactly like the eighteenth century venues del Nero recalled. Or maybe subtle, nearly incomprehensible details and flaws screamed out to del Nero alone that this was *not* the past, but some other land, some nightmare.

"How silent this world is."

This world. Indeed it seemed he knew it all.

"It was noisier when you were here last?"

"Much. But of course there's something in the walls and the glass, so they tell me, to absorb external noises."

"Yes."

"I should like wine," del Nero said, aristocrat still.

"No wine," said Picaro. "Only water."

"I think you'll find," said del Nero gently, "there is some wine."

Picaro went to the cabinet. There were three bottles, old black bottles, with sealed tops. Uninvited, someone had been in to augment Picaro's stores—unless Cora and India had brought the wine. Picaro thought the first scenario the more likely.

He uncorked one of the bottles, poured the red blood of the wine into a glass. The cabinet had correctly kept the wine room temperature, as it kept other things cool.

"Thank you," del Nero said. "You're not drinking?"

"Right. I'm not."

Unphased, (of course) the aristocrat, (son of a ducca) walked across to the Africara.

"What a wonderful instrument. You play this?"

"Yes."

"How do you name it?" Picaro told him. "But forgive me, I remember, you don't wish to discuss your calling. May I try my hand at this Africara?"

Picaro said, "I don't let that happen."

"I understand."

Picaro felt a sluice of indifference wash down him. What did it matter any more if some other—this fucking undead returnee—laid hands on the Africara? Nothing mattered. For *Nothing* reigned absolute.

"Go ahead," Picaro said.

"I may? You're gracious."

Picaro watched him, jealous yet remote. Angry. But not only at, or in, this moment. The angers of several years. And the inertia of them.

Would del Nero know how to begin even, on this black bull—a music making creature so utterly unlike anything that had existed in Europe in 1700. But yes, it seemed he knew—instinctively?—and now he put his ringed slender hands on the instrument, as if on the body of a woman Picaro had once cared for as much as his own life.

A jagged spill of notes.

The hair rose along Picaro's neck and scalp. His hands were iron fists. He felt, despite everything, a nauseous boiling rage.

And then, from the Africara—a music like a smoke, soft, half-born, uncoiling through the air. Like wings, like thoughts—almost a silence, almost far away across the sky—a music of something that had no place here, let alone there, where any eighteenth-century musician had been. A music that belonged high over any city.

All that.

More than that.

Astounded by horror, Picaro thought he had never heard its voice before, the Africara. But no, this was *not* its voice—this was . . .

The music stopped.

Picaro felt the room turn under him, as if he stood on some ancient canal flooding from a tidal sea.

His hands were no longer knotted into fists. His belly was cold. A dry electric tingling lay over the surface of his skin, which settled only slowly.

"You have been very generous," said del Nero, "Signore Picaro. That means *magpie*, I think. From the Latin?"

Picaro—no words would come. He cleared his throat.

And del Nero crossed to him and handed him the goblet of wine, still half full.

And Picaro drank a mouthful of the wine.

Cloudio del Nero said, "I must leave you in peace. Good night, signore."

Picaro stayed where he was, holding the goblet, seeing del Nero in another dimension walk away through the rooms. Hearing him at the outer door, and the door undone, and in the passageway a murmur, (as the minder stirred) and then the door shut. And the glass fell out of Picaro's hand.

He saw it fall, catching a sparkle of light; a meteor, and knew it wouldn't break, glasses didn't break here, and then it hit the terracotta, and it smashed into a hundred broken stars.

ALL NIGHT AFTER THAT, he dreamed of falling.

Next morning, it was Cora who woke him, knocking on the door.

She was alone, and laughing, in a sky-blue gown from the 1700s, her hair ornately dressed.

"We're going out on the canals." When he didn't respond, she explained, "to see the City. The UAS man is taking us." He waited. She added, "And Cloudio. And you."

"Not me."

There was a little beauty mark, a tiny spangle, pasted on her left cheekbone. Her lips were rouged like strawberries.

"You must come, Magpie. Please come. It won't be any fun without you.

"Sorry."

"But he says you must."

"*Who* says that?"

"Leon."

"Who's that? One of the UAS?"

"He's from the project. I mean, something to do with Cloudio. We met Cloudio. He lives downstairs."

"Do you know," said Picaro, "who Cloudio is?"

She laughed still. He sensed she had spent the night at a party, where there had been some very strong legal highs available—hasca, something like that.

She answered, "No, Cloudio is . . . Cloudio. I like Cloudio. But it's you I love."

"That's nice of you, thank you. Have a good time in the City."

As he started to close the door on her, it stuck.

There was CX, and the door could not ever stick. Unless, evidently, the CX *made* it do just that.

He recollected Flayd, managing to open the palazzo's main door. Some overriding key from the University . . . No doubt he could have done the same with this door, only hadn't had the gall. The University Auxilary Staff seemed to be running things. Everything. All in the cause of their project, their experiment.

Cora, apparently not realizing the door had stuck, thinking he'd had a change of heart, reached through and caught his hand. She kissed it. "I loved our night."

He took his hand from hers and went back into the

apartment and Cora followed him, because she thought she was invited to do so by the unclosed door.

In the room with the oriental lamp, she offered one of her surprises. She leapt at the lamp chain, gripped it, swung through space, let go and spun away, turning a somersault in the air before her perfect landing at the bedroom door.

Picaro pulled her into the bedroom, sat her on the bed. She threw herself back and lay smiling from the pillows up at him.

"Listen Cora, they're playing games."

"Who, most darling? Shall *we*? Let's play games—"

"Where's your friend India?" he asked.

Cora, enpillowed, shrugged her milk-white shoulders. He thought of del Nero, also shrugging. Shrug everything off that troubled you or might impede the progress of your desires.

"Cloudio," said Cora. She kicked her legs. "Cloudio, Picaro, and Cora."

Picaro could hear someone outside, in his private apartment. He went back out of the room, and saw a woman (also young and smiling) putting wine bottles into the recessed cabinet. "'Viorno, sin," she said.

The anger returned, but it was miles away. Picaro could feel it trampling through him, its hoofs echoing.

When it ended, he felt he didn't care, either. Not now. Nothing could be done, it was all out of his hands, so why kick at *this*?

In the closet he found a suit of clothes from the eighteenth century. Someone else had been in—when? —all this burglary in reverse—and left them. He took them out, carried them on to the balcony, and flung them over into the canal. He wasn't angry any more, it was simply practical.

Cora, bemused finally, stood gazing after them. But he had no intention of telling her that, in 1701, if he, a black man, had worn them, they would have been the livery of a slave.

He dressed anyway, as always, and when that was done, and he had drunk water from a fluted glass, he went out of the door, which no longer stuck.

They were waiting below in the house vestibule, three UAS that he did not recognize, another girl (also UAS) in renaissance clothes and pearled hair, and Cloudio, standing there like a tall, calm child about to be taken on an outing.

Cora darted over to Cloudio. He caught her hand, lowered his head to it and kissed the fingers. The companion gesture to Cora's with Picaro—which had been rejected. Cloudio gave Cora his arm. His eyes had the same phosphorescent-looking film on them Picaro had imagined there last night—did he only *imagine* it now?

Picaro stared at Cloudio and found that he had moved himself towards this revenant. Moved close in, Picaro looked into Cloudio's face, at those eyes that seemed to have changed, and to be changing, as if he had come up from the lagoon, with nacre hardening on the irises and pupils.

What do I see? You, Simoon—you're the sibyl—tell me what I see.

And back in his head he made out his mother's drowsy laughter, not a bit like Cora's.

Your appointment.

But one of the UAS, (not the others, Chossi, or the one dressed 1906—Leon?) was shaking Picaro's hand too vigorously. The UAS woman was fluttering them all firmly out of the building, and on the canal waited a canopied boat with velvet seating, poled by three oarsmen.

5

THERE WAS A LIGHT MIST that morning, which smoothed the water and the buildings with melted pearl. In the mist perished the last traces of a lingering false dawn. The City was dreamlike, and in its dreaminess more convincingly real than ever. So it must have looked uncountable mornings in the past, when it was fully actual and stood above the sea. Truth and Time had been an antique allegory of this place, depicted over and over in sculpture and painting. But the facsimile had become Truth, and Time had stopped. And through the resulting legacy, the boat slid like a stiletto.

As Venus woke (it was very early, not yet seven) images, sudden views, mobile tableaux containing moving human beings, leapt against Picaro's eyes. He saw them with an abnormal acuity, as if to make up for lost visual opportunities: heaps of golden oranges and apricots on stalls along the banks; green melons on a pale violet wall of some shadow palace, gothic, with thin, pointed arches; traceried balconies that seemed made of lace; hanging lanterns, catching the lit sky. Flotillas of masonry came always drifting towards them. The dagger of boat slit purely through. Under arcades that had been raised (once) in the 1300s, under the galleries of renaissance palazzos. Churches of marble and domes covered in silver foil floated on thin lines of light. Tenements towered up on rotting green stems which could never, now, rot, and unfurled a bunting of colored washing between the wisteria.

Fishing boats passed them on the surface of the lagoon. The sailors hailed each other through the mist, coral sails rigged as if on bent bows. In a great open space before the church of Maria Domina (an indigo box decorated with Byzantine goldwork from the ancient East), a puppet-show had begun. Figures danced on their little stage, from the Skilful Comedy. They looked living and animate, as the entranced crowd perhaps no longer did.

Picaro saw . . . glimpses of streets funneling through the blocks of houses, salad-green gardens that spilled over walls. Every alley, every canal, had its pet Virgin Maria, or its guarding Neptune. And the banners among the roofs were mingling with spires and conical chimney pots, flags painted with the City's Zodians, the Fishes, the Scorpion, the Crab.

All this, Picaro saw, just as he heard the soundtrack of the City, its harmony and discords.

Otherwise, in their boat, no one spoke, or hardly at all. Dividing the silk water between the banks of brickwork, stone and mist, they might have been sailing down the Styx, astonished and agog at the sights of the underworld. And Picaro thought that now Venus was, after all, a kind of Hades, for she lay under the sea, as the Greek and Roman hell had lain under the earth.

Del Nero was seated across from Picaro.

Now and then, against his own will, Picaro looked at him. And then, Picaro saw this: the City reflected in the looking-glass eyes of the great musician. And could not see, any more, *into* the eyes.

Only now and then some little murmur from the UAS people. Was everyone comfortable? (Incredible notion.) Would they care for this or that? (Yes, children taken on an outing, spoiled kids who might have anything they wanted.) Cora liking to go over to a bakery, and sweet cakes being handed down, still hot and sticky—even Cloudio taking a bite, another, smiling—and later there were almonds dipped in caramel.

In backwaters, where the shade of palaces dropped ink-purple in the wafered jade of the canals, noticing the phantoms of people behind thick-eyed windows, or white hands opening a pair of crimson shutters bright as wings.

Sometimes Picaro thought he should speak after all, though not to was so restful—to give in, to accept—restful. But besides he couldn't be bothered, hadn't the energy, lulled and mesmerized by all of this, reflecting in the water and in the eyes of a dead man who was alive.

So the morning became late, and became noon, and they left the boat, walked across the Primo Square, ate a meal in the Greek Room of Phiarello's, (where a table had been booked) under the murals of nymphs. It was food partly from the 1700s. There were pancakes, dumplings, no potatoes, and dishes of chocolated fruits. They drank an old red wine, then champagne. All of them drank this, including the four UAS. They were such a happy little party, Cora bubbling away, flirting with everyone, the UAS woman—Jenefra?—telling some story, as if she were only another careless member of their kind, something about her studies and misfortunes in some other city, when she was sixteen. (See, I was sixteen once, and made mistakes. just like you were and have.)

What did the dead man say.

Had he said anything?

His slender hands, almost feminine, yet steely strong, delicate on the fine frosted glasses, the napery. You couldn't see through his hands. But then, you couldn't see through his eyes. There was nothing in his eyes. That was, Nothing. And the Nothing had soaked outward, forming a sort of phosphorescent shine. And so you saw that.

A Victorian brass band was playing in the square after lunch.

"I love Picaro's music," said Cora.

"Oh yes," said one of the UAS men, "the Africarium —I've always admired that—"

Picaro heard them as if from beyond an egg of glass, a *dome* with which he had surrounded himself.

Why was that?

Neurasthenia perhaps.

Or the wine. Or something, something . . .

After the sociable meal they went, the happy party, to see the reconstructed Rivoalto, no longer really islanded. They rode in their boat under the Bridge of Lies, and cried out lying things, (had Picaro too? Del Nero?) and Cora cried out, "I *hate* Picaro—loathe his music!" And laughed. And beyond the Liar's Bridge, other bridges, bridge on bridge, reflections again, of each, and each also making a perfect circle with its canal self, until the boat shattered them all in fragments. The mist was gone. The City was vibrant, no longer pearl, hard-cut opal.

In the afternoon, the Palace of the Ducemae lifted its patterned walls for their inspection, its pillars ending upward in keylike traceries. It had courtyards like books of gold and gardens full of singing birds. Was del Nero to be taken to visit the palace? He had been there, presumably, off and on, when he lived. But they didn't pause. Instead, there was another palace they went to, with a ceiling ten meters high. In its center a void of sunny sky (painted) filled by winged figures, in turn surrounded by painted statuary and painted mauve vases of flowers. A chandelier hung down, every prism coiled by flowers of stained glass. Beneath that there were little colored-in creatures of plaster, hares and ducks, parrots and tortoises. They too looked real, like the painted sculpture, the flowers. Venus then had always been this way. Venus, who showed Time and Truth fondling each other, an old man and a lush young woman—which perhaps made Truth a whore after all. Venus, which had paintings of the goddess Venus herself, holding up her mirror. Venus, which displayed the Apocryphal Lion of the City, in cream stone, lying down, and upright, and high among the roofs on backdrops of Heaven—blue and sunburst stars and wheels of the Zodiac, or else presented the Lion with a sword in one paw, declaring on the carved banner that uncoiled from its lips: BEHOLD ME, THE MIGHTY LION NAMED MARCUS. WHOEVER RESISTS ME I WILL BRING LOW. And in the Setapassa—the market of silks— was a column stolen from Egypt, crowned by a black basalt sphinx, and nearby another one, dredged up from the lagoons, crowned by a sphinx that was white.

Picaro found himself then standing with Cloudio del Nero in the late afternoon, under the flaming gold dome inside the Primo.

They stood side by side, gazing up, and the four UAS were far off, and Cora had gone with them. How had they got here, Picaro and del Nero? As if a *scene* had been *changed*—even time—for hadn't they come here this morning?

The basilica was filled by people, but also by carvings, by *painted* crowds. By columns of marble and porphyry and serpentine, inlay of alabaster, sardonic agate and jaspers looted from the East. Christ stood among seven flames to open the seven seals of world destruction, against mosaics of goldleaf in molten vitreous—and a jeweled vine that represented his own Mystery. While below circled four colored horses.

Elsewhere, KARITAS read the inlaid words, (Love) and SPES (Hope) and MISERICORDIA (Mercy). As if these things existed. But they were in Venus, City of Stopped Time and Truth-the-Whore, who stole and lied and brought low—and here anyway rode the Horsemen of the Apocalypse.

"This is a city of the damned," softly said Picaro, taken aback to hear himself talk, and by what he said.

"Always it was," said the other. The other one, who had been dead.

"So, tell me about damnation," Picaro said.

Up there, Christ, a beautiful white man, Lord of Kindness, unleashing the last annihilation on mankind. (The horses seemed to move.)

Del Nero now didn't speak.

Picaro said, "How do you feel about it, what's been done to you?"

And then he found too he no longer looked at the Christ but at Cloudio del Nero, and the musician looked back at him, and there was a dazzle on his eyes now, so Picaro could not keep his own eyes on them. He reached out, the dead man, and placed his hand gently on Picaro's shoulder.

The touch felt at first warm, and then, abruptly, scalding hot. Picaro did not flinch aside or shove him off. He waited there, thinking about the weightless fiery pressure of the hand.

"Soon there'll be no more to say," said del Nero. His voice was not as it had been. Its *music* was different. Picaro was unsure how or in what way.

"Do you remember?" Picaro said, "anything? *Anything?*"

The hand on his shoulder was now so hot it burned him like frostbite.

Cloudio said, "I am beginning to remember. Inside my mind, it was like the mist this morning. But it begins to clear."

Then the hand lifted from him and a pain went through Picaro's arm, all of it, across his chest, seeming to hit his heart. And then that vanished, there was no pain, no heat or cold. Picaro found that he stared upward again, into the dome, reading over and over a line of Latin he could not understand.

And the UAS woman was there, and she was saying something about the way the westering sunlight (that was what she said, "the westering sunlight") slanted across into the Primo, and the whole structure looked as if it might suddenly fly upwards on the wings of an angel.

Picaro thought, *He* does this. He makes us high as kites. Do they know *they* are now part of their own experiment?

But Cora was there then too, taking Picaro's hand.

It seemed there was to be another treat for the happy party. Drinks somewhere in the City, and then back to the Palazzo Shaachen. An informal concert—just between friends, for they were all friends, and it had been a lovely summer's day, and sunset was still before them.

AND THE SUNSET WAS, of course, spectacular. Picaro watched it from his balcony, the whole sky in flames beyond and above the City. He watched the wanderers arriving too, five or six of them, along the Alchimia

Canal, each with about five occupants. Who got out wearing the bright festive clothes of many eras, and streamed in at the door of the Shaachen Palace. Going to the party downstairs.

Wasn't he tempted? Cora had asked him that, persuasive, adorable Cora, sweeter than almonds dipped in caramel.

But he had detached himself relatively easily from the University people—they were high enough, they didn't seem to bother now if this one subject of their study escaped them for a time. And Cora alone could not make him go.

"But it will be wonderful. He'll play for us—he'll play that old song Jenefra said "made a sensation *then*." (Jenefra—the UAS woman.) "And—he's been working on something new. And what they say he is—is he truly? Oh Picaro, aren't you interested?"

"I'm tired."

She did not accuse him of envy. Perhaps, being Cora, she didn't even think of that. But she was sorry he would not go downstairs to the party in the apartment of Signorissimo Cloudio.

Probably, in any other season, she would herself have preferred to stay with him. Maybe if he had asked her, but he didn't want her with him, that was the difficulty. Then again, some chemical sorcery was in progress. Having got away from it, Picaro viewed del Nero's attractiveness with distaste. It was more than history, more than charisma, or pheromones. What it was Picaro did not care. He wanted only to avoid it, for it had rendered him entranced, a prisoner, in a way only one other creature had ever done.

But even Cloudio wasn't like her. No one ever was.

When the sun had gone, and no more wanderers

appeared along the waterway, Picaro shut the windows. He turned up the air-conditioning, and the noise-conditioning, though already scarcely any external sound could get in.

The apartment cupboard was filled (by others) to bursting with foods, snacks, wines, aperitifs, and liqeurs. He should ask Flayd over, get Flayd to eat and drink all this.

Picaro drank water until his body seemed to him semi-transparent, just one more of the black, Venusian drinking vessels.

Outside, yellow lamplight fell like chrysanthemums on the canal.

PICARO DREAMED OF A LINE of Latin floating on gold: *Albus adest primo* . . . and then, knowing that he dreamed, that the harpsichord stood in one of his rooms. It was playing by itself, a ripple of notes too quiet to be heard, yet each note tapped in along his bones, and he became the keyboard.

He wanted it to stop.

How to stop it?

He had to get up, go out, violently slam down the lid of the harpsichord, which would be a priceless actuality, not a recx or reconstruct.

Dreaming and asleep, Picaro left the bed and walked out into the room, which had become far larger. The black cupboard with the skull was here, and he saw that first, the yellowish mask balanced up on its black perch and clung with shadow—a tall emblem of Death.

In the dark floor swirled watery reflections. The harpsichord vibrated. The melody was curious, unlike anything ever heard. But it scraped against his viscera, the inside of his brain. It made him nauseous.

He walked forward and the floor gave way and he plunged through into something bottomless and whirling—

And woke, shouting out.

Picaro turned, groaning, on the bed. As he did so, he heard the music in the outer room, *heard* it, strings not the keys of the harpsichord, and a rift of gray sickness opened inside his guts.

He swung off the bed. As he stumbled forward he saw, in the outer room, the Africara, its strings trembling, *sounding*, not in melody but at some weird disturbance of the air, which also he felt in the soles of his feet and the length of his spine. Then he was kneeling blind and deaf by the toilet bowl, vomiting, vomiting, choking and vomiting more, his whole body trying to turn itself inside out and expel him, with the sickness, into the void.

6

AND THE MORNING LIGHT made a noise, tinkling and smashing all over the bloody floor. But worse than that, the moronic knocking, thumping, the banging of a door, voices calling, feet heavy as the tramp of a mob—

Angry with it. This shaking, this fucking smell, like iodine.

The man he hit on the side of his face skidded backward and crashed against a wall.

"Now—softly, sin. Sin Picaro—can you hear me? Yes, he couldn't have struck you so hard, Chossi, if he were too bad. Can you sit up? Good, *good*, Picaro—"

He was standing.

He thought of standing in the Primo, staring up into its vaulted upside-down golden cup. His head rang, then cleared, abrupt, as if a shackle of stars had dropped away.

"What is it?"

They had broken in, through the door. That didn't make sense. Aside from Picaro, they and they alone could undo the door, or even CX-block it. What had gone wrong with the door that it required breaking? And the window—all the windows were shattered—why had they done that?

"Get dressed if you would, Picaro."

Picaro glanced at him. It was the 1906 man, the one called Leon, or Leonillo. And it was Chossi with a bruised cheek and bleeding nose.

Picaro didn't move. Not yet. He was enjoying, (strangely?) the feeling of easement—no sickness now, no writhing like a snake through his muscles and intestines. Room quite steady.

"Something happened," he said.

Leonillo said reasonably, "I'm afraid there's been a problem with the air and drainage circuits in this building. You've been throwing up? Passed out—yes. Poisonous fumes, something CX usually tackles, but this one failed. It should never occur, they tell us, indome."

"The dome is a hundred percent safe," said Picaro. "A wanderlier told me."

"The *dome* is fine. Just this one unlucky building. Get dressed, please. We want you out of here as soon as we can manage, and into medical observation."

Picaro saw some of the men had on protective visors. Leonillo did not, but kept taking a reading from his wristecx. Noting Picaro's scrutiny, Leonillo added, "All CX has been turned off here, and the whole structure flooded independently with clean air. Even so, we'll get going, shall we."

Picaro dressed.

They waited, the five men in the apartment, then went out with him. In the corridor were others. Below there came the sound of hurrying footsteps, noises reminiscent of the lugging of heavy crates, and voices buzzed, busy as a hive. And there was the whine of the flushing air, oxygenated and over-rich, going to the head like wine.

Outside his room, Picaro realized he had not seen the Africara. Had they also brought it out, another casualty? But he didn't care about it. It was no longer his.

Then he started to recall, as if after a year, long ago, the Happy Party in the lower apartment, the chrysanthemum lamps and the song. All those people. Cora.

Picaro grabbed Chossi's arm. Chossi, stuffing gauze up his leaking nose, thrust him off. Another man pulled Picaro aside.

"What about the others?" Picaro said. He felt nothing, wondered why he had asked.

The man said, "We don't go that way."

Picaro took hold of the man and flung him somewhere and there was yelling and cursing; it was funny, like the puppet theater (yesterday?) when the Commedia had been more lifelike than its audience.

Picaro ran. He jumped one by one the three narrow flights of stairs downward, veered into the secondary passageway that would lead him to the other apartment, the one they had given Cloudio del Nero.

The passage was clotted up by people. Picaro moved them out of his way and they careered back swearing. Then a man had a flecx automatic pressed into Picaro's ribs. Picaro took no notice.

He had halted at the second open, smashed-in doorway, ejected CX spangles littered winking under his feet.

Chossi spoke, as if through a terrible headcold. "Let him see, the bastard. If he wants."

The pressure of the flecx lifted out of Picaro's back.

He walked forward slowly, considering idly why he did this, what he was doing. What was the point of it?

There were men and women all over the room, and through doorways in other rooms, stranded on the wide red floor, all dressed up in glamorous costumes, from the junctures of five centuries. Also there was vomit, and there was blood. Even the red floors did not hide very much.

He looked down into their upturned faces, which stared back at him, eyelids burst open like the doors, as if from the bottom of the lagoon.

Their positions varied slightly. Where the blood had come from them—their mouths, ears, nostrils, other parts of their bodies—also varied. But their eyes were all the same. Surprised—was it that? A question—that was what was in their eyes—was it?

Otherwise the faces were blank as the most obscure, flat carnival masks.

Cloudio was not among the people lying there. Cora was. She lay across a dainty gilded chair. She alone looked still nearly happy, yet also impendingly sad. As if she saw all at once the party had come to an end. She had not bled, she hadn't been sick. Only her slim right hand, curled deftly about the stem of a cracked goblet, seemed to have been snapped at the wrist, doubtless when she collapsed, and was, doll-like, lying back-to-front.

PART THREE

Actors and Spirits

1

IT WAS BREATHTAKINGLY obvious something was amiss. Something had happened they hadn't anticipated. And their shifty, bland exteriors nearly amused Flayd, even as he tensely stood there in reception, watching how they changed when they came through and changed again, a second or so too quickly, as they hurried out.

"Yes, Sin Flayd. Please go along to the elevators, as you wish."

So his bizarre clearance at least hadn't altered. He was still permitted access. Something loosened a little inside him then. For whatever the panic was, it did not seem to involve her.

He tried again, almost lightheartedly now, with the security people along the corridor, of whom, today, there were only two.

"Keeping you busy."

"Yes," they agreed.

"What's cooking?"

"Excuse me?"

"You seem to have a kind of a flap on."

"Not at all."

Ah. Then he'd *imagined* the flurry, the running forms in the distance, the agitated sound of calls coming in, one on another, and once or twice a voice raised, sounding scared and too shrill.

Out on the canals there had been some traffic diversions, too. CX notices gleaming in the walls reassured the City that a small drainage section had somehow been damaged, there was a little minor flooding, under control naturally, and everything would be normal by 14 vv. But the wanderlier sucked his lip, shook his head. "Never before, signore, in my experience. We're clean here. What are things coming to?"

Then, as Flayd drew closer to the University Building, in the slow-as-treacle wanderer, he spotted a thinly disguised emergency crew, the kind he hadn't *ever* seen in action *inside* Venus's dome, packing itself on one of the few motorized boats. UAS? He couldn't be sure.

But what in hell had gone awry? The alarm he felt had driven Flayd into the University fast, and down to Leonillo's quaint office—vacant and inaccessible—and so finally towards the girl, his "gladiatrix"—and: no, no, Sin Flayd. Everything is fine. I will just check for you, whether you can ride straight down. And in the background, someone shouting, "*Close* the area off! Do you hear? Keep that area *closed!*"

It was a small toxic flood. That was all. Happened every hour somewhere or other up top. He was paranoid, he knew that. It had no bearing on any of *this*. On her.

The elevator reached the Roman level, and Flayd got out.

He halted, astounded.

The place had altered.

It looked—medieval, perhaps, or like something from the Age they still called Dark. Yawning pale blanks of walls, squat pillars, some lingering Roman elements, leftovers. They were bringing her up to date?

Flayd strode through the recx movie set and found a lawn where the courtyard had been. All this was more a sort of cloister now, a sheet of apparently scythed turf, with little flowers, and a basil flowering white in a tub. No more Samian pot.

Then he got the other shock. A woman came out between the pillars across the way, dressed in a dark ruby-red dress of around the 1490s, high-waisted, with heavy embroidery. There was a gold net over her hair, which was ruby like the dress, and short. She had gold lion earrings.

"Jula—"

She raised her eyes. Lowered them to his upper lip. That at least, goddamn it, hadn't altered.

WHAT HAD IT EVER BEEN for her but the life of a slave, where nothing at all was in her power, nor ever could be, where chaos was everywhere about her, her only *constant* being discontinuity. Her childhood had been severed, and never resumed. She was brought to Italy, to Rome, then north to the Roman town behind the sea lagoons, where the Eagles' Castellum stood, and the amphitheater. She was taught to be what she was intended to be, a clever animal that fought. She was offered the hope of survival through fighting. And about this rigid post the plant of her existence twined. The only say she had in anything was her right to try to live. Not everyone had even that.

So, waking under the blue ceiling, the man asking her in his peculiar Latin if she could say her own name, and finding she could not speak—or move—a state which had persisted several days—Jula was deeply afraid. But, she knew fear well. There had always been fear. It was the spur to endurance. A friend.

And this—this now? This place, the villa or school that looked so awkward and strange—these persons in their extraordinary garments—she was nearly indifferent. Her earliest memories had been of places incredible and architecture unrecognizable, and people in outlandish garb who could or would not speak her tongue, so she had to learn theirs, and learn it under beatings. She had immediately and always to do what they wanted. She was their property. And this, *now*, therefore—was precisely the same.

Thus she knew it all. She had died. They told her— she had realized before that. She knew of death—had never thought of it as an end of *being*, only another meta-morphosis. And then, reborn into physical life again, it was to her only the same life, the one she had had from the age of four. Although, like the people in it, it wore eccentric apparel.

At least this time they did not threaten her with a stick to make her get their language. No, they had an uncanny method, playing words and phrases, as they explained, while she slept. And when she learned swiftly (she had always been good at that) they were pleased with her. To her, this method was almost familiar, being a kind of sorcery. She had, in her first life, seen around her constantly spells and magical rites, which apparently worked. Even the gods must be approached via a type of magic, which was chant and prayer, and the making of offerings and promises, this for that, that for this. Accordingly, the murmur of the little pearls in her ears as she slept, sometimes half-noticed in dreams, was *usual*, though in unusual form.

She saw quickly her superiors were greatly advanced. She did not equate this with cleverness on their part, only with dominion. (As she had in Stagna Maris.)

She expected only upheaval among these rulers, as always. And that they did not seem to want her to fight in public did not disillusion her—for she sensed they *would* want this, or why else did they present the opportunity of practice for her skills, and why else did they watch her—not only in the flesh, but by some other (also uncanny) means they now possessed.

When the unconvincing villa or school changed its appearance, Jula was not vastly amazed, or interested.

Then, that morning, they brought the new clothes, and left them there for her to choose.

None of these clothes looked accustomed to her, except that she had seen some of her "visitors" dressed in similar things.

Before the clothes came in, they had also begun to modify her diet. At first the food had been like a (rather invented, slapdash) version of the meals she had eaten at the Julus school: dark bread, lentil soups and pork stews prepared with garlic, fruit, cheese, olives, a kind of wine. Then the dishes became gradually more elaborate, like failures sent her from some feast. There were spices she had never tasted, grains and vegetables she had never seen. She did not dislike them, nor even mistrust or specifically avoid them—what would have been the use? One night there had been a wine that was pink and nearly clear, and had in it a little rod with cherries stuck on it. The drink was very sweet and made her drunk after a mouthful—this then she left unfinished and afterwards seldom even tried the alcohols with which they plied her in various goblets of fantastic glass. Otherwise, the drink they told her they called *caffelatte* she did not like either. The herbal teas, rather to *their* bemusement, she intimated she already knew, dried mint or rosehips distilled with hot water were likely to be consumed in many Romanized provinces.

But the clothes were not really like this. Nor like any of it. They were *female* clothes. And until then, in the first installment of her existence as Jula Flammifer, she had been clothed always as a male.

The materials—which were luscious velvets, silks—neither attracted nor repelled her. She fingered them, found out how they fastened.

Conscious she was watched, she partly guessed they might be taking bets on her (she had always been bet upon) as to what she would select, and if she would then be able to get into it, *wear* it.

Included among the stuffs were quite simple flowing tunics, from post-Flavian Byzantium, or the Easternized chlamys.

Jula instead drew up this blood-red dress which had been designed some eleven centuries later.

Did the color persuade her? All the new clothes were highly colored, magenta, purples, flame orange, emerald. But then again, she was red-haired Jula, Fiery Jula—was it that? Some latent wish to affirm her personality? No, for Jula was not Jula, nor red-haired. She herself was well aware, even in this *second* installment of her existence as Jula, that this had not been her true name, and that her hair was, unhennaed, not red.

Why then? Why this one?

She liked it, perhaps? Just as she left the drinks that went too uncomfortably to her head and that therefore she *dis*liked. Yet was it not strange? Had she ever, in adult life before, dressed as a *woman*?

The watchers must have seen, she had negligible trouble with the renaissance dress, the same with the undergarments that accompanied it. Astonishment? Bets lost?

She put the gold net over her short hair, not spiked

up today lying smooth. And then she took the lion earrings, both of them, and slipped them into her ears.

She had worn the earrings often, one, or the pair.
They were a symbol of her status as Valuable. She had
got used to them.

At first, walking and sitting in the dress, there was a
slight awkwardness. It soon went. By the time she walked
out between the pillars and saw the tall heavy man standing on the lawn, Jula had mastered the dress entirely
and barely noticed it. Or the effect it made.

And when he strode towards her, she only stopped.
And when he asked, "Why are you wearing that?" she
only replied, "They gave it me to wear."

"You mean," said Flayd, angry again at all of it,
"they took your other clothes away and said put on this?"

"No. There was a choice of many garments."

"But—" he said.

Suddenly something in his face, tanned and glaring
under its flopping mane of auburn hair, made Jula smile.
At once, alarmed, she snatched the smile back. He too
seemed startled.

Why the dress? Unanswered to Flayd's satisfaction.

Why the smile? Unanswered to hers. Worse, dangerous. You did not smile at them, your masters. And he
was not, as she was, a slave, at whom anyway she would
not smile either. Perhaps, past the age of four, she had
never smiled at all, save in secret, when still very young.
At some unexpected beauty of weather, or some victory
she had not anticipated, some *feeling* even, inseparable
only from the springs of youth. Fleeting, all these, and
never wise; doubtless hidden.

"What's funny?" said Flayd. His voice was mild,
carefully receptive.

She heard the coaxing quality and noted her

worsening mistake. Once or twice, some man, some patrician, thinking she made up to him.

At her fellow warriors certainly she had never ever smiled. A smile or laugh could, there, be interpreted a hundred wrong ways—as mockery, boasting, as ingratiation from cowardice, as madness.

She was silent.

"OK, no, I don't think you meant to be amused. I guess you do find me funny. And you speak Amerian English now. How's that?"

"The round pearls that talk in my ears."

"Linguisticx. What else?"

She stood waiting on him, politely observing his upper lip.

Flayd said, "You're not a slave. Haven't they told you that still? Look at me. When you did, you smiled. Is that so bad?"

Again she said nothing.

He thought, I guess it's bad. Lowering the shield. Being one human with another. Or are we just creatures from another world to her, as she is to *them*?

A capital offense, equally, to murder anyone, or to bring anyone back from the dead.

He thought, What in hell do I want to do about this? What can I do?

There was a sound behind him, someone coming through the cloister, the slapping of a skirt or sleeve.

The girl looked up. Lagoon eyes—seeing something *above* Flayd's head—

He dived around, and saw it too.

It flew towards them, an impossible undone, done-up jigsaw of black and white. Then swooped down on to the lawn between them, its perfect, somehow Egyptian markings like some hieroglyph meaning *flight* or *eye*.

"Pica," said Jula.

"Magpie, yeah. That one ain't real, 's only thing. A recx or even VP—virtuality projection. What the heck. It looks good." What am I saying? Nervous as a boy on his first date, no, not that. A guy with a brand-new daughter sprung on him when he was young enough to reel, old enough to wonder—No, nor that. Not everything was that neat.

The magpie picked through the tiny flowers, its black legs, the black knife of a beak, questing delicately. On its back, among the so-white, jet-black feathers, the elusive water glimmer of alien blue.

Someone else came out of the pillared cloister.

Flayd goggled at him. Too many surprises now.

He was wearing one more set of his non-Venus black jeans and a poured dark green shirt. His body was excellent, but for God's sake, the guy was only thirty or so. He had that look he always had, so cool it froze you, so far off no use to shout, and so courteous you wanted to punch him in the kisser. But the eyes . . . they seemed a bit—dazed.

How had he got here, and again *why?*

The woman was saying something. It was Latin. Flayd understood her and turned back to gaze at her instead.

"O di magni, obsecro, intercedite pro me contra istrum—"

"It's OK, Jula—yeah, maybe you need your gods to protect you but—"

"—istrum mihi inimi cissimum qui constituit se ab me—"

"Jula."

"—vindicare et iam instat."

Flayd drew in a breath. "He isn't—*he's* not your

enemy, not like that." Flayd repeated this, cautiously, in Latin. But her eyes were fixed as her prayer had been unstoppable. Where she'd hardly ever met Flayd's glance, now she stared at Picaro, on and on. Her face was frightened, and behind the fear, the inevitable ingrained readying, the mental weapons taken in both hands, as even in exhaustion and near death they would be.

"Jula, this is Picaro. Picaro, meet Jula." Flayd said lamely, spuriously.

But Picaro too only stood there, looking back at her, expressionless, dazed (hurt in some unguessable way?)

What was it?

What it was, for Jula, was that she had just seen again after such a long, long time, the Ethiopian who had cursed her, and whom she had killed in Stagna Maris, all those several centuries ago.

2

"YOU SHOULD BE DEAD," the dead Ethiopian said, in his quiet and musical voice.

Jula stared at him, she didn't even blink.

All her awareness—on him.

"Like the other one," he said.

And then he sprang at her, across the lawn.

He was extremely fast, far heavier in build and taller than she.

Flayd had no time to react.

But she—her reactions were integral as her bones, as the ESDNA that had enabled these creeps to bring her back.

Flayd, hurtling himself forward, grabbed some of the braids of Picaro's hair, the nearest thing he could reach, but Picaro was already spinning away, going down.

The woman had not attempted the evade him. She had crouched instantly, and driven her fist, small and hard as a stone, with all her considerable compact strength behind it, directly up into Picaro's solar plexus. He was out cold.

Flayd loomed in limbo, dumbfounded, feeling grimly sorry for him, and for her, and for the whole bloody world.

JULA STOOD OVER PICARO.

It was a stance she had assumed more than a hundred and twenty times in her past. But her adversary was not dead, not now.

She looked down at him.

She remembered very well his face, the strong sculpted bones, the blackness of his skin. She recalled how his eyes, so large and terrible a moment before, appeared when shut fast. But that had been in death.

And his blood was red. She knew. No need to see it.

She tasted something too sweet in her mouth then, another recollection, like those instants in the arena. But this . . . it was a feast after victory—it was—the saffron pastry the slave had brought her, with the saffron-colored flower lying on it. But all the other flowers among the cakes and sweetmeats of the bellaria were white.

The impression was random, it seemed to have no purpose. She pushed it aside.

Just then, the tall man—called Flayd—took a step nearer.

Jula held up her hand. "Ne me attingas," she said. *Don't touch me*.

Flayd did as she told him. He waited, marooned on the lawn, as if outside a pane of unbreakable optecx.

The pica bird, Jula noticed, was gone. She knelt down by her senseless enemy, who, as she had, had come back from Hades.

And when Flayd took a half step after all, Jula said, clearly in English, "I won't harm him."

She could hear the Ethiopian breathing raggedly, see the judder of the heart in his throat. She touched him with one finger of her left hand, there in the center of his wide forehead, from which the endless ropes of hair fell back like chains of black silk and white wool.

"Quid a me quaeritas?"

What do you want from me?

PICARO LEANED ON THE RAILING, to either side of him the square-paved lungomare, stretching like a neoned chessboard, and beyond, the midnight sea done in lacquer black under stars of fire.

Another coast, another city, another time. He was sixteen. He had played a set with the Soundless Band, and the crowd had gone wild. It was an appreciative crowd. The best they'd had, in the months of traveling. It was full of women, too, some very rich and some very young, and all of them with that pleasure glaze on them like pollen. Everyone here on the shore wanted to be happy tonight, and many of them had made it, and Picaro was one of those lucky ones.

All that music, and then there had been iced beer too, and vin'absinthe, and hasca in a silver clip. Now, for the moment, all he needed was the night.

"Well," said the soft voice on his right, just behind him, someone unseen—but he could smell her perfume, and the scent of her body, warm and alluring though not especially young.

"Well," Picaro said.

That was introduction enough, maybe.

So he turned, and he saw her. She was slim, but curved like a vase, and heavy-hipped, and her breasts were big, beautiful, and her hair was long and thick like a thick black smoke, and edged with flame from the neon lamp behind her, which hid her face from him, yet gave him everything else. Even her rose-red shoes with their stalks of thin, tall, heels.

She was not very tall, even in those tall heels. A lot shorter than he. And yet, crazily, he felt—for one split second—she was the taller of the two of them, and bigger than he was. Dark as darkness and big as darkness. But there had been the hasca, and he *liked* the dark.

"I rate your music," said the woman. "You're fine."

She had cash. He could see it all over her. It hung in the gold ring around her long, smooth neck, and the platinum ring around her left ankle. Her dress was some constructed fabric, the kind that cost. He didn't care about this particularly, he had been with rich, not-so-young women, and rich *young* women, too. Only—somehow the money on her didn't fit.

"You're talented," she said. "I always thought you'd be that way. Best thing I ever did, perhaps. Leave you. Let you alone to grow."

And then her head turned so the light fell side-long, and he saw who she was. And then she laughed, and in her mouth the little jewel sparked snakes-eye green. But her own eyes were Simoon's, and she *was* Simoon.

He took a step away, and the railing pressed in his back.

"Honey," she said, "you really believed all what your daddy told you about me? Listen, if I was one little third what he said, how could I be standing here? Someone would've killed me, sure. Or I'd be in jail. Or dead. Wouldn't I?"

Picaro stayed still. Nothing moved, not even the sea.

"Listen," she said, "he and I—an old argument. I saw you were afraid, after he died like that, because you ran away. Anyone can die like that. You think I did it to him? If I even could, why would I? He was eating out of my hand right then."

"No," Picaro heard himself say.

"*No*? No what, baby?"

Picaro eased off the railing and went fast away, along the lungomare.

Light cohorts of the fortunate, the crowds were drifting over the esplanade like clouds. So they seemed to him—insubstantial.

But she was solid and present, still right beside him even though he had left her eight hundred kilometers behind.

He looked back once. She was no longer there. Where then? *Here*, next to him—

Shadow was what she could send, and what she was. Look at her, (in his mind, bobbing among the light laughing crowds). He examined Simoon. Two years older, she looked about ten years younger than when he saw her last. And she had lost weight, and her short tight hair had grown long and straight. Her skin was like that of a woman in her early thirties and no more than that. But Picaro's father had told him her age, the age of the witch, which anyhow maybe she had lied about, taking off a few years, and she had been, when Picaro was born, supposedly forty years old. So now that made her fifty-six.

He kept thinking he'd see her, in front of him, sliding out of the people-clouds, or simply stepping from the doorway of some lit-up bar. But she didn't do that. Not right then.

THERE WAS NO ONE in the big room the band had taken, but for Omberto, asleep in one of the screened-off beds with a girl. Coal's jackdaw sat on the roof of its opened cage, preening itself. Picaro fed it a few nuts it could any-way have fetched for itself from the table.

Later, in his sleep, he heard it fly out through the window, but it always did at dawn, anytime they left it free.

The next day, he saw the jackdaw had yellow in its eyes.

Perhaps this had always been the case. But he had thought its eyes were a kind of gray, like Coal's eyes.

And sometimes, the jackdaw watched Picaro—but it always had. It was used to him, as to the rest of the band, and took a friendly interest in all of them.

They played in a couple of spots. It was all right, not as hot as the first time. They talked of moving on.

"What is up with you?" Coal said to Picaro. "You don't eat, you don't sleep. I hear you up all night walking about."

"Your bird keeps looking at me."

"Sure he does. You can't play that guitar no more. Or that korah neither."

Omberto, the peacemaker, who had taught Picaro some of his own skill with the korah, drew Coal away to a game of cards.

Tuning the kissar, a recx instrument, temperamental despite its technological insides, the string burned through Picaro's fingers, so his blood dropped in the sound box.

They moved on.

AND NOW HE WAS STANDING on a roof, with another railing, and looking down at a street. Thinking back, the whole scene was somehow a whiteout. Like the magpie dream, he could only recall it in words, not images. Except for her. Her he could see.

She had come walking up the ancient redundant fire escape, which (unseen, described in words) had been painted a vivid color and had a honeysuckle grown up and through it. As she trod on the blossoms, the fragrance flared, mixing with the scent of her.

"What do you want?" he said.

(Had they said anything else first? Perhaps. Or not.) She said, "I like to look at you."

Picaro felt a kind of despair. The only exit was to jump off the roof, and he wouldn't do that.

"You keep after me," he said. "Why?"

"I have to tell you something," she said. "But not yet."

Then Omberto ran up on to the roof, and he saw Simoon, and he grinned and shook his head, and leaped away again.

Simoon said, "He thinks I'm not your mama."

"You're not."

"Who is then? Huh? Tell me, I should like to know."

He remembered all this, and remembered remembering how she had sat in the cane chair, shelling peas, and how she had made the meal, and put out the bottle of wine and the costly cola.

How did she have money for that then? And how, now, so much. For she wore a summer dress that was made of thin *real* silk. He could see her blackness through it, so like the shade of his own blackness, blacker than most black skins, blacker than his father. Black as the jackdaw, and a magpie's wings.

He thought, then, she'd put out the wine that night when Picaro was fourteen, and cooked enough for Picaro's father, too. She didn't reckon the man would die. Maybe it upset her. *And I ran away.*

In the drowsy, light-losing evening, he could make

out faint lines by her mouth, under her eyes, see the ebony string that came and went in her marvel of a neck. Not much—something. So, she didn't quite look her age. If she had money, there were ways of doing that too.

"Are you rich, Simoon? How?"

He'd spoken her name.

He hadn't meant to.

She said, "I'm not rich. *Been* rich, once. Now and then. And I keep a few things by me for great occasions, like visiting my son. Do you think I look rich?"

"Yes."

"I am triumphant. What else do I look, to you?"

He said nothing.

"You think," she said, "I look like a witch, and a whore. I've been both. Nothing left of that. It done. I'm clear as crystal. I've paid for what I have."

Then she put the bottle on the parapet, and the cork was already out.

"You're grown up now," she said, "I can bring you wine."

3

NOT UNTIL SHE MOVED away did Flayd go forward.

He checked the felled man rapidly. Saw, even in this extremity, with slight startlement, she had turned Picaro's head sideways, the recovery position, to clear the airway. So they knew that in ancient Rome? Probably a gladiator school would know things like that, teach them.

Picaro's breathing was easier, pulse slower, but he was still well gone.

Flayd stood up again. She was over by the pillars, sitting on a stone bench there. Her head was raised and her eyes set and open wide. To Flayd, it was the stance she would have adopted when waiting, under the arena, for the minute she would be summoned up on to the sand.

His other bewilderment was that no one else had come in.

Of course, they had their other emergency, whatever that really was. But was absolutely nobody able to register events down here? It seemed that right now they weren't.

Flayd crossed the cloister and went into a long room like something from a medieval monastery, through that into some other rooms that were still—to him—mostly Roman. Here he found two men in dalmatics, drinking coffee from old brown monkish beakers.

"A guy out there needs some attention." They looked at him, stupidly alert. "A little amateur practice bout with Jula Flame-Hair. He shouldn't have done it."

"Shit," said one of the men. Coffee spilled as he rushed out past Flayd. The other said, "The security apparatus has been faulty. Screens are down. You're UAS? Maintenance is on it now."

"You mean the *CX*?"

"Yes."

"Can't happen, can it?"

"It did."

"Any connection," said Flayd, "to the problem on the canals this morning?"

He saw the man decide Flayd was not really UAS. "I wouldn't know," said the fake monk. He had pressed a key concealed under a wooden table. Soon there was the sound of running feet, just like Flayd thought he'd heard earlier. He left and went back fast to the cloister. There he sat down on the half bench, near the girl, about half a meter from her, and watched as three or four UAS organized a stretcher and carried Picaro away, and Flayd thought of ants.

Had Picaro been brought here because of the other one, the bloodline related musician from the 1700s—

The cloister and the lawn were oddly empty again. Even the construct magpie had vanished.

Flayd looked at Jula.

"Their observation devices are out, it seems. You knew they watched you, I guess."

"Yes," she said. They were speaking Italian. Then she said in Amer-English, "Is he like me? Did they bring him back from death?"

"Christ—no—*no*, Picaro is—how do I put this? First time alive. Even now, after you hammered the daylights outa him. He's like someone you—like someone from *then*?"

"I fought him in the sand. He was handsome and skilled. He could have been popular and lived. But he wouldn't fight me until I made him. And they wouldn't forgive him that. I had to kill him, for the crowd. No mercy."

She continued to look straight before her. Waiting for a trumpet that now would never sound.

Instead, Flayd *saw* her hearing that punning chant from the tiers: *Jugula Jula! Jula jugula!* Kill, Jula! Jula, kill!

He said, in a low voice, "Let's get the fuck out of here."

Then she did glance at him.

Flayd said, "Some of the CX—the machines—are down. The bastards are in a bit of a bloody mess. I don't know if any of this affects the dome locks, if we can really get out—it might. But failing that, maybe we can at least get you free into the City." And Flayd thought he was mad, and she could never understand, and what was out there could, in its incongruous alienness, actually drive her insane. But he said, "We can risk it. What do you say?"

"You ask me?" she said in Latin.

No one asked a slave. Not even perhaps a fellow slave. No question marks could ever truly exist.

"I'm asking you," he resolutely said in English, in Italian, in Latin. "Come on."

And she stood up and they walked out of the cloister, and along to the elevators, of which she seemed to take no notice at all, except to adjust her balance as they rose. And when they emerged and moved through security, in all its forms mechanical and human, not a vid blinked, not a hair was turned.

Too late then, only as they came out into the sunlit corridors of the University—renaissance, Victorian—did he think, *Are they letting us do this?*

But they trod down the marble stairs, negotiated a polished floor, walked out a wooden side-door. They arrived at the brink of a green canal in the light of the noon Viorno-Votte.

Venus lay before them, under her air-and-sky-filled invisible dome. And she displayed, without any disguise, a million edifices that never, in the most lunatic dreams and nightmares, could this woman have envisaged.

But she had been a barbarian captive child in Rome, among the unimagined towering tenements and hills of palaces and temples. She had been brought to Stagna Maris. She had had to fight and kill to live.

Flayd, when he turned to her again, saw all that. Her eyes were wide again, questing now, but still not *questioning*. Not alarmed or unnerved. She was fearless. Almost—contemptuous? These glamours belonged to her masters. What could she ever care about or for them? They would never be hers.

"Venus," Flayd said flatly. He shrugged.

And thought of the goddess-face of Venus on Jula's shield, the deity favored by soldiers and gladiators alike, since she was also the consort of the war god, Mars.

And then Leonillo spoke, behind them.

Flayd shot around and saw him, composed and pallid and infuriating.

"Do you like the view, Jula Victrix?"

She said nothing. Flayd said, "I believe the lady has no strong feelings either way, on the view."

"Only on her Ethiopian?" asked Leonillo. "We wondered if she'd make that error. The first black man she sees after the last black man she saw. The ancient world wasn't noted for its racial flexibility . . . I'm sure you know what the Romans said about the British, your own ancestors, Flayd . . . They all look alike, and so ugly. She's told you all about it, I expect."

"Sorry. If your CXs are fucked, that information is classified."

"Oh my. My dear Flayd. The CX function isn't completely fucked. And we have some backup. We did hear a word or two."

"We are not," Flayd said, "about to return inside."

"Naturally not."

"So we're meant to be doing what we are doing?"

"And why shouldn't you?" said Leonillo, with a ghastly expansiveness. "Who better than you to show our favorite gladiatrix the City. To explain and accustom her, to be her guide."

"She doesn't need a guide, Leonillo. But you need your head examined."

"The need is universal perhaps."

"Go screw yourself. I guess you're the only one'll oblige."

A wanderer with wanderlier was approaching along the canal, stirring the limpidness with the oar-pole, the man easy and smiling, seeing only, as you expected, some guy in 1860s gear, some girl dressed for 1490, like a hundred thousand others. Unless he too, the auspicious boatman, was part of the general conspiracy.

When Flayd told her, she got into the wanderer, graceful and coordinated as a puma. Flayd rocked in, crashed down.

Silent Leonillo watched them float away, and raising his hand, urbanely waved them off.

4

BECAUSE HE WASN'T UNCOMFORTABLE, he stayed, lying flat, for some while. He thought that was why. But when he moved, the pain stabbed hard through his guts, and Picaro saw he had instinctively kept still only to avoid it. Muscular, outside and in, the pain. Where she had punched him. Who? Why? Surely, that had been a dream—or he was remembering that other time, that time when he was sixteen. With Simoon.

Somehow he saw his father, sitting across from him, frowning. "You never hit out at a woman, son. No matter what she does." But it was only a memory, sitting in the chair. It was an apology also, for Picaro's father had never struck the witch either—and was that ethics or terror?

"This is another kind of woman, Papa," said the child in Picaro's mind. "I never had a chance. Look what she did to me."

But it hadn't only been that. It was the sickness which had filled the Palazzo Shaachen, the thing they had said was faulty CX, bad air—that first. *Then* her.

Her . . . Who? . . . What had he done?

Picaro sat up, spat like a cat at the deadly wrench of pain, and swung off the bunk. A light melted up in the wall. Someone would be coming.

He tapped his wristecx for the time. It gave him 16 vv.

They had been observing him since they brought him in. They had performed various medical checks, not particularly intrusive—blood count, tissue sample, urine, shining pins of brilliance through his eyes, a flash scan in a medibooth. They told him he was in faultless health. And then they gave him something, some drug they said was necessary, an insurance against any future problems. And he had slept after that. Deep, so deep, like . . .

Like death.

And after—or in?—the sleep, he now remembered, thought he did, (was that yesterday?) getting up and leaving this clean antiseptic cubicle, and walking down a long hall, and a few people were there but no one stopped him. A door opened by itself, and he came into another area, and then . . . now a kind of blank was in front of him, with the thinnest razor cuts in it, through which he could almost see things, and one of these things was a woman with red hair and in a red dress, and he had meant—but she—

Picaro put his hand flat on the wall.

He looked at his hand. It was his.

The hand, and the wall, felt real. But . . . his hand a little less so.

Then the cubicle opened and the 1906 man walked in.

"You're back," said Leon-Leonillo.

"Am I?"

"Always a question for a question. Your life is made of questions. Back after your adventure."

"Which one?"

Leonillo smiled. To an unseen audience, aware of both their performances, he could not resist awarding a tiny nod. Then he sat down cozily in the chair Picaro's father had for a moment occupied. "There's a slight disorientation? That is the medication. It will wear off quickly. You'd be feeling much better already if you hadn't tried to take on the fabulous Jula."

"Not Jula," Picaro heard himself say. "Cora."

"Cora. Ah. The young woman who—"

"Yes. In the palazzo. Like the rest of them."

"I'm sorry."

"It wasn't," said Picaro, "from a fault in the CX system, was it?"

"No."

"It's something to do with him—with the musician."

"Yes, I am afraid so."

"Where is he?"

"Safe, Picaro. *Not* dead. Better concealed from you than Jula, I can assure you. Jula doesn't seem to present the same difficulty."

"Which is?"

"As yet," Leonillo flicked his hands, "the most likely cause is a form of carried germ—something latent in del Nero's bodily make-up, usual and unremarked on during his own era, not affecting his, or anyone's normal well-being, but now inimical to the contemporary immune system. He, you understand, shows no symptom of anything, except unimpaired vitality."

"How about he shows distress?"

"One must expect he would, under the circumstances. He saw them dying all around him and was powerless. Of course he is dismayed. It was very awful. Even you, isolated above, were involved. As you know only too well. And of course many of us have had continuous and direct contact with him, and so we are all being most carefully monitored. But it would seem, that particular evening at the Shaachen Palace, unfortunately—some sort of surge took place."

"Yes. Unfortunate."

"Jula Victrix, however, aside from her fighting ability, is not apparently harmful. Nothing has happened to anyone, even those most often in close proximity. Something of a mystery there. Why one and not the other one? But meanwhile, why exactly did *you* go after her?"

"Is that what I did?"

"Some of our surveillance was out of order for a while. They say it can't happen, but evidently it does. And when everything was rather lax, you left the medical area. They let you because you are free to go about as you wish. Besides which, certain parts of the section are theoretically sealed to anyone not authorized. But the inoperative CX again—you were let through into the second area, Jula's."

"Jula."

"Yes. Her master in Roman times, Julus, gave her his name, a great honor, to show her value."

"She is your female gladiator."

"What else."

Picaro said, "I can't remember. What did I do?"

"Nothing much. Rushed her with obvious murderous intent, having announced she would be better dead—like the "other one." Innocently forgetting that she had been trained to fight since the age of five in one of the most exacting sword schools of Rome's provinces. She'd slaughtered over a hundred and twenty armed men. You were rather lucky."

Staring into the mental blank, trying to pull the thin cuts in it open, and see.

Picaro said, "I actually wanted del Nero. He was the one I was looking for. I found her instead. But she is the same, even if she isn't a plague carrier. Your clever resurrection that's gone wrong. Perhaps I thought I could make do. If I killed her at least. Sent her *back*. Cleaned up your filth."

"Well," said Leonillo. "You had an added disadvantage, it seems. She thought you were the last man she dispatched in the arena. His name was Phaetho. A black man from the Africas, a Roman slave as she was. She finished him, but he had hacked her about. She was said to have died of the wounds. In fact she was poisoned, or so we now suspect."

The blank would not give way. Even the woman in red he could glimpse there, had no visible face.

Leonillo rambled on. "Both deaths are rather a puzzle. Del Nero, you may have heard, died from the action of an alchemically poisoned mask—how it worked none of the team has any idea, and in his case, no trace of a venom remains. We do know, however, it was a *beautiful* mask, half-face but with a sculpted nose, made after the likeness of a statue of Apollo. Pure white with black brows and luxuriant black hair attached. We have a written record of that, although the mask itself has never been found. What a challenge it would be if it were . . ."

Picaro, ignoring this, hearing it on some other mental level only, could feel instead the shift of new questions inside his brain. *How* had he found the way to the second area? And the faulty door that failed to keep him out—and no one trying to prevent him or even ask him what he was at—*free* to go about? Never, not in this sort of establishment. A kind of sleepwalking, perhaps induced, and *choreographed*?

Conspiracy. Plot.

He thought of Flayd.

But the drug they said would help him lined his veins heavy as lead. And then he thought, maybe *not* the drug. Not the drug, or Cora dying, or any waft of disease brought back from 1701. Not even the punch of the gladiatrix, who thought she had killed him once before. Maybe none of that.

Maybe only—*it was beginning*.

And the world opened, and nothing lay there, gaping wide.

Leonillo had finished his lecture on the mask.

"I want to leave now," Picaro said.

"There's no reason to keep you. I'm afraid, though, you can't return to the Palazzo. We can't be sure it would be safe. Your clothes and other belongings, and your musical instruments, have been moved to—let me see," Leonillo listened to his wristecx, "Brown's Guest Palace on the Lion Marco Canal. Someone will see that a boat is waiting for you by the University steps."

Behold me, the mighty lion named Marcus. Whoever resists me I will bring low.

5

THE TIME HE HAD MOVED into the room, doing that hadn't seemed so curious. It was a large, wide, airy loft, high over the streets. The walls were painted white, and there were deep red furnishings, and a splash of blue flowers in a bowl that never died. The band seemed envious. "Stick with that one," Coal said, "she got money." But that was not so. The room was rented, she had only had it, she told him, a month.

She kept her bed in a little annex, where her make-up mirror was, ringed in soft rosy lights like an actress's from fifty years before. There was still old-style electricity in the building, but sometimes, when the weather got very hot, or stormy, the lights flickered and the Intel-V screen broke up any picture into stripes. There was a wall-bed Picaro slept on, when he was there. And down the hall there was a bathroom, exclusive to this room, which Simoon had maintained, and to the door of which, as to the door of the room, she had had fixed an expensive lock that could be undone only by a personal CX-key. She gave Picaro a copy of the key. When he said he couldn't pay her for that, or put much toward the room, she laughed. "Who cares. When my credit runs out we have to move, that's all."

He hardly ever saw her use paper money. She employed plastic, like the rich. But she showed him her account statement on the Intel-V, and it contained only her large debt.

Picaro thought that perhaps she had found out how to commit fraud, running away when she was too overdrawn and her purchases were refused. But somehow she never was refused, or warned. That had impressed him. He had thought her clever in some way.

Spending time with her, even sleeping under the same roof as Simoon, seemed good. More—it was nearly exciting. It was like going traveling, or being on a stage, forming the first chord and feeling the watching listeners stir. Always a bit like that. Or, it was like a brand new kind of sexual relationship where there was no sex.

She was his mother, and he had, for two years—and more, from the first times his father spoke of her—been wrong about Simoon.

She was amusing and easygoing, and she saw things in a different way. She was young-looking, young enough, and glamorous. Beautiful. Why had he never liked her eyes? They were beautiful eyes, colored like Saké. There was white blood back when, it was that which had changed their color. In a woman less dark, her eyes might have looked less unusual. But that was all they were, *unusual.*

The flowers that never died fascinated Picaro, and also other members of the band, on the rare occasions they were in the loft. "Where you get these?" Coal asked. "A special store," said Simoon. She was frequently mysterious. And Picaro thought her mystery always alluring. She was his mother.

None of the rest of them knew this. He never said, nor she. They thought she was a wealthy older woman and they had taken up together for a while. The band was jealous, admiring, slightly uneasy.

151

But she wasn't *like* a mother. She never asked him to do anything, never demanded or requested him to, or interrogated him on where he had been, even when he was gone a month or more. She didn't inquire about women, or the band. If he told her about them, she listened, nodding, and if she said anything, it was light and casual and noncommittal. There were no traps. He woke up sometimes on the wall-bed and wondered why she had ever freaked him out, and why his father had been irrational in this one area alone. Anything he asked *her*, she answered. She always had an answer. She seemed to conceal nothing, only her body, modestly closing the annex door, wearing a robe to the bathroom. Somehow, Picaro found he did not observe this modesty himself. He even sunbathed naked on the high-up balcony, and when she brought him tea or a beer or a clip of hasca, neither of them paid any attention to it, his nakedness, her enclosure.

One morning he woke up and saw her shaking off something from her hand into the bowl of blue flowers.

"What are you doing, Simoon?" He liked her name, to use it.

She said, "Giving them breakfast. They're my babies too."

When she went into the gallery where the cookery was done, Picaro got up and stood over the flower bowl and saw in the water, not quite yet dissolved, a little coil of red.

"Looks like blood."

"That's what I give them. How else do they live on and on."

And Picaro had not minded.

Oh God, he'd probably thought she meant she bought it somewhere, the blood, ready-dried, to feed plants.

One night, when she had been to watch the band in a bar in a street named for an arrow, he met her by chance after, on the pavement walk. She wasn't always there to watch, nor available afterwards. He would look up and see her, part of the audience, often with some man paying her court, or he'd catch the firefly spark of the jewel in her mouth.

On Arrow Street he had come out with a black girl, and Simoon stood there drinking a glass of grappa, and she smiled her smile, but not showing the peridot.

For a moment he spoke to her, and the girl, his own age, young and ready for the night, stood with them, leaning on his shoulder.

"The room will be empty tonight," said Simoon, though she was standing alone, "so why don't you use the big bed? If you want. That's fine."

Picaro thought nothing much of it, except it was a generous offer. There were other places to go, but the loft was very private, and cool after dark.

"Thanks, Simoon."

When he and the girl were walking on, swinging their hands together, she said, "Who was that?" And Picaro had said, "She owns the block where I room. Sometimes I can use this apartment, if it's vacant." And realized how tactfully Simoon had chosen her words, not to alarm the girl, and now he colluded with the lie. Simoon—his landlady. (She had never offered him use of her bed before—the big bed—that would be good, with the girl.)

They had a few drinks. Only presently, when they were strolling back to the loft, did the girl say, "You got a thing with her?"

"No," he said. "With you."

The moment they stepped into the loft, something

happened. It was like—a change in the tint of the air.

He thought at first the girl was impressed by the vast room, the furniture, the fact that there were drinks of all kinds in the coldbocx, and so many music decx. Simoon's bed was large, clean, with white sheets that smelled faintly of spices.

"I got to go to the bathroom," said the girl. He showed her in past the private CX lock. "Whose is all this?" said the girl. And Picaro found he said, "She keeps it for special times."

When the girl came back, like the air tint, her face was subtly altered.

"It's her's, this crash?"

"Yes, I told you."

"No, *only* hers?"

"Maybe."

"Who is she?"

"I told you that too. She owns all the rooms." Simoon had looked sufficiently well-off for this to be true.

"What's her game?" said the girl.

Picaro laughed. He put his arms around the girl and kissed her, as they had been kissing all evening. "Forget that. Think about you and me."

But again, in the bed, she said to him, "Are you and she making a decx of this?"

"*What?*"

"I mean, things in the walls—making some movie of this, with me."

"No," Picaro said. "You've seen the Intel and the electrics—we're not up to *that* standard." He was repulsed that she could suspect him of being a pornographing her. And seeing his repulsion, the girl relented, and they made love, but not quite as they might have done, if they hadn't had that conversation.

Later on, they sat out in the loft, and Picaro played for the girl on the luta-guitar, the only instrument he kept there. But she wasn't listening. She kept looking around.

"What is it?" he said.

"Is someone in here?"

He told her no one was there but for themselves.

"How can you be sure," she said, "if you never been here before?"

"I have," he said. He frowned at her. She knew theirs was not a long-term alliance, the perfume and suppliance of a minute, as the poet said.

She didn't want to go back to the bed. They had sex on the floor, Picaro underneath, to cushion her. Midway, she stopped moving. Again she started staring round. "There some animal in here," she said. "A rat."

"No," he said. "They're careful with that."

"How? You say it's not that modern, this building, with the electrics and the unstyle screen. So how they keep rats out, huh?"

"I've never seen a rat in this building."

His erection was gone, and so was her arousal. They separated, and moodily he lay there and watched the girl begin to dress.

"I really like you," she said, contrite. "Come with me."

"You have a room?"

"Part of one. They won't mind."

"No," Picaro said. He got up and padded to the cold-bocx and the girl screeched, a high narrow wavering shriek, so he spun toward her—"What the hell is the matter?"

"Someone's here," she said. She seemed terrified, so he thought her wild on a drug, or off her head. "Someone. Something."

"Only me. Me and you."

"She—she's put something here. It looks at me. I can see its eyes—*goat's eyes*—" yelled the girl, "like she got!"

And then she ran over the loft and out the door, and he heard her feet skidding and pattering along the hall. And then the hiss of the old lift, taking her down to the street.

He went on thinking she was out of her mind. He said nothing to Simoon the next day, had only remade her bed with fresh sheets, (afterwards she said that wouldn't have mattered, what did she care?) He had never taken a woman up to the loft before. He never would again.

THE LONG, HOT SUMMER came to an end. Autumn filled the city with its smoky nostalgias. The Soundless Band met at Gotto's Bar, and discussed moving on.

"Maybe," said Picaro.

"You not gonna come, man? Come on. What's keeping you?"

"That woman is keeping him," said Coal.

Picaro said, "You don't know a thing."

"I know you're not one of us no more."

Omberto said, "Leave it."

Picaro said, "Let's move on then. City to city, nowhere to nowhere. How many decx we made this year?"

"Seven," said Omberto concisely.

"And with which company was that?" asked Picaro.

Coal said, "You know we don't have no backers. But we sell on the Intel."

"We have a *big* small minority that follows us," announced Carlo, primly.

The jackdaw, which was standing on Omberto's beer jug, made a cackling sound.

A few nights before, coming in around three in the morning, Picaro had found Simoon sitting on the floor in the middle of the loft. He had never previously met her in the room at that hour.

There was no light beyond the fat purple candle standing on its bronze dish. The candle, which no matter how often it was lit, or for how long it burned, never seemed to burn away.

"Chi', Simoon," he said. "What are you doing?"

On the floor, in the vague mauve light, a scatter of tiny things that looked nearly like a necklace of whitish beads come undone. She put out her hand and swept them up, and slipped them into the pocket of her robe.

"Just playing a little," she said. Then she said, "What do you want to happen for you?"

He hadn't thought, perhaps. Only expected it. Day by day, hour by hour. Some glowing answer, all the best that he was due. He was sixteen.

Picaro shook his head.

She said to him, "I hear you with the citarra, and with those instruments in the band. I hear you singing. You're so good."

Her praise, for some reason (like that first time) made him restless, uncomfortable.

She said, "You're better than the others. Did you know?"

"That's you talking. You're biased."

"Where do you get these words? Oh, he had you educated nicely. From there. I'm not biased—that's the way cloth is cut. Help me up," she murmured, "I sat here so long my legs are already in the bed asleep.

Somewhere in the dark of dreaming it occurred to him she had been making magic after all, there in the night, for him. He wasn't offended. It seemed more—touching.

But when the Band talked of moving on, he decided he didn't want that. And then he saw he was too settled. It *was* time to go, to get away from her. She was his mother. He could always come back.

AND SO THE DAY, scarlet flowers on the balcony throwing open their shutters to the cooling sun. What else happened? Afterwards he could never recall, only those flowers opening, and then sunset, and then going out to play the set in the street named for the Arrow.

He started with the korah, that night, but then Omberto took that up, his fingers spangling quick as rain across the frets. And Picaro switched to the s'tha. He chose this, he later believed, for the roundness of its hipline under the long, long neck. In origin, it had come from the East, and the seven strings were resined to silk—but it was a new instrument, younger than Picaro. When he glanced up, during one of the prolonged breathless races of the music, when the audience no longer made any noise, did not breathe, or blink, eyes fixed on the band as if hypnotized, he saw Simoon out there, sitting in her pale frock, watching with the rest, looking hungry and enslaved as the rest.

At the interval she came up, when they were standing at the bar, and the drinks were coming for them. She seemed to brush by no one, was only there.

In the bar on Arrow Street, the lights were chemical, high-up mercury-colored globes, but at this time of night they were dimmed. Simoon had brought the darkness with her.

"What will you have, lady?" asked Coal. (Had he ever used her name? No, very likely he hadn't.)

Simoon smiled, and said she would have a grappa.

The drinks were free for them, of course, or she would have paid, with cash not plastic.

Carlo didn't look at her tonight, and perhaps she noticed that. Coal was as courteous with her as he always was when she was there. Omberto drank half his glass, then put it down and spoke to her.

"You going to let him off the leash?"

Simoon turned her head to look at him. It was—like the movement of a snake that smiled. "What do you say?"

"Picar. You going to let him out of jail a while, so we can move on?"

Omberto had always been the most eager and flirtatious with Simoon, as he was the most rational and placatory during any argument among the band. No longer.

"He isn't in jail," she said.

"Yes," said Omberto. "You've got to let him free. Christ, even the jackdaw gets to fly about sometimes."

Simoon slightly shook her head. It was like a ripple over foliage, no more.

She kept looking at Omberto.

He drank the second half of his drink, straight down.

"You look pretty good," said Omberto. "But you're too old, way too old, for Picar. What are you, sixty, sixty-five? Old enough to be his gran'mumma. You've got to look it in the face. You've got to get your claws out."

Picaro, standing just beside her, hearing these words come out of Omberto's drink-wet mouth, as if they came out of his own dry mouth, shuddered. Picaro tried to speak, to tell Omberto to close his wet mouth.

But Picaro didn't speak, and it was Carlo, rolling his eyes, pulling at Omberto. "Don't—shit—shit—shut up, shut up."

"No. I want her to know."

"You don't—shut up. Shut up."

"Yes, she has to know. Let him go. You and he, Simoon, you can't go anywhere else. You've had him sewn on you all summer, but now it's fall."

"Fall," she repeated. The Amerian word, so apt for autumn, for the time of falling leaves of rust and yellow.

Picaro pushed his mind around into the bar, from which it had fled, and put out his hand to grasp Simoon's arm. As if to protect her—or to hold her back.

But somehow he hadn't, he didn't have her arm.

Instead it was Simoon who had reached out. She took Omberto's hand, his right hand, and as she took it, the emptied glass fell out of it, one more falling leaf, and it fell so slowly that it would never hit the ground. And between the letting-go of the glass, and the moment when it did hit, did shatter, Picaro heard Simoon speaking low to Omberto.

"What a beautiful pale hand you have, Omberto. How strong it is. So flexible. A musician's hand, and you so clever with it. Is there any instrument you can't play? And you play very well, and you love to play your music, love it like your life, eh, Omberto, with your beautiful strong white clever hand."

All that, while the glass was still falling.

And then the glass met the tiled floor of the bar and burst like a firework.

Simoon was not in contact with Omberto.

She moved away, and as she did so, she said to Picaro, "I'll just get some air. It's hot in here."

Did he see her face? For an instant. He saw, Picaro, she looked older, old as Omberto had said even, when ten minutes before she had seemed like a woman of forty. And her face, in the dimness, was so velvet black, it was like a panther's mask. And in the black, her eyes the color of Saké.

Then she had gone, and Picaro stood and looked at Omberto, who was shaking visibly, from rage or some kind of horror.

"I had to do that," Omberto said. "Didn't I? Yes. What is she? She's smothering you—"

Picaro stared at Omberto, still trying to find something to say, but before he could, the lights went out.

The whole bar reeled in a kind of liquid twilight, where almost nothing but shadows were visible. A cry or two went up. Some inebriated laughter. These lights didn't fail. So it was another ploy, some piece of fun thought up by the management of the bar. Or a trick, so watch your pocket, watch your purse and jewelry—

But they were close to the slide where the drinks were served, and Omberto slammed around and stood there, ready for the light to return and another tray of beer.

And then Picaro saw something, something so soft looking, light as a feather, or a puff ball from some seeding flower, drifting delicately down through the almost-dark. It appeared such a gentle and curious thing that Picaro watched it, captivated, intrigued—to see what it might be. It dropped just where Omberto was, by the slide, where Omberto's hand was, on the steel of the counter. And then, like the beer glass, the falling autumnal softness struck a surface too. Just there. Just where Omberto was. Where his hand was. His right hand.

The violence of the noise was impossible—so loud and harsh, full of a crack and splintering, and a spurt of silvery flame that for a second illuminated Omberto, balancing awkwardly, as if half blown over, and screaming. Until the whole bar began to scream too.

And then the lights splashed on again full pitch, and Picaro could see where the one chemical light bulb, detached from the ceiling, had fallen and detonated against the bar, smashing Omberto's hand, every bone, cutting and burning Omberto's hand, every inch—so that it was now a *thing*, not a hand, and to this blackening and minced *thing*, this other thing still partly attached, which screamed and drew breath and screamed.

NO MEMORY EITHER of going back. A gap.

Just the door open from the CX-key. And the loft, lit mellifluously by a scatter of candles.

And, in a chair. She, sitting. A cameo in her blackness and her pale frock and the candledark all around.

Was it that he hoped she could still say to him, But how would I do *that*?

Was he so naïve and spent even then in the net of the spell she had woven around him?

Like father, like son.

Did he speak? No memory of it.

Simoon was the one with speech.

"I came home. It's way too hot out there. Would you like a cold drink?"

What did he say? Nothing? Anything?

He didn't walk any closer to her.

She said, "Here you are."

He said, "He taught me to play the korah, Simoon."

"Who's that?" she said.

"He taught me," said Picaro. Then he said something about the hospital. Something about the screaming. The bones. How they had had to—

Did she try to pretend a minute, look concerned? No, she'd never have done anything like that.

Then, what did she do? From there on, like the other things, that time, her face became something he remembered in words, not pictures.

"It's time you took the lead part in your own life," she said. And next, perhaps at once she said, "You don't need anyone else. I can give you all of it. I can give you everything. You're mine."

And then the memory—not in pictures, in words— her body pressing on his, against the wall, the line of her through her dress. Her breasts feeding on him, her hand between his legs, disgust exquisite, foulness and delight. Her tongue probing his mouth, which had given way. Even the wall, giving, giving, giving way.

Fall.

Only in words. Not pictures.

"Do you like this, baby? Yes. You like this. Yes, you're mine, I made you, didn't I? I can give you everything. You don't need anyone but me."

UNTIL FINALLY THE VIRTUALITY movie was back. It was a train in the night. It was blackness and lighted halts. It was the luta-citarra on the seat beside him; all he had kept in the room, all he had brought away.

6

LIFTING HER HEAD, she looked around at them, the howling thousands. She raised her supplicant hand a second time. Seeing only the death signal—thumb compressed and hidden, symbol of a *man* hidden, *buried*. Knowing this mob would never relent.

He lay on his side, near her feet. He had pushed himself on to one elbow, elegant, like a citizen on a dinner couch. His skin, flawless black. His eyes, proud and angry, hard as the black iron they resembled.

"They won't have it," Jula said to him. She remembered his name, "Picaro—before the gods, why didn't you put up a fight? You're able—I've seen you train in the court behind the Forum, where Talio's school is. You're good. Look how you've cut me about. Not many can boast of that. We're both their slaves. What would it have cost? You fool," she said bitterly. "What am I to do?"

Above, the blue closed sky of Stagna Maris. A scent of the incense of pine-cones. Away along the paved road that began between the stone-pines, a gate to the town, an entrance to the villa of her master. Life going on.

And at her feet, just one more man she must kill.

Jula raised her short sword and the crowd bayed with a single throat, and grew silent.

Jula threw the sword away. It plummeted and landed,

point-down in the sticky sand, then toppled over, defeated. Before the hubbub could erupt, she yelled, high and savage as a bird, "*No* and *no*—and *no*—" Even the top tiers might hear it. She thought they did.

The roaring that came in on her cry meant nothing. She knew they would throw things down, ripe fruit, stones they had picked up beforehand to cast at others— never at her, their favorite. And the sticklers had abandoned her, were hurrying off to the sides of the arena, to save themselves from misdirected missiles. In a minute, the amphitheater authority would send out others, to force her to her task, or to complete it themselves. This also—was nothing.

When she turned, he had sat up. She gestured impatiently to him to stand.

"We're both disgraced now. Rat meat. They'll soon send to butcher us." She added sharply, "Stand back to back with me. This time, *fight*. Show *them*—not *me*."

He rose. He stood far taller than she did. She had not thought, fighting him, Phaetho was this tall. But his name was not Phaetho, but Picaro—for the black and white bird.

Her helmet, which she had removed as she often did when her foe was down, lay over there. Never mind that. The helmet could not save her now. But somehow she had retrieved her sword.

The far doors were opening. Men in brazen armor were coming out, gladiators, these helm-masked, unknowable. Ten, twelve, fifteen—enough for the task.

"Why?" he said, standing with his back to her, so near she felt the heat of him against her shoulder blades.

Indeed, why? Jula had achieved nothing for him, and had ended her own life. Even if they overcame these others sent against them—which was unlikely, for both this man and she were scored with deep cuts and had fought each other some while—the crowd would not allow them to leave the amphitheater breathing, let alone walking.

She said nothing. Nor did he speak again. She felt the heat of quickness from him.

They stood back to back, and watched as death came trotting, shining, toward them.

SHE REMEMBERED THAT TIME, seeing him as she waited in one of the two-horse chariots, by Talio's yard. She, and others, Julus's prizes, dressed in their well-to-do actors' garments, had been put on display in the town. Now their master had business with his plebian rival, Talio.

Phaetho fought there in the dust, near the training post, with a thickset man.

In Rome there had been black Ethiopians, and some were free men. The Emperor Narmo had inaugurated among the legions several cohorts of such soldiers. But in Stagna Maris black men and women were rare. This fighter was finely made, powerful and glorious in the dust that clouded but did not conceal him. His long hair, coarse black and thick as a horse tail, was tied up on his head. As no gladiator should, when in combat, he had no look of a slave.

Jula had noted her master's evaluating eye settle on Phaetho.

But Talio, himself a one-eyed villain (others said) would hardly be parted from such a specimen, just as Julus refused to part with the specimen he called Jula.

One day, maybe, they might be matched, Phaetho and she.

But she had not considered that then. She had seen only a man who was, as she was, a possession. And presently, because she did not think much about those who were not immediate to her, she forgot him.

THE ARENA CROWD no longer belled. She heard the sea. No, it was the sough of pine trees.

She lay across the knees of a giantess.

It must be that the goddess had her, Bhrid, Arrow of the Sun, who dispensed warmth and plenty from the earth.

Her hair, moon blonde, fell over her shoulders and touched Jula's face so mildly, like the caress of grass. She smelled too of her healthy warmth, and of pine resin, and of the blue smoke rising from the central hearth. There was a smudge of the smoke on her brown cheek. Her bright eyes were nearly shut. She rocked Jula, and sang to her in the voice of love.

Yes, I remember *this*, better than all else. I remember—almost I do—how I lay inside her. But then I am almost still inside her body now, yet joined to her, not a year old, a golden circle once baked in the oven of her womb, having her impression still.

I was not *Jula* then. What was my name? Oh, Mother, sing me my name, so I can hear it, and know.

But her mother sang instead of love.

And Jula—still not having her other name—saw how a man came in at the low door, bending, and his hair was light in color.

My mother, my father. And so—

Jula thought—Don't let me see—no, don't let me see and remember what comes three years after. And there was a flush of fire and a sound of calling—but it was gone instantly, swept away by some phantom hand in her brain. Then Jula was a woman full-grown, and she was in the forest, as she had never been.

But she stood, glancing everywhere, taking lungfulls of the balsamic wind, seeing the shafts of smoldering sunlight which rayed between the pines, seeing the tracks of deer and the white tusk-marks of boar. And then, up through the trees towards her, breaking the shafts of the sun, strode the man she would meet, as her mother had met her father in that other time, before Rome came and the world ended.

But it was impossible to see him, against the brilliant breaking shafts of light.

And it was impossible to keep hold of a world that the Romans had ended.

IN DARKNESS, JULA OPENED her eyes, to one more incomprehensible and unimportant foreign place. She was awake now, however, dreaming over, and had to stay in it.

Tears ran out of her eyes, the lament for all she had lost: land, home, mother, father, lover—never met, her own *self*.

Had she shed tears before? As a child, sobbed and been sick out of the side of the wagon taking her into Rome. Cried when she was beaten. When her monthly blood began. Not often, or for long, these economic tears. Then anyway she unlearned the recourse of weeping, as she did any wrath other than the controled fury of a swordswoman, a games girl, or any care other than for life itself.

Yet now—now, in this place, this *dark* that was also false, so she had been told—here she wept. At last. Too late.

Even for Phaetho she wept. Of course for his sense-less death and the curse he had laid upon her—not only to die, but to endure rebirth in her slavery—but also since he too was lost to her. For there had been tonight the dream of the arena, when she had done as surely she had once secretly wished to, and, like him, rebelled and given up her survival in *contempt*. And in that dream she had mistakenly replaced Phaetho with Picaro. And hav-ing seen both of them then, in the dreams, she knew finally that Phaetho and Picaro were not at all the same. Were as unlike each other as fire and water, though both were young and strong, handsome, and black of skin.

7

INDIA WAS STANDING at the top of the watersteps.

Behind her rose Brown's, the Ca'Marrone, a baroque palace from the late 1600s, its flat façade anchored along the ground floor by heavy blocks of stone, made weightless above by two stories of recessed windows, carved cherubs, masks, and horses' heads. Everything reflected in the Canale Leone Marco. Even India, and her little Victorian portmanteau.

As the wanderer approached, her head turned slowly. She didn't look agitated or distressed, or even as if she had expected him. She had that sullen expression he recollected from the first time, when Cora balanced on his balcony rail, and she, India, remained below.

"Christ," said Picaro softly.

"Ah, signore—a demisella." The wanderlier, congratulatory that this nice young woman stood waiting for Picaro by the Ca'Marrone, in the sunny afternoon.

When he had climbed up the steps, Picaro held out his hand. India put her own into it. He had seen she knew, if not how. He did not see why she was there. Perhaps simply because he was one of the last to meet Cora in the state of life.

They walked into the guest palace without speaking, holding hands, as they had that day at the Equus Gardens, during the storm.

Brown's was the remodel of a Victorian hotel, evolved, as it once already had been, within the baroque frame of the seventeenth-century casa. Maroon marble columns upheld a ceiling painted with (Victorian) Italian renaissance gods. The floor of the wide, opened-out lobby was also marble-white. You saw straight through this area to the vast courtyard remade as a Victorian exotic garden, with blue banks of lupins, vermilion stocks, gladioli, palm trees. Some tables were scattered along a terrace.

"They've given me an apartment here," he said. "You can be in private there, if you want."

"Not yet," said India. She moved ahead of him into a kind of glassed-over conservatory, up against the terrace and garden. Here there were also tables and chairs among the plants, and a handful of people eating and drinking. Everyone wore Victorian garments, it was apparently the tradition if you stayed at Brown's. Even India had dressed in a high-necked blouse and demure bulb of a skirt.

Picaro didn't want to sit down here, but he followed her.

They sat. A waiter came.

India ordered black tea.

Then they only sat, she looking at her narrow hands, now crossed one on another on the marble table, he out into the garden.

At last India said, "You know I know she is dead."

"I realized you must know."

"You wonder what she was to me? Lovers? Related, perhaps? None of that. I've always known her."

"I'm so sorry," he said. "Please believe—"

"I believe you are sorry."

Then they sat in silence again. This time, she looked into the garden, too.

171

And then she said, "I went to the University and a man interviewed me—Leonillo, he was called. They let me see her again.

Picaro's heart stumbled against his ribcage. He said nothing. He had never known India to say so much.

She said, "They'd arranged her, and she looked very sweet. She would have preferred that, to look charming. Of course, they won't dispose of the body as yet. They have to investigate. Even I was only permitted to see her through a window, you understand."

"Yes. Did they tell you why?"

"They intimated there's some illness. A virus." Their eyes met, and Picaro saw quite clearly that India, whatever she had been told, knew much more, either from Cora before her death, or from some other source.

India said, "They told me you would be coming here, the Ca'Marrone. I know you weren't," she said, "with her when it happened."

Picaro said, "What do you want me to do?"

"Do? It isn't up to me."

"Are you angry with me?"

"Of course I am," she said calmly. "I could hate you. It's your fault she was there, in that place, and you weren't even with her. But there is no use in anger or hate."

He thought, almost pettily aggravated, *You weren't with her either*. He said, "I didn't know—If I'd been there too, I'd be dead. So would you." She lowered her eyes. "Like all the rest."

"Not all the rest," said India.

Picaro focussed on her. "Who *lived*?"

"One woman. She is in isolation—in those rooms under the University Building. Her name is Jenefra."

"*How do you know?*"

India's eyes, still lowered. "You must trust me that I do. If, whenever I tell you something, you ask me how I know, or ask yourself if I am lying or inventing, then each conversation we have will become difficult and time-wasting."

"*How* do you know, did they tell you—show you?" India looked down into the marble of the table. "Why are *you* telling *me*?"

"You ask too many questions, Picaroissimo. We must live by more than questions and answers. That is what is wrongly termed Blind Faith. It means—"

"Don't give me a lecture on theosophy."

"It means sometimes we must simply get on. Have you never done anything without first asking why or how or if or when?"

"Yes." Picaro got to his feet. "I'm sorry about Cora. I wish it could be changed. Charge anything you want to my account here."

And then he saw, across the drifts of lupins, an auburn bull which had also stood up, and up, towering over the neat shrubs in its bulging morning coat and fat-muscled trousers, elaborate cravat, and hair.

"PICARO."

"Flayd."

"He thinks I followed him," reported Flayd, to India. "Listen, buddy. I always room at this place, when I'm in Venus."

"Then," said Picaro, "I was sent to room here too."

Flayd said, "Seems they want us all in one spot. You too?" he asked India. She nodded. "We're over there," said Flayd. India at once went walking across the garden in the indicated direction. Flayd went after her, leaving Picaro standing.

Picaro saw, at the table to which they went, a woman in another Victorian dress, with a combed-up mass of fair hair. Suddenly he realized it was the Roman gladiatrix. She was transformed, but not entirely enough.

He too crossed the garden, through the lupins, between the palms in tubs.

He stood looking down at them, these three people from 1888, and the English afternoon tea, (one of Brown's specialities) laid out before them.

Fantastically (in keeping with the scene), Flayd was giving India a guided tour of the dishes of hot boiled eggs, grilled coppery fish, the toasts and various butters, preserves, cakes, muffins, strawberries. Flayd, Picaro could see, had not been stinting himself. An extraordinary tea service dominated the table, a mint-green salt-swan teapot, a duck milk jug, water lilies as spice and sugar bowls—plates that were the china leaves of water-plantains or lily pads.

A terrible sense of utter, childlike loneliness swept through Picaro. Once these things might ironically have amused him, pleased him even, as they did almost everyone else. But something had happened. Simoon had happened. And what she had left with him. And now, shut out, shut *into* the frozen snow beyond the lighted window—he hadn't even the refuge of scorn.

He found he sat down slowly. He sat then, staring at them, one after another, round and round the table. It was all a fantasy. The ducks and swans, the archaeologist stuffing himself with cherry cake made to a recipe at least two centuries old, the sulky self-contained adolescent girl, who spoke like someone older, nibbling fruit from a silver fork. And the female gladiator clad as a fashionable young Amerian lady from the Boston or New York of *Then*.

Picaro reached out and caught her wrist. She stayed nearly immobile, only turning her head to look at him.

Flayd said, a tired father, "Come on, Picaro. You know what happened last time."

Picaro spoke to Jula. "What are *you* doing here?" Her eyes reminded him of the eyes of an animal, intelligent, cunning, swift, and dangerous, except for the blue-green color of them.

She said, "I was brought here."

That, of course, was the whole of this particular question and answer, wasn't it?

Involuntarily, so it seemed to him, his grip on her wrist must have tightened. Abruptly her other hand had hold of his own wrist. She was viper-quick. Though her fingers couldn't encircle it, they were pressing in at some strategic point, numbing his thumb and forefinger.

He glared into her eyes and saw waters tumbling.

Flayd got up again. A waiter was also standing there absurdly with a heron coffeepot, saying, "No trouble, please. Or security will arrive."

"All right." Picaro let go of her wrist.

As she released him in turn from her gem-hard fingers, he too got up again.

"Let's stroll in the garden, Sinna Jula Victrix."

Flayd said to the waiter, "It's OK, I'll—"

Picaro said, "Keep out of it." And to her, "Let's be Victorian. Take my arm."

Jula too had risen. She faced him. He could see her thinking, deciding to do what he said.

She was a slave. Everyone else was master or mistress.

He was afraid of her.

She reminded him—no, not of that. Not of that one.

She took his arm lightly. They walked along a path

through the banks of stocks and roses, to a flight of steps flanked by two carved urns with lavender.

"A blonde wig," he said. "Romans wore wigs. But how is the corset?"

"No worse," she said, "than the straps that bound me when I fought."

"You're a dangerous woman. A live-dead woman who can fight. Do you still think I'm that other man you killed?"

"I know you are not."

"Oh, how's that?"

"I remembered him, and when I saw him first. I remember things now I had always forgotten."

Picaro saw Flayd's responsible face peering at them through the flowers. Suddenly Picaro laughed.

He drew her down the steps into the lower garden, where there was a lily pond with golden carp.

She took her hand from his arm, and said gravely, "If you try to harm me, I'll prevent you. That's my right."

"I know that. I'm not violent."

Her eyes. She didn't look away, or lower them, as Flayd had complained she always did.

Picaro then was *not* a master? Still a slave? One of her own kind—what kind was that?

She said to him, without preface, "Why won't you fight?"

"What?"

"To survive you must fight. It's all we have. You're not Phaetho, not like him. Yet you are exactly like him. He wouldn't fight, even to live. They'd have let him live, maybe honored him, crowned him with laurel," she lapsed into Latin. He couldn't follow, heard the word *missio*—she was frowning, with thought and determination, not anger.

She spoke to him as directly as a young man his own age, not like a woman, not like a slave to a slave. They were two soldiers, in a lull between the yammering rushes of some unending war. She put her hand up and on his shoulder—he almost recoiled. It was what del Nero had done, but her hand wasn't fire-hot, it was cool. "Let go," said Jula, in her strangely accented Italian, "of death."

"That's what you think I'm doing. Holding *on* to it?"

"Fast," she said. "With both your arms."

He turned away from her and her hand's touch was gone.

I'm already dead, Jula Victrix, said his thoughts.

Carp glittered in the pool. As they swam under the lilies, her reflection failed to reform itself, her translucent shadow had vanished from the afternoon grass.

Two children came running out of a shrubbery. (Alien beings, like every other living thing.) They glanced at Picaro, diverted a moment by his height and looks. But he was stone and, unmirroring, gave back nothing, and they bounded away.

How had she known? Perhaps it was how her Roman school had trained her, to *guess* such states in others. Had *she* never been afraid, the moronic bitch? "Fight," "let go," these meaningless phrases of one who never hesitated. The brink for her had always been there, and so—always forgotten.

8

THIS FILING MACHINE CONSTANTLY clicked now. It was an irritating noise, stupidly like that of some big, old-fashioned clock exploited in the City. Maintenance had overhauled the machine. Nothing seemed wrong with it, but in the light of the CX malfunctions of the other day, it too was now being monitored.

As he walked through into the outer room, the one kept for period display, with its gilded plasterwork and typewriter, Leonillo checked his wristecx. He was due for a vitamin capsule. He took one from a pack, swallowed it with fresh apricot juice.

After a moment the hit of the vitamins would sharpen him. He stood waiting for that, gazing from the window into a courtyard with a plane tree.

There had been a lot to do this Viorno morning. Another batch of visitors wishing to leave the dome, and finding out the exit terminals were shut. They would have to be persuaded, *disuaded*, or bribed. In more intransigent cases, detained. Those who lived here as their privilege seldom departed the City (a few who had, and were now currently unable to re-enter, were the problem of the authorities on the mainland.) Most of the *tourists* had been entranced to find they were allowed extra holiday time in the City of Wonders, as the "literature" called it. They had only needed their tour agencies to reassure them that relevant employers above had no qualms. This too was taken care of. Therefore, only a minority kicked up a fuss, usually those with freelance lives, who had planned to be elsewhere. Some of those easily settled, of course still wanted to call outdome. The legend of temporary faults in the call facilities eventually had to be dispensed with. Then calls were placed with them via controlled circuits, or, in many instances, *pretended* to, with faked voices, digitally reproduced, and undetectable. (Such procedures were normally illegal.)

All this could eventually be tidied up. Which would not be Leonillo's job. He was only the one who received orders, then *gave* orders, obedient and obeyed. That was his function, not generally obvious through his veneer. He was good at it.

However, yesterday there had been three groups indome who had refused to accept the bonus of remaining in Venus. One of these groups had commitments both monetary and civilian that required their immediate return above. Fortunately some of the group were heavy drinkers, and so had enabled themselves to be made a target for false arrest. The remainder of the group were then caught up in the net. The plainclothes police—that is, they were clothed as theatrically as everyone else—were always reliable in such matters, and the incarceration facilities both escape-proof, and tolerable for any but the most criminal captives. Again, it would all be smoothed over when the time came, compensation paid, bureaucratic "mix-ups" apologized for.

Only two persons, so far, had needed broader measures. One of these had been munificently paid off. He had also been guaranteed first rights in telling his "story" to an influential mainland journal. The other, staying unamenable, had unluckily had to be hospitalized. Probably, when it was all over, and the dome open again, he would never remember exactly what it was they had had to do to him.

The nature of what went on here, the Experiment, was so monumental that almost any means were excusable. They stopped short of execution. Other governments and authorities, as Leonillo understood, would not have been so squeamish, or so careful.

Altogether, Leonillo had no quarrel with any of it. It was merely that somehow (and he would have been hard put to it to say quite how, or when) he had begun to evaluate, in his well-trained, regimented, quite near-horizoned mind, not only the enormity of what had been done, but its *outlandishness*.

Its *terror*.

He hadn't admitted this to himself. Would not. Could not. And so the creature of the terror made itself visible to Leonillo just on the edges of his close-circuited awareness—by the brooding shape of a tree that somehow upset his mood, the annoying ticking of a machine which shouldn't tick.

Leonillo obeyed orders. He kept his own life very private, clutterlessly barren. He had no one to turn to, not even a priest, for he had been born into a world where God or Spirit remained only as fashion accessories to certain psychic cravings. Among all the beautiful churches of Venus, which rang their bells and sometimes swelled with praiseful masses in the tradition of pure drama, Leonillo, on his lone nighttime promenades, was never alerted. He lived by rule of thumb. It had always been enough, and now was not.

Descending in the elevator, Leonillo compressed his

thin lips. He was unaware of this additional gesture of zipping up.

"Yes, Chossi. And how do we find her?"

"The same, Leon. It's—pitiful."

Such an emotive word from Chossi surprised Leonillo—not that the heartless clerk should say it, but say it to his superior.

Leonillo walked through into the peculiar, dimly-lit bubble, which contained what could only be called the *remains* of UAS Jenefra 19B.

The door hissed shut. Leonillo was alone with her.

He walked forward, and looked down at the narrow optecx support capsule, in shape not unlike the vitamin capsule from earlier, save this was filled by a woman's body.

Tubes and lines went in and out. Aside from the security, it was not unlike something one could find in most main hospitals.

Without the apparatus, what was left of her would not be able to exist. The support assisted her to breathe, injected her with basic nutrients, cleansed her delicately at planned intervals. Sometimes her eyes moved under the lids, but nothing else. And apparently these eye-movements might not indicate anything more than muscular spasm.

The capsule also supplied coda-morphine. She could feel nothing. That was necessary. It was all that could be done for her.

The irony was that, superficially, she did not seem to the casual eye, aside from the little medical attachments, so horribly injured. Some bruising, an ominous darkening here and there of her skin.

Leonillo did not study her in great physical detail. Again, it was not his job. He had the reports.

It was an astonishment she had survived, and soon what was left of her body would simply cease to function, despite the care it received.

Most of her bones were broken. That was, they were splintered, in some areas, *powdered*. This had happened at the scene, and also when the UAS team had moved her from the Palazzo Shaachen, despite every extreme precaution. All the corpses had been the same.

Aside from the bones, most internal organs had extravagantly ruptured. Leonillo had heard one of the surgical team remark that the inside of each of the victims, as flash scan revealed it, was like the map of a perfectly laid railway after a small nuclear device had detonated nearby. Another one said bitterly, "Jam—mush and jam, polenta. God in heaven."

Everything had given way.

This was so with Jenefra, as with the rest. Everyone who had been in those rooms, on that starry bon'Votte. All the same.

She seemed to have survived the fraction she had because she had gone to the lavatory to be sick.

Plenty of them had vomited, evacuated bowel and bladder—no amazement there, the stomach lining, colon, the liver, all of it, all, all coming undone. It had been sudden, too. But Jenefra seemed to have felt it the first, and gone to the bathroom and shut herself in—and so not caught the full final brunt of—whatever it had been.

(The musician, Picaro, in the apartment above, separated by two solid floors, and the mesh of air- and noise-conditioning systems, had received only the most brushing dose. His inner body showed a very little minor, just-observable, scarring—nothing worse than if he had had a serious alcohol dependence or spent some time as a maltreated prisoner of some harsh regime, a common enough fate elsewhere. Picaro had therefore been lucky.)

Jenefra had neither Picaro's luck, nor the luck to be killed outright.

Leonillo looked at her. He was not callous, only without imagination.

CX activated in the dimmed-out wall, lights flying up. Another door opened. Three medical staff ran in in contemporary plascord uniforms.

The woman spoke hurriedly. "Step back, please, Sin Leon. She's about to experience seizure."

Reading body signs without pause, the machines could predict this with a fifty-second margin. Now the team were adjusting the capsule lid, switching on preparatory restraints.

Leonillo stood back. Waiting, as the team waited.

He recalled how, when they had smashed in the doors of the Palazzo Shaachen, most of the windows had shattered too. Like brittle sugar. Like these bones. (Some of the brickwork, wood and stone showed, it seemed, unusual erosions.)

He thought of the other girl, what was her name? Cora? She had been the most favored by death, which had bludgeoned her heart before anything else. Her wrist bone pulverized into more than seventy-six pieces.

Seizure began in the capsule.

The team worked there, springing about, barking to each other hoarsely. Lights stabbed and poured across the walls.

Then it was over.

He returned to the capsule side as the medical staff moved away.

"Her eyes are open," he said.

"Yes," said one of the men. "That happens. There is some brain activity."

"You've told me," said Leonillo.

He looked down into Jenefra's eyes. They were massively bloodshot, and blind, he thought, but they slowly moved. For a moment they were precisely on his face. She returned his gaze—Leonillo saw, without any doubt, that though what was left of her brain had been kept alive, along with the ruined sack of flesh, Jenefra herself wasn't there inside. *This* was a zombie. For in these eyes, already, was nothing—As they had been wont to say, the building was lighted, but no one home.

BEFORE DESCENDING THE FINAL LEVEL (to the area some of the staff jokingly called Hell) Leonillo made time to look in on the screen room.

Everything under scrutiny was proceeding. Putting the four of them together had been sensible and saved some time, unless one or more of them should go out, which per-haps, at least in Picaro's case, didn't seem very likely.

He had had a dialogue with the Roman woman. Having watched a recording of this, Leonillo had found its strangeness banal, only what he would have expected. The black singer was talented but off his head. The girl thought in the manner of her former barbaric times. Flayd, the archaeologist placed within their orbit, had become almost a referee—like one of Jula's own stick-weilding "sticklers" from the arena. He trampled doggedly along, causing no lesions. The little girl of eighteen—India?—appeared to be the only composed one. There was nothing to her, he suspected, but they kept a provisional eye on her. She was enigmatic—or dumb, as Chossi had concluded.

Leonillo glanced in at them all now. Flayd working with laptop CX, Jula sitting by the window of his apartment, Picaro standing elsewhere at the window of his. India was in her own room, turning slow cartwheels, her twilight body naked as a pin, unconscious of, or indifferent to, the feasting eyes of the surveillance crew.

They all played their parts. The four at Brown's, the staff here, the population of the City. Actors. That was how Leonillo truly saw most others. Sometimes their performances pleased him—as when Flayd had inadvertantly, taking Jula from the University, done exactly what was wanted of him. Or if, conversely, they provided some informative diversion. But generally their acting was pedestrian and poor. Amateurs on the stage of life.

Leonillo drank caffelatte before going down to Hell. The vitamins hadn't boosted his mood, as he had hoped they would. And he was uneasy at what must be done next, and, not being uneasy very often, not handling it well.

THE LOWEST COMPLEX WAS THICK with safeguards. Vid banked on vid, CX thrummed, check lights flicked, and human security posed tensely, flecxs on hips and eyes wide.

The observation room, though, was empty, which was partly precautionary. It was long and circular; it ran right around another set of rooms entirely, and looked into them from windows that, from the *inside*, were not always visible. In the same fashion, no sound traveled either way, without instigation this side.

The decor of the inner rooms was gracious enough, but of a quickly thrown together type. Silk-upholstered chairs and brocaded drapes, the recxs of old paintings . . . a decorated harpsichord reflected in the tiled floor. It was the third harpsichord in as many days. Things—

broke. Strings, keys, utensils. The plaster on the walls was faintly marked again as if by smoke.

A virus? One which destroyed human tissue, and also bricks and mortar, stone and plasteel and optecx glass? One which effected also CX function?

He sat there now, at the table, writing on a sheet of apparent parchment, musical notations from the 1700s, with a pen that dispensed black ink slimly, better, he had said, than a quill, which spat, needed constant dipping, snapped in moments of composing excitement.

This was mostly what he did, del Nero. Wrote his music. The weaknesses in the harpsichords, the cittaras and mandolins—he used them up, then had to manage without them.

Leonillo looked at Cloudio del Nero through a piece of window which, from the inner side, was an opaque painting. It was just possible to trace the design of the painting on this outer side, vague delineation, as if a ghost stood there, between them. But also, there were hair-fine cracks beginning in one portion of the viewer. Again.

Everything here had to be stabilized, then restabilized. And while it was done, del Nero had to be shut into another area of the inner rooms, and besides, no one went into them without protective clothing or stayed there individually for more than ten minutes. Even ten minutes, of course, was probably too long.

They had explained it to del Nero. Some of it. Had had to.

Now he poised in front of the watcher (unaware?) scribbling away at the notation. He had that look in his eyes Leonillo had seen before in the eyes of creative artists. He was miles off—in fact, *not all there*. Despising it, Leonillo didn't find it peculiar. He himself, having no fundamental use for music, literature, art, film—any alternative reality—was quite comfortable with the Artistic Race. He knew where they belonged, and that Cloudio del Nero, despite his dangerous genetic geography, carried otherwise the correct label.

And yet.

Leonillo bent forward, squinting into that sealed room.

What was it? What?

Was del Nero such a large man? So tall and elongated? He seemed—but it was some trick of the fake light, the fake interposed painting, the flaws in the viewer—he seemed of a different size—almost of a different shape.

Leonillo blinked.

The musician had put down his pen. He got up.

Leonillo started. He stepped back from the viewing window, sweat smearing his forehead.

What had he seen?

No—a distortion—something wrong with the light, of course, the light, all the sub-University CX was eccentric now—it was that.

Look, Cloudio was only a slender short fellow, *not* tall, even in his own day. He paced towards the viewer—towards the painting—towards Leonillo—pedantically absorbed in deep creative thought.

A short small man with almost feminine hands, with long dark hair and rings and a coat of buttercup satin.

What did Leonillo see?

There had been a swirling, and a gigantic elevation that touched the ceiling, that went—*beyond* the ceiling—that filled the inner rooms, that glowed.

The illumination was at fault. The satin coat catching it, and some shadow.

And Leonillo's nerves. He must face it, he would need to do something about them, his nerves.

He moved around the curve of the window, to a place which might be cleared on the viewer's *other* side. Leonillo pressed for communication.

At the intrusion, this voice over the microphonicx, del Nero looked up at him.

His eyes—glazed with his golden dreams—were luminescent.

Tricks of the light.

"I am sorry to disturb you, Signorissimo Cloudio."

Something in the face—changing—like the uncovering of the window through which each man now could regard the other.

"It's almost a relief to me," said del Nero, "to be disturbed."

"How is the new harpsichord?"

"Alas. It will no longer play for me."

"I'm very sorry."

"You have told me. Something in my chemistry, they said. How remiss, to cause such difficulties simply by my presence."

Cloudio del Nero's voice sounded now bored and distant—yes, miles off. He was uninterested, did not bother any more. Also, as his brain labored on at his music, very evidently, the rest of him flew only on automatic pilot.

Rather like Jenefra, then. The building was lit, but *this* one, who *was* home, was locked into the attic, and did not deign to emerge for trivia.

Leonillo said, "There are some plans for you, Signorissimo."

Cloudio del Nero smiled. Automatically.

"We are thinking—we'd like you to give a recital of some of your works—whatever you wish to perform, of course."

Leonillo heard his own voice utter this.

He had been told to. To arrange it. His orders.

It was since he had had these particular orders that his nerves—

Leonillo thought of Jula. How they had told him no black UAS members must have contact with her until she was put out into the City, which naturally had in it people of all ethnic groups. Why had that segregation been deemed appropriate? Picaro, who had been allowed to reach her, was the first of his kind in her reborn world. But she had mistaken Picaro for the one she had killed. Had that too been intended?

Why think of this? It was not in his remit to consider mooted manipulations—leave that to the Flayds. Leonillo said to the man behind the viewer, "Your musical opus is already advanced, I think?"

Courteous and patient now, del Nero replied, "But since I must be kept apart like this, how can I perform any music publicly, as you suggest?"

"There'll be tight security, and containment, I'm afraid. We intend to screen you with magna-optecx— nothing like the glass of this window. Impermeable and virtually indestructible. But an audience will be present. They will witness you clearly and hear every note in exquisite exactness. Perhaps you may by now believe, we're able to achieve such things at a significant level."

As Cloudio turned, something seemed to unfurl about him, to flare in his wake—a cloak of *unseen* matter—magical. But *not. Nothing*.

"Do you find the lighting in there deficient? I'm afraid the system's reacting again."

"Oh, but recollect, I'm used to candles," said Cloudio del Nero, almost playfully. "*They* would flicker and go out. How would this light, now, concern me?"

And then he made a sort of sound, a kind of swift

almost humming noise. Perhaps some element of his composition was lingering in his mind.

Leonillo found he had danced back again. Dizzily he pressed against the farther wall.

As if a wild animal, which had seemed tame and innocent, had suddenly lashed its tail, bared its teeth, snarling and readying itself to spring.

Leonillo said something to the man behind the glass. What it was he could not remember, once outside. No doubt something else to do with the orders he had, the recital he had been told to organize.

In the corridor, checking his wristecx. Signs of slight debility. Slight hyperventilation. Nothing serious. As if he had received a small personal shock, like tidings of a distant bereavement. But Leonillo had no family, no one to be bereaved of.

Upstairs, he ordered lunch, and told others to fix the lighting in the musician's area.

9

LOOK AT ME, insisted the Africara, where it stood against the wall.

From time to time, Picaro *looked* at it.

The big black pot of it, the black belly of it, strung with its silver moon-web of strings—earth and air.

In the end, he went to it and touched the strings, and they tore. Some crumbled.

He wasn't phased. He had expected something like that.

In the curve of its hip, a crack had appeared, like the tributary of some river.

No longer his, no longer anyone's.

On this cooking pot with its antennae in heaven, seated on a roof, under a black sky assembled in stars, he had made, over seven nights, the Africarium. He and it, had made it. A symphony for the orchestra of one instrument alone.

He thought, no doubt in a while it would entirely fall apart and lie in bits along the floor of the new apartment at Brown's.

THINGS HAPPENED DURING the remainder of the year, after he had taken the train away from Simoon.

Once only he called Omberto, an Intel message which would chase the intended recipient until they were found. When no recipient ever was found, he called Carlo, and then Coal. Each also one time only. Carlo was high when he called, and wouldn't talk, kept making out Picaro was someone trying to sell him something. A girl laughed in the background, foolishly. Coal said over the wires, which murmured at some Intel storm, "What ya think he done, man, huh? What he be gonna do? You saw like the rest of us. All they could give him on his med-cred was a seesaw *robot's* hand. You don't play nothing with that."

And in that year otherwise, korah and mandolin in a darkened barroom behind a virtuality theater, an agent dropping by on a freak whim and seeing Picaro: the beginning.

It had been so easy. A swift ascent, and if not internationally glorious, good—good enough. So unlike the previous life as to be—sorcerous . . .

And next the luxurious apartimento, with its three long chambers for living, its balcony, and the use of the pool—the decx, the handouts, the moments of adulation. Best, the channel standing wide for him to pass the music through into a big waiting world.

Picaro was still sixteen. The very last day of sixteen. And that night he was going to another place by the sea.

He was loitering in Alessio's office, on the thirtieth floor, when Alessio took a call from reception.

Alessio smiled. "I don't know why I should tell you."

"What?" asked Picaro, who was looking out the high window at the rushing stream of a city and the polluted stream of a sky above.

"They say there's a fat old woman in a Dowi downstairs. She says she's waiting for you."

Picaro shook his head.

Alessio said, "Let me amend that. A fat old *rich* woman if she's in a Dowi."

"That's the new kind of CX chair?"

"Yes it is. The one that can run up stairs. The one that can do everything for you that you can no longer do for yourself."

"A fat old rich *crippled* woman," said Picaro, "in a rich disability chair."

"Yes," smiled Alessio. "Can't think how she got so far in *here*, though. Must have charmed her way."

Then something woke along Picaro's backbone.

He said, "Did she give a name?"

"No name."

"What color," said Picaro, "are her eyes?"

Alessio going on smiling. He activated the discreet intercom and asked Picaro's question. Listened. Said, "The girl says this woman's eyes are a kind of light honey. Fanciful enough?"

Picaro moved across the office. Stopped.

"What is it? Is there trouble?"

How to explain to Alessio, with his created wealth and his civility, his manicured nails and pearly ear stud and smile. How to try to convey this sensation of a building surrounded, its elevators and stairs cut off, its upper stories burning, and bomb blasts thundering at the walls.

"I don't want to see her."

"OK. Of course. I'll get them to tell her—"

"She won't go. Or she'll go—and she'll find me somewhere else."

Alessio got up. His demeanor was quite changed. "Who is she, Picar? Come on, you'd better tell me. Some woman you once—"

"*No.*"

"All right. Let it go. Do you want me to contact someone from security?"

"It won't be any use."

"Yes, of course it will."

Picaro said, "I'll go down by the other lifts."

"Yes."

"I'll catch an earlier flight."

"OK. Call me from your hotel. Tell me what is going on then. I am intrigued."

In the lift, thinking the doors would open at some floor and there she would be.

What was it? Some disguise? Perhaps facilitated by a *spell*.

No, there were no spells, no magic. It wasn't as normal as that.

It was *her*. What she was. What she could do.

The taxi got him back to his living complex. When Picaro reached the apartimento, it looked to him as if it belonged to some other man.

He had left any packing, preferring to do it himself, knowing he had lots of time.

Now, no time.

Hastily he slung things into a bag, shoved instruments into cases as if they were not fragile or important.

After closing the luggage and containers, a silence came in like a kind of weather.

Picaro was ready. He activated the security systems in the room, picked up the bag and got the instrument carriers across his shoulders by their straps.

When he opened the door, she was seated outside.

Simoon, in her chair.

The lift doors were statically together across the hall. She'd been there a while. Waiting for him to come out.

Knowing what he would do.

"Won't you ask me in?" she said at last.

His door stood wide behind him.

"No," he heard himself say. But as he said it, he stepped away, back inside the living area, and the chair, rolling forward with the softest serpent's hiss, smoothly came after him.

They were in the room. Both of them. With her right hand, reaching over, Simoon pushed the door. It sank against the wall and shut.

"Surprised?" she asked. "To see me like this?"

He thought he would never have known her. But that wasn't true. He must always know her. Even if she had come at him in some ultimate disguise, even if she had arrived in an animal costume, hidden.

She had become enormously fat. Not a tall woman, she must weigh around a hundred and twenty kilos. It was, too, a bizarre kind of fat, loose—yet oddly solid, hanging on her like creased padded clothing, folded in thick slops under the chin, at her wrists, along her arms.

Most of her otherwise was concealed by the long whitish tent she wore. It cascaded down, and out of the hem of it crept a pristine tube, which fed back into the Dowi chair. She was, then, incontinent.

Her face was round as a jet-black fruit and bulging worse even than the rest of her, swollen *hard*. Out of this face, the lemon slices of her eyes struggled up to see. Their color was now elusive, despite what the girl had said to Alessio. Her hair was short, gappy, and in tufts.

Watching him look at her, Simoon somehow *spread* herself to let him behold it all. It was as if, ridiculously and impossibly, she derived some horrible satisfaction from his viewing her as now she was.

Before she spoke again, she had to take a peck of

water from the attachment that rose up in the chair arm. Only her right hand seemed to wish to move much.

"Want to know what happened, baby?"

Picaro braced himself.

"You got big and stopped walking."

She laughed. He could recall her laugh, it was nearly the same, only a little raspy, like her speaking voice, somewhere at its periphery.

"That is the result," she said, "of what happened. Part of the result. The first *moments* of the result."

"You're sick." He was attempting to talk to her, as if there was some rationale to any of it. The bags weighed him down, but he dared not let go. They were like ballast in the air or anchors in water.

"I am sick. Let me tell you about it. It has an impressive name, my sickness: SPP. That's what they call it. Amerjargon, like most of the scientific crap—SPP. What does that stand for? Someone . . ." she said, and broke off to yawn, huge and fearful, gasping, (and he saw into her mouth, pale and missing teeth, and the peridot was gone, leaving a blackened hole in the particular tooth it had occupied.) "Someone far back, in a City they are rebuilding under the sea, in some kind of oxygen jar—she had it, this gal. They called it a palsy then. She was bloodline with me. And with your father. It affected her face. So they tell me. It's all right, unless it comes through, doesn't always. But my pa and my ma both came down from that gal. Double-value genes. That can do it. And your daddy too, his pa. Well, maybe he never let you know he and I, cousins. But it was me it came on into. When it does that, then it's like a weed, it gets a hold, and all the ground goes briars and tares, like some book says. I knew, when I called on you last time. I knew I had less than a single year. Did you like how I looked then? Sure you did. I was lovely. That's what happens, at the start. The body puts up a real battle. It repairs everything it can. Over-compensation, they said. It try to push this thing, this thing with the name away. Skin firms up, hair grows thick and long, lose a little weight, feel good, look like a girl again. For a little while. But then—then the tares and thorns are seeded all through and they start in growing. Body can't fight, not all that. Not a damn thing it or anyone can do. Tell you it's real name? Systemic Panplegia. Ain't that too sweetly pretty. Like the name of a dragonfly. Systemic Panplegia. Everything . . ." she yawned, "everything, piece by piece . . . muscles, skin, bones—hair go brittle, break off—can't burn off your fat—every joint, every nerve, all useless—and then *inside*. Heart, guts, bladder, liver, lungs, brain. Little by little, baby. Turn you into stone."

Picaro dropped the bags slowly from him.

He stared at her, *into* her, seeing the petrified vistas of her inner landscape, seeing it *happen*. It hurt him. As if he hurt for her—

"Think they'd be able to do something," she said, amiably. "Can't do a thing. Make anything. CXs, virtualities. Still can't. Not this. Found a cure for cancer back when I was a girl. Got the sexual diseases fixed. 'Long comes another new disease, can't figure it, can't do a thing. Always been there, not really showing itself anything much. Perhaps you get born with an arm won't work, or a face, like that gal back in the past. You can live with those. But it's grown up now, this one. This one has *developed*. Can't live with this one."

She sighed, and the water-tube rose again at some pressure on the Dowi of her right, moveable, hand. She bent her long neck awkwardly and drank.

"I knew," she said, "when I came to you back then. I wanted to be happy a few months. Just a few. All I had."

"How could I—"

"How could you know? Think I wanted you to know? I am ashamed of this, I am ashamed. It bring me down like no other thing ever brought me. And you. What I ask of you? Nothing. Just to be. And then for some little silly joke that you thought I did—"

Picaro felt the blood, or a poison, flare through his veins.

"I know what you did. I heard you tell him. I saw it happen. I was there."

"A light fell down and broke his hand? I did that? Coincidence, baby. Never hear of *that*?"

Picaro bit the words away inside himself. He must not speak to her, this fearsome creature, beached here like a nightmare whale, dying and petrifying before him.

"Why'd I do anything? I loved you," she said. "I only wanted to be near. My own flesh. I loved you." She sighed. She put up her movable hand and touched the gourd of her face. "All that bad stuff your daddy told you 'bout me—" then she laughed again. This time it was entirely *her* laughter. She said, "All true, baby. All *true. All true.*"

The light altered in the apartimento.

Was it darker? Or more bright? A shadow.

A shadow that was a light.

"*Omberto*. Yeah, I did it to him. He made me mad. I have done a whole lot, here and there. I can do things. Say, who helped you get your success? Who you think? Just you? Just some stroke of fortune, and you never no luck till then? Think about it. Oh I can do things, I can do everything. Save this, save get myself to cure. Only thing defeats Simoon—*herself*. Ain't that a fascination. Remember that last time, baby? Remember what we did? You and I, after I saw to that white space-waste with his white hands—remember, you and me, against the wall? You and me. So good, darling. Did you love me then, or were you only thinking of *him*?"

She was not a woman. Not a creature.

Picaro said, "You're an evil spirit."

"Sure I am," she said. "You better believe it. Listen now. This thing this evil spirit got inside her. It passes on. If the mother gets it this strong, so does her child. You hear me, baby? That was what I came to warn you last time. Just, when I saw you, I hadn't the heart. This evil old witch, this spirit out of hell—she couldn't do it, not right off. Now she can. You gonna get this, baby. What you see here, me, this is you. You, baby, in the future."

Picaro reached behind him. There was nothing there.

"Not yet," said Simoon. "A man, it mostly kicks in when he starts his thirties. That's how it goes. Older for a woman. Her blood times help keep it away. But when she stops her moon rhythm, *then* it comes. Men, it sooner. Anytime from thirty, baby. Then here you are, in this Dowi chair, if you can even get one. Here you are."

She was smiling, somehow the gourd of face allowing that. Not really a smile, not like Alessio's expensive smile or like a woman's smile. Not a human smile.

"Don't believe me?" she said coaxingly. "You never going to know till it get you. Undetectable, till you have it. Till it have *you*. No one can reassure you, no doctor on earth. No test can put you in the clear. Not even this new scan they got. You are healthy, everything shows it, then you better than most, then you get *this*. Then you are over. Won't be long for me now. Lungs starting to turn into rocks. Lucky, before the brain. That's what he said, the doctor. Lucky. Stroke of fortune. Hope you have my luck, darling."

Picaro stood, his feet grown into the floor.

The fat bulb of hanging flesh, which contained the evil spirit, sat smiling with the creases of its eyes.

Simoon said, "But I haven't done with you. You left me. You took away my last months when I could have been happy. When I'm gone, you have to live this out. You'll remember me. *I put shadow on you, Magpie.* I put on shadow. Listen now. I tell you three things. When you seen each of them, then it will be your time. Fourteen years. Maybe you'd have had ten more years after that, got to forty. Can happen. Before this thing with the dragonfly name begins. But I change that. I put *shadow* on you. Listen."

Her voice. Her voice—never to be erased—her sorcery, these words that he must keep.

"Listen to me. First thing you see, five years from now, you twenty-one years, man fall from the sky in front of you. You see that. Second thing, when you are twenty-seven years, gray dog with a pig's face, you see that. And when you are twenty-nine, you wake and a snake on your pillow, a snake coiled under flowers. You see these things. They there, in front of you. I see them clear as the sun that never shines here. Tell you. You listen me, Magpie. I *curse* you with these three things, to prove, so you know. You going to die. Hear me now. You will meet your death at thirty. You will die under water, though not from drowning. *Shadow* tells you. *Shadow* makes it be. You think I was hard on *Omberto*? That was nothing. You I *love*."

Afterwards, those other times with her, gaps coming to exist in his memory, certain sections of action he could never recollect. Not so with this. This, like her prophecy, her curse, he never forgot.

But he had begun to move before he knew it. He

only knew because the Dowi was abruptly gliding away backwards to avoid him. It hit against the shut door of his rooms.

And then Picaro stood over her and he drew her up, Simoon, his mother, this welter of fat and stone, heavy as the world must be, drew her up and up by her bulging bloated long giraffe's neck. She made no sound. He could see the creases of her eyes still watching intently. He smashed her head against the door, which the switched-on security systems had already made impermeable and hard as steel.

He heard the crack. Blood spilled, slow and too thick, from her nostrils, and trickled skittishly into all the rolls of fat, like the tributary of some river.

When he let her drop back in her chair among the detached tubing, which also spilled now, and stank, her eyes were still watching.

From the angle of her head as it dropped over, he saw her neck, as well as her skull, was broken.

And her eyes, dull now but still intent, went on watching him. Watched him as he pushed the Dowi aside, as he picked up his bags, as he went out and shot the outer locks on the door with his handprint. Watched him go down in the lift. Watched him go over the city to the airport. Watched him. Waking and sleeping.

I put *shadow* on you. *Shadow* makes it be.

IN THE DAYS AND NIGHTS that followed, somewhere then, he called Alessio. They spoke on a private line. Alessio had contacts. He could deal with it.

It was dealt with. No comment made or price exacted. Except that, after this, there were no upward turns for

Picaro's promising career. And no more meetings with Alessio.

Perhaps inevitable. Or only her success-magic, cast for him, perishing at her curse.

SO HE MADE HIS LIVING, lived. He, and his music, were known, somewhat. It was all right. It was not now he forgot—only that he forgot in *other* ways. It sat there, what she had said, what he had done, sat in his brain's back. He became accustomed to it, sitting there, in its chair.

Naturally he ceased to believe (did he?) that she had cursed him, or that he would contract an obscure disease for which he was genetically predisposed, or that he had murdered her. (He never researched any medical details, asked no one.)

When he was twenty-one, getting out of a car on a main boulevard, a suicide crashed from a high block on to the pavement almost in front of him.

Amid all the screaming, approaching sirens, the uproar, Picaro stood within a place of silence.

And at twenty-seven, on a stage with the Africara, there was a little gray dog that got up on the stage with him too, and it had on a pig's pink mask, reducing the audience to joy. And amid all the music, the amusement, Picaro played on, his hands already turning into granite.

The last time was almost the worst. He had expected it so long, but in those moments, not. The girl, who perhaps meant to frighten him those two years later, when he was twenty-nine, succeeded. She hadn't told him of the snake, her pet. He woke to find it lying peacefully between her sleeping hair and his. When he looked at the snake, it didn't stir. It was not poisonous. The flower-printed pillow cover lay half over its back.

Once he had broken Simoon's neck, all his life since, till thirty, had been a type of running down. Letting go of the precipice up which humanity doggedly climbed, clinging on, pretending that all that lay either above or below, after the fall, (as perhaps the suicide had done) was feather mattresses and heaps of roses without thorns.

When the select invitation to Venus reached him, his Proven Blood Line, (Eurydiche, *Stone Face*) the City under water—he saw what the invitation, and the City, were. By then he had anyway given up his hold. He was already dropping down through the air. Falling, like glass, leaves, angels. Like all men. Into the pit.

10

NOW IT WAS NOT A dream. Jula sat still in the dark, her eye-lids fastened shut, watching the images evolve across them.

Her brain gave up to her every last detail, as it never had in her former living of this life. Every page had finally become accessible, every line. Total recall.

And so, she watched the dinner guests at Julus's festive supper, that night at the villa in Stagna Maris, long ago.

There they were, reclining on their couches, Voluminis, the Scroll, Stirius the bald man, each lying on their left side, supported by an elbow, but Drusus, the greedy hog, flat on his belly, resting on both arms, his hands agile in the dishes from much practice.

That night, obsessed with the Ethiopian, she had not truly noticed them, or so she believed. But she had seen everything. Her eyes moving speedily over the room, lowered always at once, as a slave's eyes must be— had taken in so much.

The bellaria was laid out on the tables, the cakes and flowers, the saffron pastries crumbled with almonds. A single yellow bloom lay upon one pastry, there to the side, when all the other flowers were white or rosy.

That pastry had been for Jula. She knew she had died of it. The taste of it was in her mouth—so viciously saccharine, though veiled by the scented wines.

Which of them had wanted her to die before she could fight another match?

Not her master. Julus profited always from his own gladiators, three of whom he had paraded tonight in this very room. One of his guests, then.

Stirius was the most apparent candidate. Bald and not gross, yet somehow he sweated so heavily. His gestures toward and attention upon the dancers—the "real" women—seemed exaggerated. He had told the others how he had lost money on Jula, thinking a woman fighter a clownish impossibility.

Otherwise, the Scroll seemed quite calm and at ease, reading out to them his dirty stories of Greek gods and nymphs. And Drusus, the fat one, pawing in the dishes, selecting leftovers to carry home—Drusus who *always* bet on Jula and benefitted as he had announced . . . Could it even so have been Drusus? Someone had offered him superior rewards for a Games Girl's death?

The kitchen slaves—one slave alone—would have seen to it. He would have been given the poison and coins towards some elusive future hope of buying freedom; or else threatened with a horrible alternative—a false charge even, that would see a slave himself tortured and dead, or crippled, or in the silver mines. Slaves had no rights. This slave then was only an implement. Who was it that had wielded the slave?

Memory: Jula watched.

She saw what she had seen that night and not seen at all, for, then, it had meant nothing.

The young slave picked up the tray of pastries. He was passing first among the guests—there must be a chance the wrong hand might reach for the contaminated cake—yes, the slave was skillfully turning the tray a little, as if helpfully displaying the most succulently tempting sweets.

Stirius, intent on the dancer he had pulled on to his couch, did not take a pastry, he waved the slave off like a moth. Did that indicate his complicity?

Drusus, though, shoveled off two pastries, his fingers almost brushing even the cake with the yellow flower —so for an instant the slave's eyes widened—and then—

Jula saw what she had seen and not seen.

She saw the slave half glance behind him.

She saw precisely where his eyes went in that guilty, uncertain moment.

Away from Drusus, bypassing the Scroll, and Julus himself, slipping over Stirius—

A second, answering gaze had risen, frowning, to meet the slave's. A hand part lifted as if to take hold of time—then relaxed itself. Instead carrying a wine cup upward to a red, and white-toothed, mouth.

Clear as sun from shadow. The feaster who had bribed or forced a kitchen slave (a boy selected for the task because he was attractive enough also to serve at the tables) to end the days of Jula Victrix. *There* her murderer sat. He was a gladiator.

Her own kind, one of Julus's other prized and cosseted fighters, one of the two brought, as she had been, to decorate the dinner party.

Like Jula also, he had fought that afternoon. He too had dispatched his opponent. He too had received a laurel crown—and a sword cut, its stitchwork and binding hidden under his robe, mentioned and displayed, with his muscles and teeth, to the guests earlier. Now he lolled on his couch, drinking very deep.

Jula found she could not name him. She must never then have been told his name. As she had never been matched with him, not even in a practice bout.

This, her killer. Unknown. Nameless.

What had been his reason?

In memory, watching him fade from her vision as everything had done. She heard again that sound of rain which became the sea, *heard* the noiseless, play battle from *The Iliad*, the scatter of words around her—*heard* the deepness of the dark, and there behind her, on the vanishing land, the crackle of the funeral pyre, all that was left of her.

And he, her murderer, was gone with the rest. With her proud heartless owner, the complacent Roman diners, the frightened slave. All gone.

Why had he done it, that nameless man?

Jealousy? Some bet that would bring him, in turn, greater wealth? Fear that he could not match her, and one day soon, put in with her on the sand, she would finish him? She would never know.

The slave would have set the tainted pastry specifically before her. Yes, look back, and she could see he had. She did not like sweet things. She had taken only a small bite to show the lie of her appreciation of her master's food.

The taste—piercingly, singingly, yellowly invading her mouth and throat.

One small bite. The poison must have been so very strong.

AS SHE CAME OUT OF THE bedroom, Flayd glanced up. He had given himself the other bed, in what he called the store closet of his unlarge apartment. His, therefore, was the less comfortable of the two rooms, and he had chosen to stay up and go on with his notes and filing, seated by the open balcony window, which gazed out over the canal and the starry, warm-cool night of Venus.

Jula looked at him. Flayd put down the pen he habitually used before tapping at the machine.

For a second, he thought he saw her about to ask permission of him to leave the rooms. But he had told her to ask was no longer desired. Fleetingly she met his eyes. She said, formally, "I am going down to the garden. For a while."

"Can't sleep?" he said. "Neither can I."

He wanted to go out with her and was aware he should not. She had dispensed with the Victorian dress she'd worn for dinner. Despite Brown's unwritten code, she had on jeans and a loose shirt, things that, once she had been made conscious of them, she had seemed persuaded to ask for. Her short silky hair, unwaxed, losing its henna from constant washing in the shower, was the color of a faded orange geranium. She stayed barefoot. Her tough arched feet had no need of shoes.

She was not a child.

Don't look on her as a child—let alone as a liberated young woman who might make choices, or could be *led*.

"I'll get on," said Flayd. He turned back casually to the CX and heard a door softly opened, softly closed.

BLACK ON BLACK, the night wasn't dark enough to hide him. He stood out against the furred shapes of ornamental trees, the indigo sky with its freckled pathways of blue-milk white clouds that seemed to summon the brain upward, flying.

There had been a late ball, circa 1880, in Brown's chandeliered ballroom. That had been over by the twenty-seventh hour. By the second hour of the new Viorno, the final stragglers, pissed on punch and alcoholic fruit cup, amorously entwined, and with candle-wax splashed shoulders, had departed.

The garden was empty, even of its tables and chairs.

Somewhere a fountain sounded, a thin silver-foil of noise drawn through the dark.

Jula, on the steps between the urns, stared down at Picaro.

He had been smoking hasca. He cast the dregs on to the lawn and rubbed them out with his foot.

He walked up the steps and stood beside her.

At once she turned as if to go away.

Then did not go away.

She said, succinctly as the water noise, "I dreamed last night I lived in a city like parts of this one. I was wearing the long red dress. Tonight too I dreamed memory."

"Why are you talking to me?" he said. "Telling me things?"

"I don't know. Don't you dream?"

"Yes. I dream. Everyone dreams. So they say."

"I pray to the gods," she said, "I never dream the memory of my mother's death."

Picaro started. He cursed.

She looked up at him.

"I'm sorry," Jula said, "what have I done?"

"Hit a nerve," he told her bitterly.

"Everytime I hurt you," she said. (It was the strangest conversation.) "You cause me to do this in some way I don't grasp." She added two or three words in Latin. Then: "What is between us?"

"Nothing."

"Yes. I know that there is. I think of you so often, and then I come out into this garden, and you're here. Something. Some fate."

Picaro half smiled. She observed this, wonderingly. The expressions of others often drew her attention.

He said quietly, "You talk as if . . ." then grew silent.

They stared away from each other.

The garden, for a moment, might have been anywhere, belonged in any era or area. A nocturne of vegetation, faintly susurrous to a fragrant breeze, was gilded by a sinking moon.

"Why are you wearing modern clothes?" The hasca asked this, idle, loosening him.

"Flayd found them for me. I wanted them."

"Out of costume at last."

"Like you.

"You're interested in me?" he said. "But I'm afraid of *you*. You knocked me out, remember. So I think you'd better not be interested. In me."

"What do you mean?"

"You don't know? You're sure you don't know? Nothing like that back in Roman times?"

She had fixed him once more with her eyes.

Was she a child? Barbarically naive?

Perhaps . . .

She didn't seem to know what she had been saying, or what it might imply—that she was keen, and inviting him, as if she were a normal woman in some bar. He had heard it often, responded often. But her feral awkward innocence was daunting.

He didn't even consider if she attracted him. How *could* she? Even if he had been sane and had a life before him, even if none of the past had taken place. This lynx in the darkness. With her fists and her young man's way of standing and speaking to him, and her slave's ignorance, all the paucity she had brought with her out of a grave. How could anyone, any lover *ever* approach this flesh of hers?

Jula said, "There is a hill in Rome, one of many. It's covered with temples. They took me there. I don't know why, but I remember a place underground, and they were burning incense. A man came, and he was blind. His eyes were shut. He was old. He put his hand on my head and he spoke to them, the ones who brought me, but not to me. Now I know what he said because I can hear it, and the language is the one they taught me in those years after."

Picaro heard himself ask her, "What did he say?"

"*She is yours*. That was what he said. He gave me to my masters—or to one master. That must be who they were. The ones who sold me to Julus. I don't know what it means. It seems to come clearer. Perhaps it means nothing much. Some custom there."

Before he could say anything else, or move off, her hand caught hold of his.

In all the garden, all he could feel was the firm still grip of her cool hand. His entire awareness seemed to center on it. He couldn't pull away. Or let go.

"What do you *want*?" he asked her harshly.

"Where I was born," she said, "there were pine trees that held up the sky. We baked bread on the fire and my father would bring raw meat from the hunting. There was beer in a clay pot in the thatch. The firelight shone. My mother's hair was the color of the moon, there, where it's going down. The Romans came and killed her. I can see it, and how it was done, though I look away. My father died elsewhere."

"What you are," he said. "How can you stand next to me and talk to me—don't you begin to *know*?"

"I am what you are. A living thing."

"*No*. You were *grown*—not even born."

"Once, I was born. The first time. I think I've begun to remember that too, the battle to live, the sudden light."

Unable to let go of her hand, he shook the hand angrily in his.

"In Christ's name—*what are you?* You're not like the other one—del Nero—but you're not a human being. You're not like her. She was . . . a demon . . . You're not like her but I'm afraid of you, like her. Why are you telling me all this?"

"There is a fate between us," she said.

"What are you saying? You *fancy* me? No."

"Fancy?" she queried. She appeared, for an instant, puzzled, nearly laughable. "No, it's that—I have *found* you here."

"You haven't found me." After all he shook her hand out of his. After her touch, the air stung him. It was, like the garden, rife with vacancy.

"I'm going in," he said. He moved. She took a step. "Don't come with me," he said. "What do I have to say to make you stop?" Then she raised her head, put it back. Her eyes on his now made him veer from her, turn his back on her to walk away.

The moon slid down and was lost among a net of tree boughs. The sky grew for a second more luminous, and then more somber.

He himself hesitated. He looked round at her.

In the dimness now she might be any girl, a tanned white girl, with funny reddish hair and fashionable, uncomplex clothes. Something seared inside him, not anger now, not sex.

Picaro walked back to her, took her face between his hands, like some new instrument he must learn to make music with.

When he set his mouth down on hers, there was neither resistance nor response, in either of them.

He kissed her, noticing randomly her clean young healthy mouth that was centuries too old, too old for him, too old.

Then her arms coiled around him. She was strong, of course. She *held* him. It was familiar from a million other ordinary times, but only as if every woman he had ever embraced had been some version of this one. Yes, even that *un*woman, the evil spirit, out of whose womb he had been spat like a burned star.

"Let go," he said.

She let him go.

"All right," he said. "That's enough."

"Only my mother and father kissed me. And I've seen them kiss each other, as you have kissed me."

"All right. Let's leave it there."

"Why?" she said. Her voice was frank, undemanding.

But now he strode off across the garden, alone.

He walked quickly, until he came up on the terrace, to the doors. She hadn't followed. Unlike Picaro, lighter skinned, she had managed to disappear into the night. He crossed the paving, under the fluttering, guttering paper lanterns left from the ball, which, CX motivated, could never go out.

11

A SMALL RIOT, ONE OF FOUR that morning, was taking place all along the Blessed Maria Canal. The others were located, one in the silk market, another in front of the Temples of Art and Justice. The last was out on the lagoon, near the restored church of Maria Maka Selena, inside which a group of the agitators had barricaded themselves. The disturbances were all to do with those who wished to leave the City, and who had found this would not be allowed them. Soft-soap was changing in heavy hands. The main concern—at no point must any of Venus's reconstruct buildings be damaged. Detachments of police, clad as henchmen from the times of the Borgian Alliance or the masked 1700s, their natty garments CX-proofed, armed with flecxs and cannisters of lacrimogeno, massed ready in the wings. The University Auxillary, Flayd noted, as the boat chugged slowly through police-audited channels, were not openly involved.

Jula hadn't seemed concerned, her impartial face turned to take everything in. When he asked her what she thought, she said she had seen a riot just outside Stagna Maris. It had been brutally put down. She described legionaries from the Aquilla, shields locked, swords ready, marching forward in phalanx, to crush and slice men, women, and children, against the town walls.

She wasn't inclement, or uninvolved, only pragmatic.

Pragmatic too about the other thing. Some turmoil he could see behind the gemstone luster of her child-perfect eyes. What was it? What had happened to her? Something had.

Aside from themselves, no other passenger was in the boat. The tourists seemed mostly off the waterways and alleys, scared of the rioting—the smashed chairs slung at CX-impervious windows, the wrecked wanderers by the Primo steps, with their swearing, raving wanderliers—either that, or they had themselves joined the riots.

Who had called them riots, anyhow?

It was just guys trying to get home.

THEY WENT THROUGH A CANAL named Fulvia, for the lagoon. Under the watersteps close to the Centurion's Bridge, their boat stilled its engine.

She had said she wanted to see the real animals, in the Equus Gardens. Flayd had been glad that she wished to do something and had told him. She'd progressed well, but he wondered how much of *that* even, was simply due to her slave's essential ability to mimic what she was instructed to be.

They walked along an arched arcade, and went up into the Gardens. Cypresses, transplanted and tampered with, and already with a growth of several hundred years, towered from the terraces.

He spoke to her about the past—it was always mostly unavoidable, though he tried sometimes to curb it— wanting to wring every last droplet of authentic remembrance from her, then scurry to the laptop and make notes. She seemed not to mind his questioning, to expect it. Occasionally she would add another detail she said had just come back to her. She spoke English absurdly well, along with her excellent Italian. Linguisticx could only take credit for so much. She was intelligent and versatile.

Now and then, however, in the clarity of her eyes, that newly disturbed movement came. She had said nothing about *that*.

By the groves where the lions were housed, they stood at the low, CX-protected fence.

Flayd thought her like a slim young lioness herself.

The lions, of course, were still in slavery.

She began to speak to him (without a prompting question, maybe only to please him) about the lions used in the arena. How they were kept hungry and savage—they were only for killing men, or being killed by them. Unlike these pampered icons, swishing their tails against their lean, dieted, pale flanks, a male lying on his back to sun himself, taking no notice of the human audience, which came and went at the outer limit of lion life. Then Jula told Flayd about Playful, the lioness who had survived so many fights and finally had been pensioned off in the Roman town.

Afterwards they ate ice cream at an umbrellaed table. Then they walked down and viewed the horses, trotting or galloping about a wide meadow, apparently railed off only by laurels.

The big roan horse reminded Flayd of himself, though it had not a spare molecule of fat.

He had ridden, years back. As a boy, with his mother, Rose, and then again not so long ago with his wife.

Surprising him, his eyes filled with tears.

That hadn't happened, tears, thinking of these two women he loved, not for a decade.

She had seen. This quick, ancient Roman daughter of his.

God, Jesus, yes. Yes, she was *like* Alicia. Ali could have been her mother. Perhaps. Or was it only one more self-deception?

She looked at him, the girl. Then she touched his arm. That was all, nothing said.

"I'm fine," he said.

"Yes."

"I just remembered someone. Sometwo. We lose people, then we lose ourselves. All tipped down that fuck of a drain. Nowheresville, Death County."

She was silent. He sensed her forming a question — of *him*. And he was embarrassed by himself, at speaking out in this manner. To her, of all people in the world— she had enough to deal with, without his neurotic tantrums over the Inevitable—which she, anyway, had already experienced. (He could recall what she'd said before. *I went elsewhere . . . yes, I know that I did.* And to his blurted *Where?* she had replied, *I don't remember that. Only . . . nothingness.*)

Now she asked, (shaming him further) "Death County—is this your name for Elysium?"

"No. Not for Elysium. *Elysium* would be kind of wonderful." She stood looking at him, as the horses bounded around, uncaring of tomorrow. Flayd said, apologetic, "I was just mouthing off, Jula. About total bloody annihilation—Elysium, Hades, afterlife—wishful thinking."

He, now, did not meet her searching gaze.

Jula said, "But I have been in Elysium."

Flayd shut his eyes. Opened them. Saw horses. Dully said, "What?"

"I was in Elysium. Heaven is how they say it now, is it?"

"You have been in—"

"Where else? I'd died."

Slowly he turned and stared at her. Her face was so damned honest, so composed and—almost ordinary. "All right, Jula. OK. Tell me about—heaven."

"But I don't remember," she said. She smiled. (Since that first time, she had begun to smile on occasion. Generally it would have cheered him. He wanted, now, to shake her.)

"If you don't remember, lady, how the hell do you know?"

"Because I've been there, and the other places."

"Other? No, I don't buy this. You don't *remember* anything else because there's nothing out there. You went and were nowhere. Sorry."

"Flayd," she said, "have you never hoped for life to go on beyond this? For the *freedom* of it?"

"Sure."

"Why did you hope?" she asked.

"I'm a coward, I guess. Can't face personal obliteration. Like most of us."

"No," she said, "I mean, how do you know *how* to hope—for anything else? Fear doesn't give hope. Fear takes hope away."

"OK. How did I think to hope. We've all been told, over and over. The great blue yonder. Sure we have."

"Who told you?"

"Priests, preachers. All the teachers they claim have lived—Christ, Mohammed, Buddha. The whole list."

"And why did they tell it to you?"

"To manipulate—to help—who knows? Because they made it up, a nice fairy story. Or they just plain hoped for it themselves."

"How," she said, "did they know to make it up, or to

hope for it? How could they—*imagine* it—unless somehow it was there and they knew? Without that—such a thing—isn't to *be* imagined."

"Imagination is the word."

"How can you even know to imagine," she said quietly, "something of which you have no knowledge *at all*?"

"Riddles. We're going round in circles."

"Flayd, I can't remember—that other place—because while we exist in flesh—the *flesh* of us doesn't go there. Things here, even if we forget them, the brain memorizes everything it experienced. I've heard you say this. But how can the brain memorize a place it's never been?"

Flayd heard himself breathe. "Jula. Oh lord." He took hold of his mind. "Unrecorded data," he said.

She said, "It's like these languages they taught me. Until I learned them, I couldn't make words in these languages."

"Heaven is a language we forget how to speak," he said, dreamily.

"And yet, something remains. The idea that Elysium is there. I can recollect," she said, "the passage into death . . . It wasn't empty, only dark, like the River they told me of—perhaps that's why they thought it was a river. But it wasn't a river. The light of the pyre faded behind me, and something else began—but then I was *free*. Only that freed part remembers. But it uses images I can't see, words I don't understand."

Flayd thought of the teachers and saviors, of the gods. He thought of Rose and how she had *known*. And of Alicia who hadn't. Alicia and her fear. And of a dark river that became something else, and Alicia was free, and speaking another language.

And then he took a firmer grip on his heart or mind

or, God knew, his soul. He said, "Listen to me. Don't say any of this to any of them—Leon, that crowd. They'd never let you out of jail, even this little distance. They'd want to test you, find out a whole lot more." And thought, *But they'll be watching, listening in, somehow.*

"They had no interest in that," she said. "They didn't think of it perhaps. Only you ever asked me anything like that."

A black and white horse, streamlined and dangerous, ran up the meadow—was it like Picaro?

"Tell me this," Flayd said, "if you knew all this, why did you fight to stay alive in their arena? Why did you bother?"

"That's why we come here," she said, "to live. So we must fight to do it."

She had been calling him Flayd. Had she done that before? She wasn't the same as she had been. Or perhaps, rather than change, she'd simply become *more* herself.

The religious beliefs of ancient peoples—unshakable? "Jula, if—"

She interrupted him. She had *never* done *that* before. Maybe never to anyone, in her slave life.

"The man called Chossi is walking along the path toward us."

12

FROM WHERE HE LAY, he could see it moving about. He wondered how it had got in, but the windows at the Ca'Marrone were sometimes undone, in old-fashioned style, by the rooms' human cleaners.

A magpie.

It must be real. Picaro thought he had seen one already somewhere else in the City.

Like Shaachen's bird, called Beloved, or Darling, so the disc had told him when he was a child.

Darling—*Caro*.

It was a big bird, with a round solid body tapering to a long black tail that, when the light caught it, glinted with smoky green, just as the sides of the white and black wings sheened blue. Its head was all black, as if hooded, the beak black, and the eyes pale, so he remembered Coal's jackdaw. It strutted, arrogant and unsafe, across the floor.

Picaro sat up.

(How late was it?)

He could call the room service that Brown's supplied, ask them to catch the bird and release it back into the City.

Picaro had wanted a magpie, once, as a child.

And the magpie could write?

The murmur of his father's voice, *Says so . . . but you can't have one . . . magpie's a wild bird.*

And her. Her voice—*I put shadow on you, Magpie.*

The signal went in the outer door.

At the noise, the bird spread its fans of wings and flew up through the high-ceilinged room.

Picaro thought it would be Flayd at the door. Not the Roman girl, surely not her. India?

He sat on the side of the ornate canopied bed, looking into space, considering whether to admit the insistent (still signalling) visitor. And then the door was opened. And in walked the UAS clerk, Chossi.

"I knocked," said Chossi, uncaringly.

"So you did. But I didn't let you in."

"Oh, I have a key."

"I thought that must be the case."

Chossi scowled. His nose had entirely recovered from the blow Picaro had given it, but not his demeanor. "Leonillo sent me. I'm to give you this."

Chossi came forward and threw a thick late-Victorian-type envelope, thinly lettered in gold, written over apparently by hand, on Picaro's bed. Picaro left it there.

"Better open it."

"Whatever it is, I'm not interested."

"It's an invitation," said Chossi. "I've already hand-delivered several others, one to your friend here."

"I have no friends here."

"The fat archaeologist who thinks he's so unusual. Sin Flayd."

Picaro did nothing. Chossi stamped from one foot to the other, urgent for response. "Tonight," Chossi said.

Picaro got up and walked across to the bathroom. He stood by the bowl, urinating, as Chossi fidgeted in the doorway. When Picaro turned to the basin, "I say invitation," said Chossi, "you are *requested* to be there. A gala occasion. The Orpheo Palazzo—the auditorium seats six thousand people, even allowing for the security equipment. Many more persons have been issued tickets for the square outside."

Picaro shut off the faucet.

"What are you talking about?"

He already knew, and a sound began in his ears. It was far away. Unrecognizable, unspeakable.

"The great musician, del Nero, is to perform some of his works. That is, works written *since* his rebodiment. It should be worth an hour of your precious time. Of course, the general public aren't aware of what he is— they believe he's some composer who has chosen the medium of the 1700s to express his genius. None of them know what a crucial affair this is to be. The security, of course," officiously chatty, Chossi letting go of some of his resentment now that Picaro was his audience, "the administration—we've had to work all nights. Indeed, ever since we were told. There's never been anything like this. What will the music be? Astounding? Boring? What a magnificent gamble. Personally, I believe any health problems are now sorted out, and the screening is only provisional. The most up-to-date medical scans reveal nothing wrong with him. Is he a carrier? I doubt it. None of the rest of us has displayed the slightest symptom, even those who spent the most time in his vicinity. No one's even sneezed. They were unlucky. Jenefra. The others. Whatever it was, they took the full force of it and now it's over."

Picaro came at Chossi suddenly. Once again, Chossi hadn't expected it. Squawking invective, he ran away across the room toward the door.

"Leonillo—" Picaro shouted. But Chossi was through

the door and gone. To the apartment, Picaro said, "Leonillo is—he *saw*—and *that* one—*saw*—what happens—"

Then he in turn had reached the door. Two Victorian men, not UAS, police probably, stood casually just across the passage. One nodded to him.

Picaro went back in and shut the door.

Standing there, something made him look up at the plasterwork around the ceiling, the top of the bed, the carved armadio.

The magpie too had gone, though none of the windows had been opened. Perhaps it had followed Chossi, to peck out his eyes.

ANGERS HAD BEEN REVERSED.

"*What?*"

Flayd, a red bull of rage, bulked in the entrance of his rooms, confronting Picaro, (and the idly draped, parasol-bearing policewoman who adorned the top of the stairway.)

"Let me in, Flayd."

"Why? What the fuck for?"

"*Do it.*"

Flayd gave up. He tramped away, beating his arms on his body. "Be my guest, buddy. Everyone welcome. Just walk all over me. What do I care?"

Picaro glanced about.

This main room was smaller than the one he had been allotted, scattered with pieces of antiquated equipment, books, box-files, discs. At the table the laptop, hot technology beyond many dreams, slender as a wafer, a fey machine crammed with a universe.

"What is the matter?" said Picaro.

"Jula," said Flayd. He thumped on to a sofa. The

room, designed to oldness, shook. "We were in the Horse Gardens and up slides that prince nonce, Chossi. Time for her to go back to the University, it seems. Back to whatever it is they now want to do with her there."

Picaro said, "She'll be safer there."

"Garbage. Out here had gotten her so she was starting to be a person. She thinks she's *their* slave. Leon, all that shit-shower. Now she's back in all that—slavery. And I couldn't do a fucking thing."

"Listen, Flayd, where did they invite you?"

"What? Invite me—oh that crap. Their other *protégé* —their musician—what's he called? Nero—some recital. Yeah, it'd be an education. But not *now*."

"No, not now. They haven't told you what happened, at the Shaachen Palace—or have they?"

Flayd's face cleared, a screen at the activation of some override.

"OK, OK. No. No one tells me a thing. So you do it."

Picaro told him.

Flayd sat listening. The blank screen lost color, settled, heavy.

"And this was some genetic viral episode, right?"

"No."

"But—"

"They have no control over it, whatever it is."

"What do *you* think it is, Picaro? You tell me it killed everyone in the rooms below yours, and worked you over two floors up."

"One woman survived. So I was told—not by Leonillo's mob. India seems to have found out. But I don't know why or how this woman could survive. Like me, maybe, shut enough away—insulated."

"You know what it is."

"I—a guess. I may be wrong. It makes no sense. Every sense."

"Then what *is* it?"

Picaro said, "Just don't take up their invitation."

Flayd said, "There are going to be over six thousand human dupes crowded in that hall that do. I know the Orpheo—it's the biggest concert hall in Venus."

"Not limited to six thousand people."

"You're saying it'll spread—*how*? This guy is going to be screened off by magna-optecx—*radiation* can't get through that."

"I know."

"Then—"

"The recital is part of their experiment, Flayd. It is a *conspiracy*, Flayd. And we're all just laboratory material. No one can intervene. The police are already in position everywhere. Hadn't you noticed? And even they don't know what they're up for. Anyone's only chance is to avoid it. Pretend you're ill, drunk, stupid. Stay put."

"You have to have made a mistake. If not—all I gotta do is to *stop* it."

Picaro smiled. It was the old smile. Flayd no longer meant a thing, only someone to be polite to, from another planet. Picaro walked out.

Alone, Flayd paced. The new rage was warming, almost comforting in a foul and deranged way.

While he did this, he had no notion that Picaro was talking to the police, now three of them, hanging about on the landing. Flayd did not know Picaro was suggesting to them that Flayd might have plans to upstage the recital the University had arranged at the Orpheo. Flayd, with his crazy paranoia about conspiracies. When the policewoman asked Picaro, easy, "And are you invited, Sin? Yes? Will you attend?" Picaro said, "I play music. I'll be there."

A little later, when Flayd (unknowing of all this) marched to his door, mind made up, he discovered it refused to give. Though it was Victorian in several aspects, it still contained CX, and the CX was fixed. Presently a call came through to him, assuring Flayd that the "fault" in the door had registered on the main system and would soon be seen to. And much later, another call, just the same, the same as the stuck door was the same.

By then, Picaro was back in his own apartment. He had begun to drink the alcohol left there for him and to eat some of the snacks. Sometimes he considered Simoon, Simoon the sibyl. *Your appointment* she said, over and over, in the back of his mind, where she sat, reeking of sulphur, in her Dowi-chair, with her neck broken and her lemon-slice eyes. *Your appointment, baby, tonight.*

SHE HAD SEEN TOMBS BEFORE. Along the Graculan Way, for one. But also that time in Rome, when they had taken her down under the temple on the hill. That had been partly a columbarium, a dovecote of death, the boxes and vases of ashes arranged in their pigeonholes. But also great marble edifices were set in the walls, porticoes wreathed in cut stone, and by paint, with stone faces looking calmly on, or the gorgon's mask set there to protect them. The area was part of a catacomb, one of many. A mystic, mysterious, and occult vault.

Who had they been, the two who brought her there? She thought now, perhaps, she knew. She was left in their house a little while, before the wagon bore her away from Rome for ever. The house with the peacock in the courtyard, which had frightened her so. But the woman had taken her hand and said, gently, in a Latin which, then, she scarcely understood, "Nothing to harm you, little girl. See how he spreads his beautiful tail. He is the symbol of the Risen One."

And then they had told her they dared not set her free, not from her mortal chains. But they would try to free her in another way.

And so, almost four years old, she had gone down into the stony underworld, and the old man had appeared. His skin was brown with age, and his hair clear white as the garment he wore. His color scheme had an extraordinary clarity. His eyes were shut because he was blind, yet he seemed to see. And then there had been a trickling of torchlit water poured over her, and his mild old hand, resting on her head. And he said above her, "She is yours." But he was not giving her, she now saw, to the couple who had brought her, nor to Rome. It was to another one.

This tomb, amyway, under the University Building in domed-in Venus, was not really like the patrician tombs of her past.

This tomb was her own.

In addition to that, it could not be physically touched.

The most important master here, Leon, had told Jula, when he informed her she should visit this viewing room, and that what she would see there would be a reconstruction, a CAVE, or CX-Assisted Virtual Environment. It would appear three-dimensional from every side or angle, might be walked around, into and through, and anything there that she wished to examine would be fully displayed for her. But it was not real. The real tomb, Leonillo had said, was on the mainland, rebuilt in the Roman Museum.

All the while he spoke to her of her own burial place, explaining its technology, advising her to see it as if conferring a special, and much-wanted favor, she sat impassive.

The facts of the technology were meaningless to her, therefore redundant. Otherwise, she knew that she was studied. Flayd had informed her of this, confirming anyway her own impressions. (As a slave before she had only been watched.) She knew too that she must do as she was told. Even after Flayd's instruction in her own autonomy, she retained her credo that resistance to the unavoidable was as foolish and wasteful as not to resist what might be overcome.

And so she was here. Another tourist, she stood and read of her victories, inscribed on the tomb-side, and of her last fight, and the lie of how she had died. The engraved motto, *Even the gods, who grant glory, cannot hold back death*, left her unmoved. It was a truism.

Jula spent an hour inside the tomb, or its CAVE. She was rather interested to see what had been buried with her—the honors that had been shown her. What had been deemed necessary.

At one point, she puzzled over the burned remains of her own body. Fragments of charred bone were revealed to her, when she requested it, lying there spread out among the coins and lamps, and Jula leaned down to see. If they had been tactile, she would have picked them up, these pieces of herself.

Those who observed her, the advanced machines that monitored her and her reactions, and stopped short, just barely, of being able to read her mind—per- haps decided she was blasé about her own former death, since she had been brought back alive. But if she was *blasé*, and maybe she was not, it came from the knowl- edge that had grown in her. This was the battleground, *always* you came back.

HAVING SCRUTINIZED JULA in the CAVE, looking at her own reproduced cadaver, Leonillo went up to his private rooms.

He required something, he thought, but having reached seclusion, couldn't recall what it was.

Leonillo believed this abrupt forgetfulness, which was unlike him, had to do with the narcotics the University pharmacy had supplied. True, he had slept a great deal better than he had been for several nights. But one was left with this tendency to mislay, omit . . .

Tonight, of course, was important.

It was the night Cloudio del Nero would perform for a large, selected audience, his (as some poetic memo had termed it) post-awakening opus.

Apparently the sheets of (fake) parchment on which he had been writing it out had corroded in some form. But del Nero seemed confident that the notation was established, flawless, in his head. There remained the slight worry as to whether the new harpsichord supplied for his performance would hold out—none of the other instruments had. But it needed only to persist an hour or two.

No one had yet heard his music.

To those who enjoyed the arts, it would be an epic event—save that very few of those engaged to be present realized the nature of the recital, or *what* they were going to hear. Revelations would come later. When everything was finished.

Leonillo frowned at his own choice of word. Finished? There was yet a vast amount to accomplish on this project; it would not end tonight.

Really, he wouldn't have known where to begin, left to himself. But the orders he received were unfailingly explicit.

Leonillo himself would not be attending the concert. Although naturally he would closely observe it, here, in the University, with other UAS.

The security arrangements were excessive, complex, and by now all in place.

The venue was considered charming, a palazzo itself in the mode of the 1700s, full of little curiosities and delights. The auditorium had been constructed years back. The tiers of gilded seats were of velvet. Gardens were depicted on the ceiling, which conveyed, it was well known, every whisper of sound from the performance area, even of that quietest keyboard, a harpsichord.

Though hedged in by his impenetrable screens, the magic of CX audition would ensure that none of del Nero's score was lost.

Some of Leonillo's staff, he had seen, were very excited.

Leonillo opened a sealed container, unwrapped a disposable syringe, and gave himself a skin-surface injection of vitamins and caffeine. Probably that was why he had come up here.

Probably also it was the sleeping-pill tiredness that made him, now he was in this private room, not wish to return below.

AS THE TWENTIETH HOUR of the Viorno-Votte approached, soft, along the lagoon, the canals, the sky, Venus readied herself for sunfall, and the night.

Over her lovely spires and cupolas, her walls like spice and crushed pearl, her glimmering veins of liquid, the westering of a sunless sun threw all its limpid nets. Transfixed in the fetters of this murmuring light, the City—unreal, encapsulated and immersed as it was, yet became, as always it had, feminine, and surreal.

She then, Venus, lay dreaming below her sky, and drew the sky colors down upon her countless mirrors. Windows and canals flashed gold, sank with cinnabar and purple. Masonry, in cliffs and ravines, flushed blood-bright, and let its dyes seep down into green water. Every tower was roped by fire.

Out on the lagoon, the constructed sunset, a massed fleet of architectural clouds, scalded madder, scarlet, cochineal. And this was only like a million genuine sunsets, over which Venus had presided, bathing herself in them to gain immortality, when once she had been throned above the sea, and *only* the sea, and heaven, contained her, and the darkness which came was a *real* night, full of sighs and winds and spray, and the moon, when it rose, another lighted marble palace.

Bells rang. Birds flew. Boats folded their sails. As, in an endless past, over and over, they had.

Then the sunset fell into the sea. The sky smouldered. Stars appeared.

And night, no longer real, had come.

PICARO WAS STANDING in the dusk on the wide terrace of Brown's, which looked out along the Lion Marco Canal.

Various guests were there, going about, preparing themselves for pre-dinner drinks, or another of Brown's nightly entertainments. One group detached itself into an arrived wanderer.

He heard one of the women cry eagerly, "But he's the *newest* composer? The one they were talking about?" "Yes," said one of the men. "He's modeled his music on another man's from the eighteenth century." They were going to the receital at the Orpheo.

Picaro was vaguely conscious of the fashionable Victorian lady positioned along the terrace arcade, half glancing at him, to see how he would react. He did nothing.

He *could* do nothing. And now—had no urge to.

They were all bound for the same destination, and finally, at last, he didn't care.

Then he saw India coming briskly out from the lobby.

She wore an off-the-shoulder evening gown of darkest red, and what looked like golden chandeliers hung from her earlobes.

After all—

Picaro stepped in front of her.

"Where are you going, India?"

She halted before him. "Where do you think I am going?"

"The recital," he said, indifference bursting apart inside him.

She said, "No, I'm not. I wasn't asked."

"All right." The terrace shifted under him like a boat. He took no notice. "A lot of people were. But you won't be missing anything."

"Won't I?"

He looked down at her. Her eyes were strange tonight. Perhaps she had been smoking something— something better than the clips he had consumed.

Then she turned her head and looked at the canal and said, "How bright the darkness is. I'll see you later, Picaro."

I doubt it, he thought, *I doubt if you will.*

And then he saw the wanderer which had come to pick him up. There it was, slotting itself in by the terrace.

As he stepped away from her, he heard India say, "I'm sorry I was harsh. Cora always loved you. She always wanted to meet you, and to make love with you. You made her happy, Picaro.

He hesitated. He said, "You helped her fly up on my balcony."

"I always helped her fly," said India. "Even the last time. We were lucky. That I was there."

Something divided in Picaro's brain. He saw, as if from one eye, the wanderlier ready in his unavoidable boat, saluting him, and the policewoman over there, slightly less languid, alert to see what Picaro would do next. And with the other eye he saw India behind him in her evening gown.

"You said, the last time."

He faced the canal, lifting his arm to wave, friendly, to the waiting wanderlier. (The policewoman relaxed.)

Then he turned around to India. He took her hand, partly to demonstrate his excuse for lingering.

"What do you mean, India? After she died, in the morgue?"

"Oh, no, Picaro," said India, "*as* she died."

The terrace *shifted* again.

"You were in there with her?"

"I came to be."

"You were *with* her?"

"Yes. She didn't suffer long. Not like the rest. I held her. She trusted me. The others. They thought they were on their own. That was the terrible thing."

"How," he said, "if you were *there*—how—how did you—"

India regarded him with sulky gravity.

"We'll talk later."

"There won't be any later, India, not for me. If you were *there*, you *know*."

She lowered her eyes. It was very dark, despite the dawning lights of Brown's, the profligate stars.

The other woman was beside him. "Time to get in the boat," she said. "Or we'll be late for the show."

FLAYD HAD CALLED FOR the eighteenth time. As usual, Brown's was apologetic. They had never known such a persistent fault, at least, not in a door. It had affected the windows too, he said? But at least the guest cabinet was full of food and drink he had previously ordered, and the air-conditioning and other CXs worked. They would of course refund his entire bill for this one Viorno-Votte.

Why had he troubled to call? He knew what had been done, probably why. Had figured it out.

He was afraid. Not for himself. For the others. The ones who would be there. For Picaro. For Jula. He tried to think of young-man ways to escape the rooms, or failing that to alert the citizens of Venus, while bypassing the UAS, the police, and any other security units now operating.

The riots had been quelled. The wall screen told him that. It was a peaceful evening.

When he got tired of pacing, he put quite a lot of chicken, sauce, and pasta in the heater, retrieved them and began to eat. The food, and the wine, helped to distance him, to make him heartless and fatalistic for all of thirty minutes.

He sat by the laptop and read over the piece of Latin he had put up there yesterday, copied with a mass of other inscriptions, years ago, from the mosaics of the Primo. On the goldleaf, Christ and the flames of seven angels, and the warning of the apocalypse.

ALBUS ADEST PRIMO MACRO PALLENTI ET OPIMO ET ASCENSORUM SEQUITUR PAR FORMA COLORUM. The script, when he spoke it aloud to her, had confounded Jula, because it was in medieval Latin, rather than the classical tongue of Roman times. "They're called Leonine hexameters," he'd added. He asked her, curious, to suggest a translation in English. She considered, and announced, "The white one is by the first, the thin one, the pale one and the fat one, and of those who mount upon their horses, there follows a like pattern in color."

"Approximately it. But this Latin depends on the reader also looking at the mosaic picture and drawing conclusions. See these guys on horseback? They're the Four Horsemen of the Apocalypse, predicted to bring war, famine, pestilence, and death. Something high on the agenda of the early Christian mindset. So, from the picture and the words together, we get, The white one stands near the black one, the pale one and the one large in size, and the same style of color holds good for the knights."

Looking at it now, across the wine glass, something darted through Flayd's consciousness, quick as a speeding bullet. He couldn't catch it. It was gone.

He wondered why he had brought the words back on the screen. Solely to show Jula the discrepancy between *her* Latin and that of fourteen centuries after? No, he'd been looking for something else—the emperors, he thought now. Checking the dates of the Flavians. Though what that had to do with a Christian apocalypse he wasn't certain.

Flayd frisked the buttons.

(This was what you had to do. Carry on with everyday matters. Research, your work. Kept you from wondering, wondering how insane Picaro was, how true what he had said, why the door had jammed, what maybe you yourself should really—)

Names appeared. Proud names redolent of Roman power: Vespasian, Titus, Domitian, Narmo . . .

Again, something flicked at the edge of Flayd's inner eye. Vanished.

He opened another bottle.

PALAZZO ORPHEO LAY ON THE Canale Magnifico, which sprawled beyond the Rivoalto, in parts almost one fifth of a kilometer wide.

Orpheo had never really existed in the past. It was a modern edifice, built to resemble another of the reconstructs and recxs, and ornamented with recx artifacts, sculptures, mouldings, and art from assorted historic palazzos that had been lost to the sea. Among these was a great white marble Apollo, a re-creation of a statue located under the old Aquilla Lagoon. Birds circled his head, for he was a sky god to whom birds were sacred. But also, the brass plaque told one, it was Apollo who had invented music.

In the amphitheater, tiers of seats, their velvet midnight-blue, crimson, chartreuse, rose from the room's center like banks of flowers. And Picaro thought of the snake, coiled under the flowers. But all that was there, poised on the flat stage, (and visible as if unscreened, through the crystalline magna-optecx) was a harpsichord, patterned over in some gold, silver, and azure design.

The audience of tourists, of PBS citizens, music-lovers, sightseers, milled leisurely up and down like creatures trapped in a tide (as if helpless), swimming into their seats and becoming anchored there. They had been gathering busily outside, too, all through the lamp-lit square, where the tiny speakers hung like fruit—

altogether perhaps, a second crowd two thousand strong.

Picaro hadn't yet gone to his seat. It was far up, miles it looked from the central area where the music would be made. A bad seat, yet given the current excellence of CX audition every concert hall employed, poor only in the visual sense, for not a note would elude even these upper tiers. He had heard the audience discussing, in pockets, and with some enthrallment, the supposed importance of the optecx screening—in *perfecting* the sound system. They didn't know the screen was to protect them from the performer. Nor that it would be useless.

Useless . . . Everything. Life.

The hasca and the alcohol, an opaque rough spirit mixed with Seccopesta, had blotted her away. Blotted away Simoon. So she was just a shapeless muttering amoeba, the wraith of a demon, in his brain's back.

He no longer heard the words of her curse. No longer heard her tell him how he would die, underwater but not by drowning.

He could almost grin, almost laugh. Almost be happy. He had fled so long, fought so hard for ignorance. Now, the release of total surrender.

Yet too, having already seen it, how it must be—he was *afraid*, and only the drink and the drug had moved him slightly above his terror. But he had had enough of both. They would last another hour. And by then—nothing could make any difference.

WAR—A FIGHTER. Famine—a dearth. Pestilence—an unseen spy. Death—the bringer of changes.

SOMEHOW HE HAD HIT the wrong button. Flayd gazed tipsily while the list of emperors elongated, incorporating now the forerunners of the Flavians, the Julio-Claudian Caesars.

Almost amused.

Almost convinced. Picaro was nuts and had either hallucinated events at the Shaachen palace . . . or exaggerated.

Flayd had his own detection to do anyhow: Why he seemed to have connected up the Roman state with a medieval interpretation of World's End.

Using *voice*, he told the laptop's CX to correlate the listed emperors with the apocalypse. If there was any link, CX would suss this. He sat back and drank his wine, ready to be intrigued.

JULA HAD SAT DOWN by the door of her tomb.

Tonight, very few human staff were at their posts to watch her. Most had gone to the other larger-screen monitors, to enjoy the relayed recital at the Orpheo.

In any case, she appeared to be doing nothing much. She wasn't upset or nervous.

She only sat there.

Her hair was no longer hennaed, and the red was fading out to a Gallic blondness.

None of her small audience thought her attractive, or even a woman. She was an exhibit, a canny white rat in the lab.

THE LARGE AUDIENCE WAS settling now, all seated on the glamorous velvet chairs. They rustled programs, chattered. The noiseless air-conditioning filled the atmosphere with meadow fragrances, to compliment their perfumes.

Picaro looked at them, these people about, as he was, to die horribly and in immeasurable pain.

They were nothing to him. Less than flowers scattered on the flowerlike seats. A cast of extras.

And then something—the gleam of a woman's silver dress, a man's quiet laughter—something, unbearably and unforgivably, made them all *real*.

Each a living thing. Each trapped in his or her vessel of being, a body which moved and talked, and thought and felt, and might be needful or loved.

Not flowers. Not actors given only minor parts.

They, each one, as he was, hero of their own life.

Something leapt inside Picaro, clawing and rending him with its teeth and very nearly he stood up, to shout, to scream at them, to grab their hands, their arms, to push and force and throw them out into the night. To send them running as far as the prison of the dome allowed.

"Why, you're crying, Sin Picaro," said the flirtatious policewoman beside him, "and it hasn't even begun."

And then a storm of applause rose all around them. And she too, poor living heroine, clapped, smiling. And of them all, only Picaro was not applauding. And Cloudio del Nero had appeared, rising upward in the bubble of the optecx, stepping out of some contraption, through the opened floor of the stage, bowing through the invisible screen, in the manner of 1701, elegant and handsome in his aristocrat's coat of white brocade.

FLAYD'S LAPTOP HAD STARTED to tick. He wasn't sure why this should be. (Maybe breathing on it had gotten the damn thing drunk.)

It had been shuffling a kaleidoscope of data across the screen. Now the soup dispersed. Decided as a mathematical equation, it showed this:

> **Re:** **Emperors of Rome connect Apocalypse.**
>
> *Nota*: **Revelation of St. John the Divine, disciple of Jesus Christ.**
>
> **Forecast of destruction of the earth. Rev. 12: The Beast, generally supposed to be the fallen angel Lucifer, or Satan.**
>
> *Nota*: **The Number of the Beast, which is remarked as follows:** *Let him that hath understanding count the number of the beast: for it is the number of a man: and his number is six hundred threescore and six.* **That being more simply rendered as 666.**
>
> *Nota*: **The early Christians, who were savagely persecuted during the reigns of several of the Julio-Claudian and Flavian Emperors, ascribed this number to one of their most ardent persecutors, the Emperor Nero, who is said to have ordered the crucifixion, upside down, of the Apostle Peter.**
>
> **This emperor then assumed, both in the then-contemporary Christian mind, and in some later medieval theology, the status of Antichrist, potential destroyer of the Kingdom of God on earth, and subsequently of all things.**
>
> *Nota*: **The number 666, however, refers less to a man than specifically to the** *name* **NERO.**

A block of numerals and letters in Greek and Latin followed, demonstrating the interpretation of the name *Nero* as the number 666, the Number of the Beast. From the advent of which being must proceed the end of the world.

JULA HAD LEFT THE AREA of the CAVE, and travelled up in one of the lifts. Hardly anyone was about in the sub- or higher corridors of the University. She understood, from Leonillo's earlier words, they had gone to witness the relay of some entertainment.

Something drew Jula up through the building. It was a definite and concrete urge—perhaps only to reach the open air. Even though Flayd had told her about the air, and the dome that held it in.

When she emerged from the University Building, she stood a short while on the terrace of the Blessed Maria Canal. Honeycombs of ancient palazzos lined the water. Small lamplit craft were going up and down.

Above, the sky was darkest blue and radiant with stars, the moon not yet up.

She had grasped all this was a counterfeit. But might not anything be that, for all she knew. And a freshening wind blew in from the lagoon, bringing with it a spiky and electric smell, as if a storm were coming, unannounced, to thrill the City.

LEONILLO SAT BEFORE THE enormous CX viewer, behind and about him, his staff, fired up and high with expectation. There were some two hundred people crammed in the room, which was authorized, as a rule, to hold only one hundred. Due to the shortage of seating, they perched on stools, crouched on the floor—willingly.

As in a virtuality theater, the lights had been dimmed, to maximize the effect of the screen.

Again he was reminded of the theatrical aspect of life.

FLAYD WAS ON HIS FEET. The chair had gone over. He lurched toward the laptop, glaring at it.

He was still drunk enough that his head was muzzy, but the wine had also released him. It was as if abruptly he could *see*. His brain sped, running with the bullets now.

If anyone had been watching, which probably, right at that instant they were not, he might have given cause for alarm. Justified.

Without any other preamble, he picked up the table. All the way up. And hoisted it over his head.

Strong, Flayd.

His face engorged with blood, the laptop, the books cascading away in a shower of paper and sparks, the green flare of some socket detached.

With a smack that rocked the whole apartment, and caused some comment on lower floors, thrown furniture slammed into the shut-stuck balcony windows.

The optecx glass rippled. But didn't give.

Then Flayd roared, a brazen boom of wrath, frustration, and despair, like the sounding of trumpets.

PICARO CLOSED HIS EYES.

Others did the same.

It was so silent now, in the Orpheo.

Like an opened door.

"A CARNATION OF AN EVENING, sinna," crooned the wanderlier. "Are you off to a party? There's a big event on at the Orpheo. But not for everyone, signorina. Not everyone likes such formal music. Me, I like the Victorian songs. Or the songs from the south."

He began to sing to Jula.

He had a fine voice.

She looked away along the canal. They had come some distance. She had said she wanted to go to Brown's guest palace. He had been surprised, seeing her modern clothes, shaken his head, informed her such a pretty sinna should wear the historical dresses, they would suit her so.

Jula thought perhaps she had worn them, such dresses, somewhere, but not truly here, garments from the renaissance, or skirts that had ended far above the knee . . . and other things. At other times.

The moon was coming up, blonde as her mother's hair.

THE FIRST PHRASE, tinkling like silver coins, delicate as raindrops dappling metal. A million drops, upon a million knives of steel—

Was it only a harpsichord? These diverse and mingling sounds, this harmony—surely some orchestral overlay began, unless—

SINCE IT WAS THE NINETEENTH call he had made out to them, he thought they might not take it. They took it.

"I need help—" he groaned. To pant and sweat was easy, after the table. Possibly he'd even given himself what he was describing. "'S bad—heart attack I think—I need someone—real quick—"

And cutting it off right there.

Crashing back, so the voices gabbled, and then a light starred on in the wall.

Flayd, not lying dying on the carpet, rolled over, in case any unseen close-up camera might reveal the faults

in his acting skills. And the notebook always kept in his jacket pocket stabbed him in the ribs.

THE FIRST TIME HE HAD ever heard . . .
Music.
When, where, had that been?
Only a nothing surrounded it, yet out of the nothing, which perhaps was night, this incredible element had drifted, like water, like smoke, like air—and *made* from the nothing, as fire was struck with an old-fashioned match. And, as he later thought, as pleasure and orgasm were created inside a woman's body. Touch—friction—magic. Something miraculous which came—from nowhere.
Like life itself.
Music.

SO MANY LIGHTS IN this City, so bright. Not like the Roman town, with its intermittent candles, torches, beads of flame in oil, ordinary stars.
Snatches of sound. Scents.
The glutinous, caressive *clokking* of the oar through water, wanderliers hailing each other, lit boats out on the lagoon, the jewels of churches . . .
Wind blew back her hair.
"Rough weather coming," said the wanderlier, and winked, for here rough weather never came at all, unless intended and authorized.

AS THE MEDICS BENT over him, Flayd parted them like curtains. Across their toppling, he lunged at the two security men, punching one out cold, cranking his elbow back into the other guy's middle hard enough to remove him from the action.

Out in the corridor, a girl with a flecx.

"Pardon me," said Flayd and knocked her hand, and the gun, separated, ceilingward. He hoped he hadn't hurt her.

He could almost hear Ali laughing. Yeah, baby, you don't expect this kinda stuff from some big fat slob works all day at his desk.

They forgot the excavations, the aqua-diving. The fury.

Ignoring the elevators, filled up anyway with over-dressed guests going down to dine, Flayd took the stairs. Leaped them, one stack of steps at a leap.

It was beautiful. He had not thought—it could be—
Beautiful.
So—
Beautiful.
It
Was like
It
was like—
This sound, this
Music
It
It was
Was—

Affronted, the wanderlier protested.

"Sin—signore—what are you doing—my *boat!* You could have upset her, and the lady—"

The large man, his hair a fiery banner, had erupted from the doors of the Ca'Marrone, pounded across the terrace, and jumped straight down into the wanderer.

"Jula—" said Flayd, "you're perfect. She's my pick-up," he added to the wanderlier. "We're late. The Orpheo. Fast. Get going."

"But signore—"

"Can it, buster. Use your fucking engine."

"*Engine*, signore? But this is a wand—"

"I know you got concealed fucking engines, buddy, you all do. I'm UAS, that OK for you? Now rev her up."

The wanderlier pulled a face, reached down along one side of the boat.

The roar of an outboard CX split the electric night.

"Hold tight, Jula. Oh Christ am I glad to see you. I thought you might be *there*—"

Up on the terrace, disapproving or tickled guests watched the slender wanderer shoot away along the Canale Leone Marco, at the end of which it left the water to leapfrog a jam of boats, before plunging on, missile-like, into the waterways beyond.

PICARO OPENED HIS EYES.

Unless, by now, he could see through the closed lids.

Everything had become sound.

Everything had become the music.

He sensed, but did not see, a rustling undertow, like leaves driven by a wind—

Or the sea, coming in.

But what he heard, heard in completion, and what he saw, and what he smelled and sensed and felt, and had become part of—

Was—the music.

And it was the music, not of earth, but of the outer spheres, the music of a world beyond worlds.

Its beauty and eloquence showed not only in the plangent ecstasy of its sounds, but in the shifting rays of a supernal light, now white, now gold, now topaz.

The music was full of wings, and it carried him upward as it must carry everything, up where the heart knows it must fly, and tries to, and never can—

But now, it could.

The sheer beauty was its joy. Joy beyond belief and hope and dream, joy that had no place in an earthly world.

It was the music

of the sky, and of the realm the sky signified. Of the blue vast airs, thin as gossamer, strung with planets and clouds, where images came and went, and which, no longer, had any end.

It was the music of Eternity.

It was the music that played about the Entity of God, when the stars sang together.

Picaro knew.

No wonder it killed.

How could flesh and blood withstand it? They were not equipped to sustane this flame-struck and orgasmic fire from heaven. From Heaven.

There was no pain.

Peeled like the apple of knowing, the soul was drawn from its skin. Naked, and without thought or word, it stood in the sky and did not care for the dropped soiled costume it had left behind.

Once they had put on bodies to conceal the nudity of their souls. Now they pulled them off, cast them away—

There was no pain, but the joy *was* pain. It was a glory beyond expression or endurance.

And the light. Alabaster, aureum, jasper, orichalc, sard . . .

Through the pulses of it, Picaro, no longer Picaro, no longer a man, or anything at all, saw out to where a towering burning creature was, making from *itself* the outspinning gold of

The music.

That then, Cloudio. This the true essence that had filled him. Not himself in any way. Not human. Another element, which had entered his regrown, vacant flesh.

The opened door.

Love, love—greatest of all—this was what the music was. The love that cannot, (here) be understood. Or borne. Yet here it was.

There was no pain. No fear. Nothing mattered. Only the music.

Picaro saw, through his lids, without sight, the creature that lifted now, up on its titanic wings.

It was too large for the auditorium. Too large for the City or the world.

Its beauty more burnished than the morning star, called Lucifer, or Venus.

The wings spread.

Not like any bird.

Picaro heard, the length of the earth away, his own screaming—orgasmic, joyous, blessed—one solitary crying among thousands, as the roof became undone, and the end began.

THEY WERE ALMOST AT the Rivoalto.

The speeding wanderer had jetted through a maelstrom of shouts and maledictions, water syphoned, stars in streaks. And then—a kind of silence was there, beyond all speed, all noise.

"Cut the engine," Flayd yelled.

The wanderlier obeyed.

Suddenly they were in an ink-pool of utter stillness. And through the still came a wire of sweetest agony that pierced to the brain—

They stood upright in the boat.

Everywhere around—

A sort of unheard humming, a sort of image that was invisible—

An assortment of boats were standing also stock still in the channel, and somehow no lamplight was anywhere, the fake gas-globes along the arcaded bank all out, the wind blowing buffets and yet—

Not a hair that stirred.

There were no people. All these boats, these walks, were empty.

Where had the curses and the laughter gone?

Abruptly, up there in some palazzo, a window shattered to a puff of glittering spores.

And then a score of others.

And then—

They were lying in the boat, where they had been standing.

Flayd, Jula, the wanderlier, all clutched together, like frightened children—Blood, in the mouth—a smell of blood—

But another sound was coming.

It was like thunder. Then like water.

Then like light. It was the *noise* of *light*.

The sky went white as snow.

From everywhere came a gush and sigh, a falling of things like soot from the darkness that the whiteness made.

After that, something was, which rose up into the air.

It was the yellow enormity of a dawn. All they could see of its shape, to recognize, was the gigantic outspreading of its wings, one behind another, and another, and another. And yet, they could see it smiled.

The canal heaved. It threw the wanderer, and all the other little empty craft, upward, threw them at the sky, after the angel. But even as they were flung against the stars, the stars went out. The sky went out. And the shrieking screaming they had never heard was finished.

LEONILLO RAN. A man of straw inside his nutshell.

He had seen—he had seen—

For an instant, before the sound relay failed, the CX exploding outwards in razorblades, he had *heard*—

Blood, that was the color, the splashing redness, all the blood, and the yellow of the light—

Even in the screen room, the screaming, crying, the vomiting—

Noises in the ear—

Leonillo ran against the elevators, which would not respond. The doors stood wide, and down the shaft he saw a cage, with something smashed in it.

Leonillo ran up the stairs.

He knew why he ran, and to what, he hadn't forgotten. To the sleeping tablets in his room. He could taste them already, each of those sugar-coated pills he must swallow quickly, quickly, before he no longer could.

PART FOUR

The Gorgeous Palaces

1

SOMETIMES SLEEP WAS as nourishing as food. You woke, and for a moment a great happiness and serenity were all there was to know. But then, you remembered all the rest. The balance tilted. A kind of fear commenced to flood, unencumbered and swift, familiar with its way— the hollows of the mind.

Picaro's eyes had opened this time on an unexpected height. It was unaccountable and rich with color.

For a while he lay still, gazing up at the vivid yet inexplicit chaos of it. Until gradually its structure and explanation became apparent.

It was an exceptionally high, vaulted ceiling, which in one area had parted, revealing another, less solid, ceiling beyond. The first and nearer ceiling had painted figures on it, dancers and garlands, but the rich panoply of red, black, and a curious, pinkish ochre, had been flung across it, so that very little now of the painting might be seen. Glad faces, robust limbs and floating draperies, were stranded among banks of abstract color. As for the second ceiling, it was dull, less dark than obscure. It seemed perhaps to tremble a little, Picaro wasn't sure.

He was lying on a jumble of something, uncomfortable, a soft rubble he did not identify.

He could hear a slow thick dripping noise. At first

he was used to it, and then he realized he was not. But he wasn't ready, as yet, to turn his head, or to sit up.

What came last to him (unbelievably, considering its omnipresence and intensity) was the smell. A stench so horrible, so noxious and indescribable yet—*describable*— that in the instant his brain accepted awareness of it, Picaro choked, started violently to gag. The spasm tossed him after all off his back. As this happened, he felt a looseness all through him, vertigo and misplacement. But then he was kneeling, and, amazingly, the sickness retreated utterly. And then he saw, without even the armor of animal nausea between him and it, what he had woken to.

This was some cathedral in Hell. Its walls were built of freshly torn flesh and offal, of intestines and hearts and bones. Its floor was really paved, just as, in painted form, the ceiling was, with scattered faces, limbs, torsoes, pieces of cloth, all under a coverlet of blood, and of every liquid eruption that bodies, so volcanically discharged inside out, could eject. It was this too, this bomb-blast of evisceration, which had splashed over the ceiling fresco. But it was the Creature that had risen up, that had melted and next fused the palazzo roof, passing through like a plume of white-hot gas into a darkness now also despoiled.

Picaro stood. He stood on faces and breasts. On the body of the policewoman who had flirted with him, what was left of her—but he couldn't even ascertain that much. Only here and there the edges of the gilt and velvet chairs, midnight, crimson, chartreuse—torn open also, broken, caved-in, half dissolved, like the tiers which had supported them.

Where the sunken stage had been was a twisted shapeless place. Nothing remained of the instrument.

Music.

It was the music.

*Am I alive? How can I be? Am I imagining it? Am I really
down there, under my own feet? Are all of them standing here as I
am, each of us unseen by the others—*

Over the clangor of silence, the dripping, the creak
of some disarranged masonry preparing to give way,
Picaro heard an unconscionable noise. Like footsteps.

At the rim of the melted ceiling, a woman's face
appeared, not painted on plaster, not dislocated, inverted,
and dead. A tail of blue-black hair hung down through
the opening as she peered through it. She still wore her
sumptuous evening gown of red, but now she seemed
designed to match the cathedral of Hell.

India saw him there. He saw her see him.

Then she swung right over the opening, fearless,
indifferent, and set her narrow bare feet against the
brickwork.

Picaro watched as India, one hand holding back the
hem of her gown, walked easy as a fly down the wall of Hell.

"TAKE MY HAND."

He took her hand.

Her hand was slim and cool, the nails very pale and
clean.

Picaro, holding her hand, turned to look around
him, to look and look, and then he turned himself bodily around, (still holding her hand, so she moved after
him, like one of the dancers from the fresco.) He didn't
care that she could walk down walls.

"We should go now," she said.

"Why?" he said. "Where are we expected?"

"Somewhere."

"In a minute," he said, "something will give way."

"Yes. The ceiling will come down soon."

"No. I meant myself. I meant—this—will happen to me."

"If it were to happen, it would have done so." India pursed her lips, impatient now as a busy mother with a toddler who delayed. "Come."

She helped him climb over the soft rubble.

He didn't know how she did this, either. Most of the tiers had dropped inwards.

At a pair of doors that were melded together, she turned aside and offered him a broad, cracked-open slice through the plaster.

He did not want to leave Hell.

Hell was where he belonged.

But she wouldn't let go of his hand, and he knew, if he failed to go out, she would have to stay here too.

Behind them, as they maneuvered into the invented tunnel, came a sound of slapping hands, one last commotion of applause—

Picaro craned back.

He saw, circling through the pinkish dust, against the bled-dead sky, a black-and-white bird, its wings and tail luminous with peacock green and blue.

Then the roof began to crumble and crash in, and the magpie, like a cast spear, hard and invulnerable, flew upward and was lost in the nothingness beyond the nothingness.

OUT IN THE BODY of the Palazzo Orpheo, the dead lay around. Their state was not quite so complete as that of the dead in the auditorium. Most were almost recognizable as human. Some were worse than others. Perhaps they had possessed better hearing.

India and Picaro, hand in hand, picked across them.

He was crying, and his nose ran, and he wiped it on his sleeve, which was stained and ruined like everything else.

Once he stopped, he tried again to throw up. But he wasn't sick now. It wasn't that. Nor so simple to be rid of.

There were stains like acid on the walls. Vats of acid. Near another smeared door something lay jerking.

"*No,*" said India sharply as he tried to go to it.

Then he pushed her off. He stumbled to the flapping squeaking thing and stamped down upon it, where the neck must be.

"I couldn't—" he said—"leave—"

"Very well."

"Not like that."

"I understand. Give me your hand again, Picaro."

He cried, now and then making a wrenching stupid sound that filled the total dripping, shifting silence like the gulping of an engine. Through room upon room.

"Here is a way out," she said. "The square's outside."

"Yes."

"The square is also very bad. And the canals."

"Yes."

They went out.

The square was bad. And the canals.

In the middle of the square he halted. She tried to pull him on, she was extremely strong for so slender and unmuscular a young woman. Not like Cora, who had been so tender, a blithe featherweight.

But he refused to move.

He looked up at the sky. It truly was no longer a sky. The lights had all gone out. No stars hovered, no daylight came.

Only there, out across the static roofs, hung a vague reddish smoking ball, which was Venus's fake moon, glued to the horizon; like him, currently unable to move on.

"Why am I alive?" he said. "Am I the only one alive?"

"From this area, yes. Beyond the radius of the music, ninety percent have survived, but everything is touched a little."

"Why not me, why not you?"

"Come with me, Picaro, and I'll tell you."

"Promises," he said.

They went on over the square, teetered over the stacked-up bodies in the canal, not needing the small collapsed bridge. Fragments of window-glass lay sparkling everywhere, as if all the faked stars, which had gone out, had shed their dying tears on the City.

2

HERE, THE WANDERLIER SAID, they must leave his boat. He was sorry, they must find another route. He could go no further.

He wanted, he said, to get out to the La'la district, where his wife and baby were, and his uncle and grand-father and aunts.

He shook Flayd's hand. Then they embraced each other. The wanderlier hugged Jula. "Take care, sinna—for the love of Jesu Christ—take care of her, sin, and you, sinna—you take care of *him*—I must go back."

They had all clung together in the narrowness of the boat, and become married in some infallible, perhaps not enduring fashion.

Obviously the outboard motor no longer func-tioned. As he poled the wanderer off, back across the Rivoalto, he shouted, "I am called Chuseppe! Remember! I'll give you free rides—" Ludicrous. Who could ride the wanderers now? But they waved him off, Flayd and Jula, standing on the watersteps, under the stone sky.

Then they climbed up to the doorway of a dark, dumb house.

"It's that way," Jula said.

"Yes." He didn't ask how she knew, she who had seen such a limited amount of Venus. Anyone would know, as if arrows of icy uranium pointed in that direction. Towards the Orpheo.

The door of the house, when they thrust at it, gave way, as they had both known it would. No one seemed to have been there, or they found no one. They ran through a lobby, a courtyard where a frothy acacia tree had bent over in a tortured bow, its black leaves out on the paving. Loose cobbles, and bits that gushed from walls, impeded them only momentarily.

On the far side of the house, was one of Venus's compressed squares, where a fountain played, still played, dismal and bereft. The roof of a building had come down across the square, but it was negotiable.

Flayd thought, as if logic had, at all costs, to be fumbled for, some things resisted, were able to, tougher in construction or in some other manner.

Everywhere, intermittently, the irritating flashing of CXs jabbed the eyes, smashed or shorting out. Sometimes bizarre and eerie sounds echoed out from houses or streets, yet none of these were human, surely, but high-tech indestructible mechanical systems going all to shit. There was only slight evidence of human curtailment, some of this easy to overlook, others—

They raced from the square and out into the tangle of alleys beyond.

At the end of a corkscrew of walls, where Flayd glimpsed the bloody-colored moon stalled at the sky's edge, they reached the fringe of the ZMI—the Zone of Maximum Impact.

Presently Flayd puked, leaning one hand on a wall that for some reason did not collapse.

Jula waited.

Unspeaking, they went on.

They didn't need to cover all the distance to the Orpheo.

Through the fogged miasma of dusts, and cold dry stinking smokes, suddenly the only impossible and insane thing: two figures upright, alive, and walking towards them.

Jula was gone.

Nonplussed Flayd came to a stop, and watched her, self-fired, like a flexible dart, landing on the ground only a meter from her target, Picaro.

He was covered in filth, in the debris—of what had once been human.

Jula held out both her hands, and Picaro was fixed there, staring at her. Then Jula took hold of him.

Despite her smallness against his height, his thin, wide-boned body, she seemed the greater. She wrapped her arms about him and held him close as her own skin, looking up into his face until he put it down to rest, forehead to forehead with her.

That was all. They were motionless, seemed likely to stay that way.

Only then Flayd began properly to see India, the Asian girl he had met at Brown's. He noticed that she alone, in all the shambles, was entirely unmarked. *Clean* in her *clean* evening dress, clean in her *expression*, which was temple-carved, like that of a kind yet sullen god.

THE JANGLE AND WAIL of sirens and emergency vehicles began to come when they were some way down the wider canal, leading out on to the lagoon.

India had found a boat, a tourist vessel, with non-CX engine, left at a quay as if waiting for them. But there were boats everywhere, many empty, and, by that station in their journey, some not. Flayd noted methodically at last the intactness of these bodies, though blood and excrement attended them. The empty boats provided the other clue that probably their occupants had fallen or jumped into the water. There were people lying on the streets, also. And at one palazzo, they hung from the balconies, a score of them, like gaudy washing. But by then none of the four in India's found boat gave any sign of reaction.

Beyond the major zone, and its lesser rings, they went through an area where no one, again, seemed to remain. But here and there Flayd spotted momentary, shadowy figures, wandering, half-glimpsed, aimlessly. He didn't see enough to know what state they were in. Perhaps they were merely stunned and could survive once the medics reached them.

Then India's boat was among high, standing walls, still whole and solid, with no view or intimation of damage. Here, instead of dead or dying or dazed human things, they began to see dead animals and birds. Flayd debated why they had come across none before. Soon it occurred to him that these creatures had *known*, as the human animal had not, apparently until too late, and tried to get away. (There were no projected recx birds either. The CX capacity of the City was well and truly down.)

In the end it was Jula who first made out the black gulls, hundreds of them, crowded on the roofs, hustled in with pigeons and doves, all alive, none of them avoiding or seeming to mind the other species.

They had gained the borders of the ZASP—the Zone of Anticipated Survivor Potential.

And Flayd saw he was using war-room terminology. And that it seemed applicable.

Picaro and Jula sat, side by side, their arms pressed together, otherwise not touching. It was India who steered the boat through the water and the desperate obstacles, although Flayd had put himself forward to do it.

Finally they could see the walls opening out, and the broad sheet of motionless stone that was now the lagoon.

And that was when they began to hear the sirens.

It was at first a relief to Flayd. Had he thought, despite what India had earlier said to them, that no one else was alive in Venus?

FROM THE LAGOON, they had a sort of sidelong overview of the City. But in the dull and dispirited twilight, every lamp was out, save for the flash of wrecked CX systems. Though seemingly standing, the City looked bomb-struck, and lost.

(Flayd had thought they might try to make the subvenerines out by Maria Maka Selena—but his wris-tecx too was dead, and the dome locks, already shut down, were doubtless now doubly impassable.)

Jula spoke. "I've heard this described. The lull."

Flayd glanced at her. "I guess. Then we're in the eye of the tempest, whatever the tempest is."

India had cut the manual motors of the boat.

They sat, in the leaden, re-gathering silence.

Flayd said, "I saw it. I thought it was an explosion. A firestorm. But it wasn't. I don't know what it was. But I do know, don't I? You just know. Something I've heard of. Something I reckoned just can't exist. I—*recognized* it. Christ, that's how. I *knew* it, the minute I saw. And not from any picture, not from any statue."

"The Christiani called them the messengers," said

Jula. "When I was a child, I heard some of them speak of this once. Angelos, or angelus."

"Angel," said Flayd. "They exist in every religion, in every mythology, in some form or other, thinly disguised. Angels, and demons."

"They are the same," said India.

As if none of them had expected her to speak again, they all stared at her. Even Picaro did this. But India now was once more silent as the pervading silence. Her eyes were down. She might have said nothing.

"Maybe," said Flayd. "OK. Whatever it is—that thing—it could cause all this by *sound*—"

"Music." Now it was Picaro who coolly spoke. "It was the music. Anyone who heard, anything in its path—and then the shock-wave spreading."

"Listen," said Flayd, "am I being too basic if I feel the need to ask—*where is it*? Where'd it *go*?"

And then Picaro, who was evidently in the cool and level stages of madness, stood up in the boat. Staring at Flayd from a face hard as a rock, Picaro lifted his right arm, and pointed, straight up, into the granite sky.

"Up there. Where else? That's where they go, where they fall from. *There*."

Silence again. And from the City emerged a low slow booming that swelled and died. Nothing was visible of what it was, or had been. Only the distant mindless cries of sirens that were themselves growing infrequent now.

Flayd said, "But that *isn't* a *sky*—are you saying it's gone?"

Picaro laughed.

At the blinding, insulting whiteness of his teeth, Flayd wanted only to kill this laughing man, but there were enough dead already.

"No," Picaro said then. "Not gone."

And then India spoke again. "It's lying up under the dome, above the sky. It lies dreaming and brooding on its game. That's what the lull is, and the storm's eye. Soon it will begin to play again, with the new toys."

Picaro sat down.

The water seemed so congealed, the boat scarcely reacted.

But unheralded, across heaven, there wavered the glorious flambeaux of morning, yellow-gold.

The City was made golden too, waning lights drained to nothing, the laguna an animate floor of flame—over the water the other way, the church of Maka Selena blazed like a rising sun.

Everything held its breath. The City. The unknowing world above and beyond.

The dawnlight flickered, curdled, and was folded in behind the costive darkness of the unreal sky.

Flayd found he was shuddering.

Jula reached across now and pressed his hand. Her eyes were steady still, over the rim of the shield she had been so wise never fully to lay down.

India said, "Don't be afraid. Not yet. After such pleasure, it will wait a while. It needs no rest, but has learned of rest, as it's learned music. And so it rests."

"That was the angel," said Flayd. "That light."

"That was the angel," said Picaro, "turning over on its bed of sky. Because angels live above sky, somehow, and they're evil, and they fall. I found that out when I was sixteen."

Flayd said, "When it starts up again—"

"The rest will go," said Picaro. "What the fuck else, do you think? Maybe even me, next time. Good."

"No," said India, "not you."

267

She had raised her head, and once more they all looked at her, as if at a signal. And Flayd, not seeing why he did, pulled from his jacket the paper notebook always kept there, the outdated pen. For it seemed India was ready now, to tell them all she knew.

3

"*WE ARE THE* fallen angels."

India, her words, there in the boat upon the water.

As Flayd wrote them in the book, end to end:

This is not Hell, yet Hell is here, nor are we out of it.

You must understand this. The story of a rebellion in some upper sphere is a mistranslation current everywhere. God is not rebelled against, for God is all things, even rebellion. So how would it be possible?

It was a departure then, not a rebellion, which drove us out. A *decision*. Our own, which naturally was allowed us, since God is also freedom and we are free to choose.

So then, some of us came to live in the world. Not where we fell, for the Kingdom of Heaven is not above any sky, but, as we are told, *within* us. (Which, while we are here, is no more explicable than to explain the shape of the wind.)

In this way, those who live in the flesh, as they have chosen to do, carry their muddled memory of a fall from grace or from sky, which is untrue, but inevitable, for symbolically we have *descended*.

Also, you will recognize angels, if ever they are seen. How could it be otherwise? Although their form, on earth, even if etheric, is changed, yet they are analogous to what they are when elsewhere. And this other *actual* image is that which belongs to all of us, when we have left the flesh behind. And of course, they appear winged, too, for how else can they fly?—except that, there, they and we need no *wings* to fly, and so that as well is the *translation* of a truth, its analogy.

You must understand . . .

Among our kind, yours and mine, there are two races.

There are those who come out to the earth often, and enter in, are born, grow, live, and die, in the flesh.

And there are those who seldom come to the earth save in invisible ways, to solace those who, living their earthly lives, so often fail to see us, or, without physical sight of us, to remember.

To that first category, the three of you, mostly, belong.

To the second category, I.

But sometimes, my kind do come here in the flesh, are born and grow and live a selected time as human—almost as human, for special abilities remain to us, though at a glance we seem the same as any fleshly other.

For myself, I was born here to be with the woman we call Cora. I did not want her to live all her earthly lives without me, for she and I are like two unmatched twins, in that other place I cannot begin to describe to you, since there are no words for it.

So Cora was born, and so was I, and I lived as a baby in the very apartment that lay next to Cora's own. When Cora baby cried, India baby cried. When Cora child began to play, India child went to play beside her. There was never any need to tell her who or what I was. She always knew me. Even at her life's end, when I had walked up the walls, slid through the pipes of the air-conditioning, when I had reached her—I had only to be seen by her and she knew. She went from me smiling, back to the lands within. Where all of us go, where all go, all. And though I must wait now in this body, until my day comes to return, I know her to be safe. I am glad that I was here. Glad, for I have seen so many die that think they are alone, and in terror, but they are not.

There are others of my kind, among your kind.

Our kinds are the same, in the end, when we are gone from here. And *there*, our powers, of your kind and mine, are those of angels.

But among our two races also, there is *another kind*.

They too have come down in flesh. And they have learned to love that better than all else, even better than the other worlds beyond. The pleasures of the physical sphere ensnare them. They are tempted not by demons, but by their own demonic greeds. And so, they *become* demons, to fulfill their wants.

The man we call Picaro, listen now. Your mother was one of these, the woman we call Simoon. A fallen angel in the truest sense, for she dashed herself to earth and took on a physical life, while refusing to forego her spirit powers. And it has never usually been the aim of physical life to live by the magical powers of spirit—or why else are mankind born to and limited by flesh? But these others, they wish the most to combine flesh with uncanny *power*, and enter this world to *play* here, like greedy and cruel children.

Even so, the action of birth, infancy, childhood; of confinement and growing in the flesh, still constrain them nevertheless. They are kept by it *small*. It curbs their liberty and their sorcery. Rarely do they recall they are unhuman. Even the woman we call Simoon did not. And for this reason, their abilities, although sometimes supernatural and very great, are ultimately rendered down, as Simoon's were rendered down. Indeed, they turned upon her and became disease. And since her body itself could also die, death threw her away, back to her own country—which is also ours. Though if you were to compare them, her homeland with mine and yours, though they *are* the same, they would seem as unlike as light to shadow. (And from this recollection come the two notions of a Heaven and a Hell.) For her kind *color* what surrounds them. Just as that one, who is lying in the upper dome, colors the make-believe sky.

You must understand . . .

Never before have any come here, into flesh, who did not have first *to be born*. Who did not have to *grow into flesh*, constrained by it, and kept within bounds, so even Simoon, a spirit of vast and cunning malignity, as she—*it*—has come to be, was held in chains by her body, and could not do even seven sevenths of what otherwise she might have done. While, when in purely *etheric* form, none of us, we, or her kind, beyond a given effect, can tamper with the physical world. It is less we must *not* than that we *do* not, not even the ones like Simoon. If you like, it is a law of balance, God's law, for God is also balance, as God is everything.

Yet now, your people have themselves made flesh in this world. They have *made* it, like a cup. Not born, nor grown through a time of years, with the angel which is called Soul inside it, but instead created *fully* grown, adult, strong, and *unoccupied*. And to this vacant casket, an invitation issued.

You must understand that never before has such a thing ever been.

Now I will tell you this. To the full-grown body of the woman who fights, and that we call Jula, her own soul, which is her angel, came back. It came freely, since it was not elsewhere here in the flesh. The woman Jula has lived many lives in the world between the time of her first incarnation as a gladiatrix, and these, a little, she recalls now in fragments, as many do. Although the life *between* lives remains always generally unknowable. So she has secured her own body, for a second term, as is proper and lawful, in the sense of True Law. Also she brings back to it all that was learned since by her, recovering it piece by piece, as she becomes accustomed to her flesh, gained in such a sudden and preempted way.

Jula, and the man we call Flayd, know too the legend of Lethe, whose water is drunk to take away the memory of our other life in Elysium. Though Lethe is a cipher, still to forget is necessary, for without forgetfulness, what human would otherwise stay in the physical world until their purpose was accomplished? Only my race, when we are here, linger in partial recollection, which makes us sometimes sad. But such is our payment to ourselves, for giving up the greater worlds to be with those we love.

For this world that is the world, is required. See it how you will, as the only paradise, as exile from a garden, as a harsh school or a battleground, we come to it for our own purposes, and of our own choice, and for this it was created.

Now as with Jula, if that soul too, which had been the man we call Cloudio, if that, as I say, had been enabled to re-enter its former body, no awful harm would have come of it. But that soul is engaged elsewhere in this world. And therefore, the flesh of that made body stood empty. Then that which fell, or came outward, it went into the man we call Cloudio, whose other name is Nero, But Cloudio it was not. That one which came is one like the mother of Picaro. It is of her same type, though less wicked than she. For it was more curiosity, more a selfish, grasping *innocence*, which drew it in, irresistibly, to assume the body of Cloudio, and to pretend to itself and others a while that it was he, even as it forgot, and so *remembered* what truly it was.

For the flesh could not restrain it. It had not *grown* to and *with* the flesh. Had not selected the flesh, only been offered it and tempted in. It was as if a night-flying moth beheld a candle, and must rush into the flame. But in this case it is the flame that flies, and the candle that is the moth and is burned up.

It is, in the terminology of the earth, *air*, this thing, sheer air from the worlds beyond worlds. Air like fire, like radiation, and like everlasting night.

It has played that it is human, as do we all, but it is unrestrained and has come to relish, more than usually, the *being* of itself as a man, adoring to eat and drink, to sleep. But more than all else, *to make music*.

For in the physical brain of Cloudio, which had been the brain of a genius, this angel found great skills, and learned them in a second. How it loves to make *his* music—but the music which it makes is also its own, a music translated in this instance in *absolute exactitude* from the music that is not music, but the essence of its own supernal elements.

You must understand . . .

It is as if a sea were poured into a jar, or the whirlwind poured there. And the jar bursts to let out the tidal wave and storm.

And now it lies overhead, resting because Cloudio would rest after a performance, readying itself the while to play once more, out of itself, the detonation of its melody, its harmony, the symphonic of the power of a soul made just barely present in the physical world through *flesh*, and made also *fatal* by its raw link to the psychosmal Heart. An angel-soul that has no empathy with mortal man, and does not see the horror it has unleashed. It will not stop.

There are so many stories of this. Babel fell, Phaethon plunged into the sun. Semele was consumed. It is not possible for human things to look on the face of God unless that Face itself is shielded from them by the mask of human flesh. Nor to *hear* the *Voice* of God, unless it speaks in a wind, or a lightning-bolt, or from the made-mortal lips of messiahs.

And now, a splinter of that Voice is *heard*.

Do not suppose it spells destruction solely for this city. It spells the destruction of all the physical world.

Nothing human or animal can stand against this thing. Only my kind can stand, and I, because I am of the second race, may not, for my kind, beyond a certain point, must never actually engage in war.

However . . .

The man we call Flayd, who believes always in conspiracy, may perhaps observe that a psychic conspiracy has also been at work, to bring to this place at this time the three of you.

Jula, the fighter, who has come back as others do not, equipped with forethought from many lives. Flayd, the guide and anchor, whose mother was a psychic, and who is able to write down now, therefore, what I say. And Picaro, who is the half-child of the demon-angel Simoon.

Picaro must closely listen again, now.

That which is above the sky has recognized, in turn, *him*.

By which I mean the angel loves Picaro, as brother loves brother, or father loves son. For Picaro, to this thing, is partly of its own kind.

And to this end, it has scaled off some of the weakness of humanity from Picaro.

Picaro will remember, perhaps, how it touched him with its burning hand, and gave him to drink from its cup. And how, when first he heard its changing music, he was made ill. Picaro may recall the act of immunizing against a disease by means of giving a little amount of that disease itself. The illness which then assailed him is the last one he will know in this body he now inhabits. The angel we call Nero has *immunized Picaro against itself.*

How else has he survived?

Only my race can survive, and we must stand by.

Now Picaro too is armed, as we are, and without our restriction.

You must understand . . . for this too has been misread.

It is Picaro who is to be the black knight, hungry for his life, consecrated by his half birth. As Jula is the fiery white knight, consecrated by that which she has begun to recall. And Flayd is the great knight, also hungry to be filled, who opens the way and holds earth and air together by his weight and strength.

But the fourth knight is still death, the changeable and pale with being hidden, who is also pestilence, the secret spy, the air that kills.

Understand me, for you must.

It is the hour, and the gates are undone.

The prophecy has been centuries read, and so will be fulfilled as it is seen to be, and by those symbols. As all things have become what they were taken or mistaken for, since first men darkly saw with mortal eyes.

4

FLAYD HAD HEARD INDIA speak in his own native language. He had spontaneously written her words, however, in a slightly different format—though still in English. He understood, without discussion, that Picaro meanwhile had heard her speaking in Italian, and Jula either in Latin, or (who knew?) her own original Gallic tongue.

When he looked up from the notebook, (which he had filled with huge erratic writing, readable by him, but unlike his own) he saw that India was gone.

Something made him squint over the side of the boat. Was she walking under the water—or merely *on* it? Neither, perhaps.

She had simply, modestly, vanished.

Her kind kept such abilities, so she had warned them. But even so, they were *all*, ultimately—*her* kind. Was it *possible*?

JULA THOUGHT HOW THE manipulative element, whatever it had been, which had kept from her all those who might have been, here, forerunners of Picaro, and so sensitized her to him so highly in the wake of the man she had killed—Jula thought that this in the end was

277

irrelevant. It was a fate that had bound them, taut as a rope of steel.

She began talking softly.

She was speaking of the catacomb under the Capitolium Hill in Rome. About the old man who had placed his hand on her head.

"They called him Cephus. Of course that meant nothing to me. I could hardly understand their Latin. But I remember it now, and know what they said, and how they named him. He had another name too, which was Petrus."

Jula glimpsed Flayd, frowning across at her.

Flayd said, "Those two names were given to the Apostle Peter."

She nodded. "Yes, that may have been it. He was a man of great importance to them."

"Peter was crucified at least thirty years before you say you met him," Flayd paused. He added, "Unless that was only a story. Some other guy took his death, died instead—and it was allowed because Peter was of such vital significance to the Christians. My God, Jula—he'd been touched by Jesus Christ."

Jula half smiled. She said, "The old man was over ninety years of age, yet he had the face of someone, lined and *old*, but *young*. And wise. I've seen children like that. Except then their faces were full of pain. His face was full of something better. It was so clear."

Picaro said nothing. Flayd, now, was also silent.

Jula said, "I have heard of the Apostle Peter—some other time when I—somewhere else—not in Rome or this City as it used to be. I think he blessed me. That was it, what the water and the hand on me meant. And I forgot the blessing. But I see now it was part of what made me able to *live*. Naturally, if he created me a Christian, dedicated to peace, I should never have fought or killed—but I didn't know any of that. Yet my strength—perhaps I took it from him with his blessing, when he gave me to his Christos. And that was what they meant, the Roman couple, when they said they couldn't free me of actual chains but would try to free me another way.

"And does—the body you've been returned to—"

"Yes," she said. "The blessing has grown back, like the memory. Like one more scar. A *beautiful* scar."

Picaro sighed.

Jula noticed India was gone.

Then they looked, the three of them, toward the abject shore. When Flayd moved along the boat and restarted the motor, no one protested or asked foolish questions.

PICARO HAD WATCHED, uninterested, India turn sideways in at a doorway in the air and vanish. Next he found himself thinking as if he hadn't thought for many hours, days, months. He thought, without an iota of incredulity, about how all his life seemed wasted, or at least warped and *forced* towards this moment. This Now.

Jula had been made sacrosanct by some ancient supernatural contact. And he by his demonic half-blood.

And India—was an angel.

But Flayd, with a psychic knack he had never known, was the medium in which everything of theirs now took place, a kind of walking petrie dish.

Meanwhile the real petrie dish was the dome. That was how they had used it, whoever they were that had wanted to pilot this particular research. Live subjects had abounded here, and the environment was safely closed. Of course, all other dome environments were already directly connected to governmental projects thought to be of use. Only Venus was a holiday area, finally dispensible, a superb test tube, sealed tight, so nothing of the disaster which had been made, so wantonly, could escape.

Except, it was apparent, now it *could*. The dome couldn't contain a being of the sort that Nero was, any more than the magna-optecx screens had shut away his music.

Picaro thought: *Simoon sent me here.*

He thought, I didn't die, but now I shall. Soon, over there, somewhere in the dying City.

EVERYWHERE, ALONG THE walls above the canals, or those that ran about the buildings and beside the alleys, the shattered pieces of a CX message fluttered, came and went.

Please—has been—explosion—no need—alarm—residue —clean—all keep inside—further—will be—

There were fewer empty boats—here and there you saw one that had been staved in and was going down. There *were* emergency crews in motorized boats. These men and women were overalled and suited-up, belying the story of the "explosion" having been "clean." But there weren't many even of these. They signaled to the boat Flayd had brought in, told him, through loud-speakers, he and his companions should get out and immediately return to their apartments. Flayd by signs assured them that this was exactly where they were headed. No one stopped long enough, or got close enough, to argue, or demand ID checks and details.

Barriers had been erected at certain points to prevent any but official vessels from going through to the Rivoalto district or beyond. The barriers were of the old kind, mesh, and generator-powered, no longer seen save in the remotest parts of the Amerias, the Africas, or the sub-Antarctic.

The sirens had fallen entirely quiet, exhausted.

A great stillness lay, heavy and necrotic, split only now and then by some far-off, unbearable cry you prayed wasn't human or animal.

Groups of people stared out from windows. They looked anxiously down at the boat, but without any comprehension or apparent urge to ask of it questions. All doors and windows were shut fast. On the terraces, banks, squares, in gardens, under the arcades of the palazzos, no one stood. In one spot only did they see a solitary woman, positioned, seeming petrified, her hands up to her mouth as if to hold in a scream—which never broke from her solely because she could never lower her hands to let it out.

Flayd wanted to go over to this woman. Jula shook her head. "She won't hear you. Let her be."

Flayd thought Jula, even in her one acknowledged life (evidently she had recalled episodes from *others*) had probably come across such casualties. (He recollected her burned village and the military massacre she had detailed in the Roman town.)

This world, this bloody world. It had always been Hell, would continue to be—despite its painted-over beauty—till everything ended.

And then a numbed and bitter almost-relief laved him, for very soon that end might have arrived. All this horror and struggle would be finished.

But even in that instant he thought of their words—

India's, Jula's, his own mother's—the necessity of this venue, which human things had chosen and themselves created, (obviously they themselves, for it was full of mistakes a true God never would, or could, make) even though they soon forgot their part in that. The battleground.

They were going toward the University. By mutual consent, he believed, though they hadn't discussed it. UAS might have answers. However, he'd seen none of their personnel to recognize among the police launches and ambulance craft.

As they came around into the shipping lane, behind the apron of water under the Primo Square, Flayd, Jula and even Picaro glanced up. Above the tilted, dulled colors of sails, birds were flying in, and around and around on the dead sky, in a thick maelstrom of black, blue, and pearl—pigeons, gulls, doves, some duck with mottled wings.

Down on the square stood a small group of white-suited men, and one, his facemask raised, was blowing through a soundless bladderlike object.

It must provide some other-frequency signal that attracted the birds. Flayd supposed it would normally have been CX operated but had a manual back-up. The man was red in the face from his efforts, but now the birds were swooping down and landing in the open cages Flayd noted standing ready on the square.

"Yeah," Flayd said. "They've always had emergency plans to get the animals out. They're valuable. Birds, lions, horses—and bureaucrats—first to the subvener-ines. Only I doubt if anyone can work the dome locks. Try the emergency escape hatches, maybe, they can be blown—use good old antique gelignite. Which won't help the rest of us much."

Picaro, surprising Flayd, who had reckoned him in a trance, said, "The dome can stand up to a small atomic strike." He laughed quick and deathly. "It was in the 'literature.'"

"Sure," said Flayd, "but if they can blow the emergency locks, which is possible, they're designed for that, the lagoon levels in here will fill up from below. Take about three hours before it gets hectic. Maybe give some people time to get out, but there aren't enough subvens for everyone, not the entire City at once."

"Outside the dome, is it possible to swim up to the surface?" said Jula.

"Could be. We're not down so far. Better with oxygen and a suit. They've got some of those at the University. One of the reasons we're going there." (And hearing himself say this, Flayd thought, But that won't be any use. Nothing will be. There's going to be nowhere to run to.)

The Primo, as the birds flew past it, down into the cages, seemed like a model in a kid's paperwight, after you shook the glittery snowstorm and watched it settle. The great white dome of the basilica came gradually back into view, this second dome, with its internal message—still clearly to be read, unlike the failing CX jargon on the walls—Apocalypse and Terminus.

They had to leave the boat. Some women in white plascords, with flecxs, (presumably in working order) came and told them to get out.

"Where are you going? Haven't you seen the announcements? Hurry to your hotel or apartment. Wait there. There's no danger now, but there will be an evacuation. Hold yourself ready. Stay calm. Listen for voice-relay instructions."

Flayd almost said, *Sure, since Phiarello's is shut.* Actually he said, "Just where we're going. Thanks. That's what we'll do."

They marched briskly and obediently across the square. Another two women, in suits and helmets, were leading up a chain of horses. The animals were restive, not docile and deceived like the birds trained to a whistle and rewarded with food. The horses rolled their eyes inside their blinders, frisked and snorted, and the women called to them uselessly through the now-distorting helmet microphones.

The Primo Square seemed set as the point of departure.

Flayd and Jula glanced along the ready-to-be-loaded boats that were gathered there.

They had passed the Primo, and were under the great bell tower (named for an angel) which cast no shadow from the lightless sky. (Sun into darkness. Moon into blood.)

Right across the Blessed Maria Canal was a barrier, five meters high. There was no other sign of life. These facts combined were indicative.

"Christ—shit—I hadn't *thought*—they had a direct relay from the Orpheo—Jula, do you know how to swim?"

"Yes." She did not add she had never learned when she was Jula.

Picaro was, changed so much, already diving off into the canal.

The water, which was not water, was full of chemicals, weird irritants, but so what, the whole of the City had been poisoned.

Flayd lumbered last into the canal, and like a hippo—unknowing—became instantly graceful and coordinated.

They swam, the three of them, deep under the barrier, and came up by an acacia growing down from the walls almost to the water. The tree was still alive. And on the arch beyond, the hyacinth-blue wisteria still fronded. Not so bad here then, despite the barrier and the desertion.

Seemingly unobserved, certainly unchallenged, they pulled themselves onto the steps, and walked up into the University Building.

HAVING GOT OUT OF THE worst area, (the so-called ZMI) perhaps not expecting to meet this again . . .

The dead were concentrated in one place. They had died cruelly, like the people just outside the edges of the Orpheo Square, or the people in the lower rooms of the Shaachen Palace. The corpses were less physically astonishing and fearful, but their longer-lasting agonies were also more apparent.

The center here had been the room with the relay-screen. CX and optecx glass lay everywhere and the windows had imploded, raining in not out.

But not everyone had died.

Some had been stronger, in varying degrees.

They were wandering about, several only like the shocked and internally, invisibly mutilated survivors of a bomb-blast, persistently shaking their heads, staring without sight at all things and themselves, their eyes wide open. Others crawled, or ran. But there was little noise. It was as if they had absorbed all the sound they could ever take or know. As if the *music's* noise, heard in the fraction of a minute, heard sometimes better (worse) or longer—or through earphones, or from some way off—heard like a glimpse, had deprived them, too, with everything else, of the ability to make a sound themselves.

Sometimes there were, about the corridors and lifts and stairs, rustling notes, or thumps or notes of falling, or a note like a kind of breath rushing out forever. That was all.

There had not been, Flayd thought, so many people present in the University that night. Perhaps most had gotten out, sane and alive.

But the sights they saw—

The sights they saw, Jula, Picaro, Flayd, were now anyway so terrible and *terribly* familiar—that they did not hesitate—save only once or twice to hasten death for what must have death hastened, since it had now no chance but to die.

Each of them was able to do this. Jula because she had been trained to do it. Flayd because he had been trained, long ago, to know *how* to do it. Picaro because he had killed once before; but more because death itself had lived with him so very long, he had learned its ways, he had learned its inevitable and utter omnipresent banality.

There is, too, in the heart, always that dread, that what is seen must afterwards always be carried, just as what's *done* must be. And now—how short a distance they would have to carry it. Any of it. Anything.

FLAYD FOUND LEONILLO in his private rooms. The security-laced door gave at a push. Leonillo had not managed what he had tried to do, his easy barbiturate death—the evidence of the attempt lay everywhere. Along with its failure.

But Flayd spent no time on that. He searched for and found a computer wafer with codes, code-keys, and official overrides. He had known such things must be here. The thing might be useful. But again, this dichotomy. For Flayd was simply acting something out, as if escape were feasible, or mattered.

JULA STOOD ALONG THE passage, by a window. She looked across the inanimate roofs, out to the Primo's pinnacles. And beside them, the crown of the Tower called Angel.

She recognized the Tower.

Not from having lived here, or from any picture ever seen in whatever other life.

The Torre dell' Angelo was a symbol, and to a mind once Roman-trained, along with the stuff of the arena, to an everyday sensitivity to omens and portents, the Tower, with its fateful name, rose sharp as a sword on the flatness of the sky.

And even as Jula watched the Angel Tower, there came a spurt of dazzling daffodil light, a lightning flash, across the smoky nothingness above. Nero had stirred again in his sleep. Turning on his bed of human-educated dreams, the flesh-formed demon was, as would a human man, slowly preparing to wake up.

PICARO HEARD SIRENS, a burst of them, somewhere. Then they too became dumb.

He thought of the ambulanza which had borne Omberto away, his arm closed in a sort of half-bubble; the rush of a city night, and they in its midst, outcast in calamity, and held static as if already ended.

He thought of his father's dead body, lying motionless among the musical instruments.

Then Picaro went through a door in the here and now, in Venus, what was left of it. And he *saw* musical instruments, hung up on the wall of this chamber in the University. And one of them was a s'tha.

It had been, he'd believed back then, like her.

Like Simoon.

The long giraffe's neck, the wide round hips that held the core of its music-making. Since that night, the night on Arrow Street, Omberto's night, Picaro hadn't played a s'tha ever again.

From the East, they said it came from there. Now he read the non-CX printed label, which told him that, too. He touched the silver lines of the seven strings, (like seven thin flames). They sang a curious, wiry sound.

He lifted the s'tha by its strap from the hook. (CX security lit and niggled feebly in the wall, powerless to stop him.)

Picaro held the s'tha across his body.

The wood was smooth, oiled and tended to, the whole body nearly flexible, the strings supple.

Picaro thought of holding her, his mother, the demon, of fucking her, with her breasts against him and the snake of her tongue in his mouth—flexible, supple, singing a curious wiry sound—

Kissing. Making the music.

And in that moment, for a moment, the sky flamed again, yellow, (like Saké, like wine, like the flesh of a rotten apple.)

And as the sky went dead again, Picaro found his hand on the s'tha's long neck was intense as that of a strangler. And only then –

He knew.

5

Jula had found and put on the carefully-crafted replicas of her gladiator's armor. They were based exactly on accoutrements placed in her tomb and had been brought to the University no doubt in order that Leonillo's team might get her to wear them, and so conduct some further psychological archaeological test.

These things felt known. (Their remodeling was that good.)

Helmet—whole head covered, tiny eyeholes like bullet holes, thin slits by the ears. The *Fishhead*. Silver-skinned.

Straps binding breasts in firmly against her torso. Beadwork of snakes.

Greave on the left leg, chased thin bronze, figured with Minerva, the warrior goddess who was also sagacious.

Bands of bronze and leather on her arms.

Shield. Rectangular. Scarlet. Central boss the head and face of Venus, lover of the war god Mars.

Feet bare.

Knife (iron blade, reconstruct ivory hilt) in belt (ropework and linked bronze).

Sword. Iron-steel compound. Short in length and with a point like a sharpened thorn. The hilt bound for grip, fresh, yet seeming used a hundred and forty-seven times and more already.

Kilt, thin linen, narrow, unimpeding.

Narrow leather drawers.

Her scars: on arm and below ribs, (latter partly visible) left foot. Upper thigh, (not actually visible.) Scatter of smaller thinner white scars, some less than six millimeters in length and hair fine, here and there on legs, arms, and trunk, especially the left shoulder.

Red hair (now almost blonde) concealed, as was the face.

Fiery Jula Flammifer, Jula Victrix, walked out into the Primo Square, as so many times into the arena named for its burning sand.

To fight. What else? But why?

Because she had become, maybe, the symbol of the fight all mankind must take on, the battle of the battleground. And because, like the fleshly thing once named Cloudio, and possessed by an angel, she too had come back out of a grave. Like Picaro, though in such a different way, Jula also was *kindred* to the demon. Her role was fixed. She must defy it, on whatever level and in whatever way. A fight to the death. As it always was.

She stood, looking up and up the length of the Angel Tower.

Now Picaro walked back into the square, with Flayd directly behind him.

Flayd was a tower himself, so tall, bulky, solid. The earth giant who, felled to the ground, was only revitalized by its bruising contact. His hair was tied firmly back. He had thrown off the Victorian coat and cravat and resembled a beefy gentleman going out for some amateur cricket on a village green. He carried nothing.

Picaro was in new clothes pulled on to replace the

soiled horror of the others. A magpie costume, white shirt from the 1600s, black leggings, and boots. His hair not tied back but hanging out its daggered stream-lengths, with the white striping among them. And on his body, balanced from its strap, the instrument of music, the s'tha, with seven strings that gleamed like water.

He did not, alone of the three of them, look at the Tower. His face was serious and empty. Indeed, as they had once said of him, cut from a coal.

A flash of light, brilliant as an erupting moon, blasted around them. They were, the three, blasted out gold-white, their shadows slashed away and away, black as voids.

Then the flash dying down. Then the flash waking again. Dying. Waking.

It was close.

They reached the Tower of the Angel, from which, once, bodies in cages had been hung to perish. Under which men and women had strolled, argued, lovers met, destinies crumbled. Saints given their blessing and brought down fire from heaven.

The sky back across the dome lagoon was darker, it seemed, against the wakening light show. And out there, there was trouble in the water. As if the ancient serpent, always rumored to haunt the under-lagunas and canals of Venus, were rousing itself, the great Leviathan.

The lagoon was high, if you looked. The water had just begun to slop in on the paving. The ships, most of which had remained unfilled, stood up heavy on the risen tide, as long ago in the real first City they would have done, in times of winter storm.

As he climbed up inside the body of the Tower, along ramps, then stairs, Picaro considered how his father had taught him music, sitting there in the store. And of the enormous lutas and sombas, which gradually, as Picaro grew older, grew themselves *smaller*.

Could he remember the first notes he had struck? Yes. And his father's voice, "That's good." And the sound of his first name, the one his father gave him, which, for so long, he had never used now, so it wasn't his any more.

The outside of the Angel Tower was the way such Italian towers were—towers for bells, campaniles. The Angel Tower had no bell. The clock, and the decorative horses that moved, were up on the Primo's spire, not here.

For what had the Tower been built? For angels to alight upon?

The brickwork was brownish red. The pointing top, which possibly had not always pointed, dragon-scaled with verdigris. But that was above the gallery. He would not be going up quite so high.

It was a long climb. But he was strong, he was quite young, his singer's lungs were excellent.

When he reached the gallery, he walked around it, slowly.

The general light was so dulled, a kind of *deafened* light. (Not when the angel stirred, of course, not then.) Picaro stared through the deadness at a checkered floor, and at the parapet railing, which was a stone balustrade, cut with the distinctive keyhole-shaped arches that formed arcades and windows for so many palazzos.

Once, you could look out from this place toward the distant mountains marching at the brink of the Ve Neran Plain. But now there was only the mounting surge of the lagoon beyond Venus, and the emptiness that earlier had been the seeming perimeter of a summer sky.

On the other side of the Tower, down in a trough of shadows lay the Primo courts, formerly always swarming with tourists, deserted. Over there, the chapel and the barracks of some ancient order of knights, roofs of silver and gold-like lead. A fountain basin in opaque marble held up by lions in dead bronze.

Who had ever stood up here? So many.

Now, not one in sight. As if death had already entirely come and swept them up, crying and pleading. Swept them all away.

Above, the sky blazed up again. No longer lemon yellow, now it was yellow-golden and blinding white.

Picaro sat on the broad top of the balustrade, and began to tune the s'tha. And the plastivory pegs felt like hard fingers, resisting his own.

He had forgotten the other two. He was quite alone.

Below him by one long floor, Jula the gladiatrix, having stood aside to let him enter first, had reached the area where a closed-in gallery ran under the open one above.

She paced around this square space, which only the stair split and occupied, entering from beneath, leaving to ascend to the higher floor.

This was her station.

She knew it, as she had known the feel and inevitable dimension of an arena.

Having put on her fighter's gear, she had nothing else to do but, as in the centuries-ago past, wait.

And so, as then, she sat down on a wooden bench. She began to rinse her mind, as her instructors had told her to.

But now there was more clutter in it. She must dispel the images of this City, and other fragmentary cities—a garden here, a street, a building. She must turn even from the sweet sight of her mother in Gallia, bending to the smudgy fire in the dusk, with a star behind her head through the open doorway—

And lastly Jula must put from her Picaro, who in her mind she saw, walking up between the forest trees, barred with sunlight. He could never have been *there*. He could never have been that one. She had never *known* enough as Jula to know that she loved him. But different women—and different men—that somehow, since, she had also been—*they* knew, and had, little by little, told her. The sadness of her love, unrequited, unwanted, unique and total, this too, last of all, must be poured out from her thoughts.

Jula poured it out. And was vacant of it.

Now truly only the waiting remained.

She was no more frightened than, after the first few times in her youth, she had ever been of combat and always likely death. But she was only Jula now. She had made herself forget.

Through the window slits of the under-gallery, she saw the yellow-white fire flare up in the sky. Flare up and stay. It was like the sound of the trumpets. Once more Jula got to her feet. She was ready, and alone.

When the fire burst out again, and lit the whole inner scape of Venus, igniting the sky end to end, and turning the surging tumult of the lagoon a nuclear flaxen, Flayd had been thinking about Alicia, his wife.

About how she had died one pleasant evening, in his arms, by the subway at the corner of Dale and Charity. (The words from the Bible had for years after become awful, and tortured him, *Faith, hope, and charity, but the greatest of these is charity*, until Rose had pronounced that *Charity* was better translated as *loving-kindness*.)

The guy who snatched Ali's ID credit chip, and cut her hand open to get it, also stuck his knife in her when she resisted. Flayd had been up the street buying them both a mint cola. By the time he had whirled around, dropped the cola and run, it was over. She held on to him so determinedly he thought she might live. He told her she would. In terror she argued, knowing she couldn't. In the end, she had to let him go. He watched her pulled struggling away from him along the remorseless river. He couldn't hold her back.

But if all that didn't ultimately matter—then—

Oh Christ, then—

What was he doing here, in some way expected to defend, by means he could not guess, the world of pain and death and horror?

But then the fire came in the sky, and it was here and now. It was going to happen.

And Flayd, not knowing why, lay face down on the floor of the Tower of the Angel, holding fast to the ground —the earth—real or false.

He heard from far away the prayer begin to come out of his mouth. It was, to start, the sort of prayer his mother had taught, the Eastern prayer that had to do with God and gods, with the Infinite, with dharma, karma, the ever-turning Wheel. Yet mixed in it presently began the calm cadences of a medieval and renaissance Europe, a Christianity paramount at its inception.

And then Flayd heard, still coming in his own voice, which did not and *could not* know them, the words of the Koran, also pure and paramount in their birth—

And too the words of ancient beliefs he had, per-haps, or not, studied, but whose languages he did not know how to speak—

The orisons of Babylon, of the Inca, of Africa's most secret heart, of ancient China and Rus, of Egypt, of each hinterland, height, or depth.

Every empathic god, these Faces of a God otherwise invisible since It might not, without incineration and surcease, be physically witnessed. To every benign Power the world had ever claimed and clung to (as Alicia had clung to him) the breakers of chains, the gods of compassion, of love and loving-kindness—

For there is no god save only God.

And all things therefore are God—are part of God—the gods among them.

To these, Flayd heard himself praying, in a great, loud organ-note of voice, which, even as the cracking sky began to loose its thunder, the City to shake, the sea to rush upon the land, made the larger noise, a noise of trumpets.

And Flayd, praying for the world, forgot the world, and was alone.

AND SO THEN, as the light of darkness came, the Tower.

It was so black now in silhouette against that vast radiance.

At its base, prayer, the anchor, spirit's essential communion with Source.

At its upper center, fight, the guard, endurance and the body's battle for its rights.

At its head, music, the magician, creativity, the nearest echo in the flesh the soul can find.

Heaven opened.

SEATED ON THE PARAPET, (in a position that, in the chakras of the body, would approximate the Third Eye) Picaro began to play the s'tha.

It was—peculiarly, aptly—as it had always been.

Despite the surrounding volcanic disturbance of all things, he was instantly in private with the music.

The instrument, (until then unplayed?) gave up a rough, rich tone.

Only over this, kilometers away, the groan of the rising sea. The wind.

A smell of sulfur stank out of the plum-yellow cloud mass. Where it had broken, it bled. A sort of rain was falling (fall). Grayish, yellowish rain, blackish rain. Stinking. It was the false weather-system of the dome, ruptured and going wrong.

But the smell itself was ancient as Hell, the underworld, prophecy, and damnation. The rainfall added to the churning overflow of the lagoon.

And the s'tha played a song. This was old, too. It came from a region Picaro had only ever been in his mind, the back of Africa, beyond mountains made of moons, beyond the blackness of forests and complexion.

Picaro sang.

He had a freak gift with his voice, not often used, sometimes not always attainable—now it was. An upper range, and very deep lower range, and between the two no disparity or friction.

He slid his voice upward, downward.

Up into the collapsing sky, and down into the Tower and the roots of the earth under the sea.

All that while, *he* was there. The angel. *He* was hanging there, perhaps still invisible.

Picaro didn't look to see.

He knew how an audience was, listening, attached to every phrase, heart beating in rhythm. Like sex. Waiting on the magic, on the music, on the magician, to find out the orgasmic core.

The angel too. For he and the angel, he and *he*, were *kindred souls*.

No wonder Simoon had wanted Picaro, and in every way. He was so much more than her son. He was her own *kind*.

All this was also in the song, which spoke of searching over scalded plains of land and anatomy.

And in the twanging purring of the s'tha.

Come to me now, said the song. *Here I am*, said the song.

Picaro was no longer afraid of anything, in the world or out of it. Nor of *her*. Nor of himself.

Here I am.

Above, *everywhere*, a form now merged out of cloud and water. Blood-red snakes of energy tore the upper atmosphere, like birth-blood, running, dripping.

And from this chaos, the angel was made manifest, clad in its electric, interminate, semi-bodily yet un-bodied form.

It was at first limitless as the horizon, yet now, from being the whole sky, it condensed. It became only a giant.

You might see its face at last. Which was exquisite, and of a gorgeous, *gentle* ferocity, pitiless and mindless nearly as the mask of a hunting beast. And its eyes you might see, *beaming* down. It was all sheening, flame-wet brilliance.

A spear of razored lightning struck the head of the Tower.

Then, the angel opened all its wings, of argent and brass and orichalc, of sard and chrysoprase and corundum. One behind another, another and another. Another.

It dropped. Like a hawk.

To the pointed apex of the Tower.

The Magpie played on.

What do magpies do?

THE TOWER SHOOK, and to Jula, the lightning flash, the roar of wings, demonstrated what had arrived there.

Into her mind, one thought.

I will, if need be, die for you. As part of my repayment for all the ones I have killed.

The thought was gone.

Virtually sexless and mindless as any angel, a machine, the gladiatrix stood and raised her sword.

She had not reasoned it out, instinct only. But an instinct coalesced from all her almost-recollected pasts.

The demon was mortal clay made ether, energy *embodied*. And so it was both, neither, something new— and yet, as India had told them, without the getting of that body it would never have come to this.

Now, in some esoteric and integral way, it was possible to stretch the essence of it *away from itself*. To place it therefore, in *two minds*.

She was no positive threat to it, could not be.

Yet, as a man only, in that body's first life, and since in its beginning as a man here, when it played at believing it was only mortal, *then* she could have been.

Picaro's music, unheard by Jula, thrumming and singing through the storm around the Tower top, engaged the psyche of what the demon-angel was.

Jula, by her presence, and the nature of what *she* still was—fighter, defender, *pursuer*—(and in her placing in the Tower, between the chakras of heart and belly, sheer *guts*) she called to some other part of the demon.

Immaculate though it was, what was physical in it

could not ignore her, if what was spirit in it maybe never even *noticed*.

And so (physically *threatened*) that element of it, *physically* descended.

The sword in her hand seared crimson, white.

Through the four narrow gallery windows sprang four shapes.

She knew each one.

The Gaul was a blond man she had killed when she was only sixteen. He was clad merely in his kilt, a dented metal helm and greaves and armlets. It had been a make-shift bout, a trial of her, not even in the arena at Stagna Maris but some other little nearby pit. Second was a man from Talio's school, a Neptuni Retiarius, with net and tri-dent. She had killed him in her third fight with him—when she was about twenty. The crowd had not liked him that day and not allowed him the Missio. The third man was Phaetho. Oh yes. Phaetho that she had killed, her last. He was kitted out as a murmillo—a *shelled* fish. The crested, round-rimmed helmet, with its lowered vizor, hid his face, even the eyes behind their lattice—which now she knew resembled the faceted eyes of insects—the greaves, padded and thicker protection on the left leg, as on the right arm, the four-foot length of shield, the short sword. Above his bared torso, a sculpted artwork, she noted, without amazement, the scar of the death-wound she had had to give him, across his neck. The fourth man was a challenger-provocator. Despite the closed, rimless, and uncrested helm with its feathered points, the rec-tangular breastplate, the concealment of shield and greaves, she recognized this man too. She had *never* fought him, never killed him. *It was the other way about.* He was the nameless gladiator at the feast, who had seen to her poisoning.

She understood all four were dead. That these were not—*themselves*. But she too, what else was she but one who had been dead, and who was *not*.

They came at her together and at once, of course. All four.

There had been such times—past images of built bridges above water in the stadium, fighting against three men—a fight with wolves made terrible by hunger and mistreatment—a free-fight, seven against seven.

Then the longer sword of forged ferrum, the nameless provocator's weapon, arced inward, and for a second she felt its shrill claw on her ribs, before her shield was there instead.

Already dead, Nameless was not afraid to fight her now.

IN THE OPEN GALLERY ABOVE, Picaro was aware of, yet did not hear, the clash of blades below, could not hear Flayd's trumpet-voice thundering—

Could not hear the storm, the curdling wind, the waves smashing in over the Primo Square, driving before them the wreckage of crushed ships, the crashing of glass and brickwork no longer CX-protected—

Could not hear rewoken, limping sirens, the shouting, the screaming of fear throughout the City, the pandemonic of despair—

Could not hear the sky falling.

Picaro played the s'tha.

A pleasing sensual heat, like sunlight or the hot fur of a cat, bloomed up against his face and throat, his chest, his hands that danced on the strings—

A marvel of effulgence was there, sunlike and wonderful.

Something

leaned towards him—

He felt its touch.

Not a hand now, nor a cup against his lip, not jealous pain and sickness—

No, this was the infatuating brushing of an unearthly aura, *stroking* against him—

In union—

Like—

Like *then*—

with *her*. Simoon—

Breast to breast.

Just like that.

Not even sex. Never love.

Stronger.

An emotion that should never have existed in the mortal world, and which never had, till then.

Till now.

Picaro, as sometimes he did with a captured audience, half glanced up, toward it.

So he looked directly at what hovered there against the roof and the parapet of the Torre dell' Angelo, and against *him*.

Probably its blissful glow would blind him, like the sun it had copied. Which wouldn't matter.

Its ethereal splendor.

He too—*he too*—was partly this—

It was shining and so bright. He could not look away.

(Unfaltering, his musician's hands raced on.)

And—with things so bright and shining, what do magpies do?

ABOVE NOW, JULA *HEARD* the music, and the singing and the sizzling like a conflagration in the air. Below her the howl of the sea, the quake of the City, Flayd's bronzen calling in a hundred different tongues.

She had killed the Neptuni Retiarius, as before she had, evading the net, taking the trident against her shield, slicing upward through his side. But the others were at her, circling. . . . The Gaul, eager now as he had not been in the past, struck her in the side.

Jula paid the wound no attention.

This combat could only end in her death. So she believed. She had no care.

And above Music, and below Prayer—

Instinctively turning, she ducked under the longer sword of the provocator, the short thrusting sword of Phaetho—she stabbed the Gaul through and through—he tumbled aside.

She too sprang away, and saw, unstartled by it, how the two upright adversaries she had evaded were suddenly entangled with each other, blade on blade, ignoring her, cursing—believing themselves—not brainless automata of an angel, but actual gladiators, matched together, muddled. For a stupid minute they fought, murmillo with provocator, an unusual pairing. Then that was over.

As they pulled away, turning to fix their hidden eyes again on her, the new-killed Gaul, and the retiarius, like the remade warriors of the Dragon's Teeth, were getting once more to their feet.

In her closed-shut helmet, Jula grunted. It was a laugh.

This was not Phaetho, and the nameless one who had poisoned her was not himself, nor the Gaul, nor the man with the net. *Things*, that was all.

She ran at them, the sword swerving, now here, now there, her metal-edged shield tilted, weapon not defense.

The flawless face of the angel poised centimeters from Picaro's own. Its breath was on his skin, transparent and glittering—*visible*, and unadulterated as virgin honey.

What do magpies do?

The angel

Spoke

to Picaro.

Come to me, said the angel (as the song had said.) And then: *I can give you everything. You need no one but me.*

As Simoon had said it, long ago.

Picaro ceased to play the s'tha. The angel was the music, and he, Picaro. It was they themselves now who played, without any musician.

"Come to *me*," said Picaro. He smiled up into the wondrous face. The longing to throw himself against it, to become absorbed, was very strong, ecstatic, almost— sexual—*not*. "Come to me. I can give *you* everything. You don't need anyone but me. *You're mine.*"

And

It smiled. The angel smiled.

In all worlds, there, here, nowhere, never had there been a vision so peerless, or so irresistible. It was what mankind clandestinely dreams of. The love of God.

The nameless provocator engaged her, while the other three, temporarily, were again down, stunned or slain, believing it themselves.

As fighters sometimes did, but never wisely, the provocator began to talk to Jula.

"Why did I have you killed?" asked the provocator. "*I* wasn't fearful of you. No. I too was simply paid to see to it. You were discovered to be a Christian, even if *you* didn't know. And to our masters, the Christiani were intent on overthrowing all earthly authority. And where most Christiani were passive victims, you, Jula, were not. You had been *trained* to fight. Have you heard of the rebellious gladiator called Spartacus? He led a revolt that made a cavity in Roman might. Those men he inspired could win against the legions. Rome never forgot Spartacus. They thought you might be one of that kind. And you were so popular, too. Nor did they dismiss you for being a woman. Rome knew women more deadly than any man—all those foreign queens that had hammered against their empire. I was paid. I bullied and bribed and buggered the kitchen slave into doing it for me. Poison on a cake. You died."

Unwise to speak. She had no care at all.

She knew she had heard all the truth at last. Even in this extremity, it intrigued her.

"How do you know?" she said.

She had thought too, This thing knows nothing. It is I who know, have known—this voice talks inside me, and is mine.

Were these *things*, then, dissembling as gladiators, also hers? Her own demons, which the demon-angel had brought to life—*through her*?

Cephus, who was Petrus, had blessed her and given her to his Christ. She thought, to the Christiani—ultimately *not* to fight was the one true battle.

She thought of the peacock in the courtyard, and its colors. Green and blue. What did it mean, any of it?

Jula stood back.

As once in a dream, she let go her sword.

The Gaul was standing. Phaetho was getting up— absurdly, for a second, assisting the fallen retiarius—

Jula let her shield topple down.

She looked at the gorgon enameled on the breast-plate of the nameless provocator.

"Again, kill me," said Jula. "I have done enough. I won't harm you any more."

As she said this, a colossal quietude rose within her. She had never felt in all her life—her lives—such still-ness. She drew off her helmet and discarded that too. She lifted her head. She looked at the four things that were spatters of etheric dough, bits of a demon-angel. Ghosts.

She heard the old man say, blind and clear as clarity in her mind, out of the catacomb of death: "*She is Yours.*"

WHAT MAGPIES DO IS steal what is bright and shining; for that act they're well known.

Picaro sighed.

As he reached to embrace the angel, it too, now enormous, now only the size of a tall man, put out its arms to him.

Breast to breast.

Molten.

Not a cup, but its lips on his own.

He had kissed Jula.

That had prepared Picaro. *Taught* him.

The kiss of the angel was not like the pressure of a mouth, but like a mending. Nor was its proximity like anything of the body. It was so healingly warm.

Yet the mouth also—was still a cup. Picaro parted his lips. He was parched, always. He must drink. No water, no alcohol, no drug, could help him. Nothing would do—but this.

He breathed inward, opening wide, like wings, his singer's lungs. And drew in the glowing scintillant breath of the angel.

Drew and drew. In and in.

He and it—one kind.

Nor was this *inhalation*. It *was* drinking, and devouring. It was *thievery*. And truth.

Only then—*then*—did the angel abruptly stir—move—begin to resist him. Too late. They were linked. He could not stop now, even if he had meant to. For all these years of waiting had formed him to this split second. Made him so hungry and thirsty, so desperately empty—a vacuum, which by mere pressure of its vacancy, *would be filled*.

Picaro was a bottomless vent into which the brightness of the angel was *sucked* down.

Breathing in and in and *in*—

Picaro felt it fill him. He was the vessel. He drank the sea, and the whirlwind.

The flaming airiness of it was spangling and kindling through every vein, artery, nerve, channel. He felt his organs catch colorless fire and burn, painless, black as his outer skin. Felt his inner self, of which most was almost the same material as the angel's own, grabbing and pulling and swallowing down and down and down—*Greedy. Hungry. Famished. Fill me to the brim.*

Picaro heard himself far off, the music he now made, as he died, as the demon that was an angel, and his brother, and the end of everything, was dragged and drawn and poured and trapped fast inside him.

It had itself made him vigorous enough to do this. (It, and She.) It had meant them to be one. But never in this way.

How small it was, the angel.

It was only like—

A man—

Full.

Picaro dropped backward.

He lay on the checkered floor of the gallery. He was saturate of nebulae, a nova. It was possible to see this, and the fires, behind his open eyes. The s'tha, snapped in two, lay over him. He was dead.

Cloudio del Nero, naked and fair as a statue from the dawn of Venus, still leaned, staring, staring, trying to pull back into himself—*itself*—the radiant immanence Picaro had, by a fellatio of the soul, *sucked* away.

Cloudio was taller than any man. He was like the sculpted god Apollo from Aquilla, (patron of birds, inventor of music) upon whose marble face a mask had once been modeled. The very mask that, when Cloudio once wore it, ruined and murdered him—

Picaro's lips had remained slightly parted.

A glimmer, like lit smoke, pierced out between them. And flew up.

It was a bird, which had come from Picaro.

It was a magpie.

Black and white, black head and body and wings, white-collared at the neck and white-fringed at the wings' edges, and wounded white across the breast.

It flung itself straight into the face of the statue which was a man, which was not a man, which was an elemental demon-angel, which was the Beast, World's End.

The magpie slapped full against the face of the angel, and as it did so, all its black and white changed places on it, its beaked head, its long-feathered tail, the out-fanned wings.

It was no longer a magpie stuck against the face of an angel.

It was the *Apollo mask*—the half-mask, with the noble brows, the thick attached hair, the classical nose, all the black of ink, and the white of snow.

Picaro's magpie had become the alchemical mask that had destroyed Cloudio del Nero in the Year of God 1701.

An angel built of flesh—and the flesh *remembering*—
The fair statue wailed.

It tore at the mask. Which would not come loose.

Ran across the parapet on human naked feet. Hurled itself off, off into air, as once into a deep canal. It fell. It fell. Screaming. Flightless.

It fell.

And when it hit the water and the stone beneath, it broke into a thousand fragments.

And the light—

In the lower gallery, Jula felt the phantoms of swords, trident-points, knife, pass through her. Unhurtful, unreal. The four aggressors disappeared.

She saw instead the lightning-bolt that hurtled by.

The Tower juddered.

Beneath, (the base of the Tower, the lowest chakra, cleansing and release) Flayd opened his eyes. He had missed the light but he too felt the impact, and saw the second lightning-splash. And then, a light beyond all light—

He did not get up, knowing it was redundant.

Across the City swelled one incandescent shriek. Million upon million voices—

And then Venus, all Venus, burst like a star inside an eggshell, and the eggshell too, her poreless, impenetrable dome, (a goblet of Venus crystal) blew inward, outward, with a sound so immense it was entirely silent. And through the shattering of all things, the toylike, shaken, pretty sparkle, the sea fell in. Falling, falling.

And soft as a flower head, the City separated to petals and fell also, upward, into the abyss of the waters.

6

PICARO . . .

The water closing over my head, my body—I seemed to see through a bulb of obscure glass. And in that fashion I beheld the church of Maka Selena pass, drifting away, and then I saw the bottom of the lagoon . . . all at once I felt I need no longer suffer this, and felt myself let go . . .

Like a ruined pile of brushwood, trodden on, the mess of sails, brave flags, crests, burning, burning, on a water poison green and streaked with oil and fire. Loose spars and floating corpses. And men swimming or going under . . . mortal voices . . .

Like the Flood. The City looking up. Safe under the sea for ever. Streets and domes, towers and squares. The boats grounded. The beautiful faces under green drifting layers, a paving of lilies, or masks. All struggle done . . .

IT WAS A SEA OF glass mingled with fire.

Under the light morning sky of the upper world, a sky unbroken and whole, seamed only with delicate cirrus clouds.

Everywhere on the water, wreckage, breakage. And glass, fractured glass, and islands of fire.

The dead went idly by. Their faces scanned, with no anxiety, the real heaven, which was blue.

Some kilometers off, a host of subvenerines, stabilized and mostly intact, were rising up through the surface, with their cargoes of animals and personnel.

There were other survivors. They held to unintended rafts of furniture, wood, sails, carpets, pillars, pipework—Some were in a bad way. Others seemingly untouched.

Here, there was scarcely a noise anywhere.

High up, up in the real, blue, unharmed and now unthreatened sky, real black gulls circled, calling crankily, disturbed by this strange upheaval of the ocean. And on the distant sweep of the mainland, sirens now were beginning to hoot, and a swarm of VLOs just now cumbersomely lifting.

As yet, perhaps, *they* had no notion of the magnitude of the catastrophe. (None, of what it might have come to.) Bizarre forces had somehow kept the event localized. No quake had rocked the mainland, no tidal wave had cast itself across the shore. That they had not was inexplicable. Given the scope of the disaster, nothing—no one—should have survived the dome, or its upper environs. And yet.

Jula and Flayd, unscathed, as others were, save by the smallest nicks and abrasions, sat together on one of the endless, crowded, improvised boats. (It had no motor, let alone CX. The passengers, those that could, took turns rowing, using any oar-like flotsam.)

Picaro watched Jula and Flayd a brief while. He took in their speechless communication, the way the faint morning wind combed out Jula's wet blonde hair. Picaro saw that Jula and Flayd were crying. In silence. Like many hundred others.

For a moment then, he wished he might have gone to them and spoken.

But the moment didn't last. It never does. It never must.

He went from them less visible or felt than the breeze. Curiously, however, when this happened, Jula turned her head and gazed after him. He noted that. Her eyes on his, as he moved away inside the unseen door. Her eyes, peacock-colored, vivid blue and green, were the last he saw of the world he left.

"Look," Jula said. She leaned a little from the boat. A dove, dead, the color of pearls, lay on the water. She took it up in her palm and held it there.

Flayd wiped his hand over his face. Then, an afterthought, jettisoned the computer wafer (useless) of codes and keys over the side. "I guess they couldn't send all those birds up in time. Like the people—down there." He stared at the dove in Jula's palm. At the epicenter of the cataclysm, they had been, like heroes in all myths, flung clear. Only he couldn't remember much about it. And Picaro hadn't come up with them. Picaro was—*down there*, under the sea. Down where the drowned City was and all the rest.

"They'll build the damn place over," he said to Jula. "I guess they will."

"Yes," Jula said. "We always rebuild. Even ourselves." She held out the broken dove, "Even this will rebuild itself. All things, always."

"I'm sorry," he said, "you and Picaro—I'm sorry."

Jula laid the dove gently down again into the cradle of the sea.

The pale wind was freshening. They rowed towards the shore.

Our revels now are ended. These our actors,
As I foretold you, were all spirits and
Are melted into air, into thin air;
And, like the baseless fabric of this vision,
The cloud-capped tow'rs, the gorgeous palaces,
The solemn temples, the great globe itself,
Yea, all which it inherit, shall dissolve,
And, like this insubstantial pageant faded,
Leave not a rack behind. We are such stuff
As dreams are made on, and our little life
Is rounded with a sleep.

Perhaps.

Tutto crolla, ma nulla crolla.
(Everything collapses, but nothing falls.)
                                             —TRADITIONAL

GLOSSARY

Amerian: A native of the double continent formerly
            known (as in the time of del Nero) as the
            Amarias.

CX: Super-advanced computerization of a type
            not yet feasible in our world, and generally in-
            corporated. Any new or apposite word there-
            fore that includes (normally at the end) the
            letters cx, indicates that this is exactly what the
            object so named also includes: as in *optecx*,
            computer-strengthened glass; *decx*, music
            disks with CX function; or *recx*, historical or
            other reconstructions facilitated by CX.

ESDNA: The type of isolated DNA obtained (at the
            time of the book) for use in genetic and
            archaeological study, and finally in the
            "return" process of the Venus experiment.
            The letters stand for Elective Specific DNA
            (deoxyribonucleic acid.)

Flecx: As with the above CX, a CX-permeated gun,
            primed to reflexes.

Intel-V: Computerized world-link TV, already mostly
            obsolete by the main time frame of this novel.

Plascords: *Plas*, at the start of a word, indicates use of a form of advanced plastic in the item so called. Plascords are plastic-invested coordinations, that is, materials incorporating the new plastics, and so highly resistant to wear and soiling. (Plastivory meanwhile is a type of faux ivory derived from a plastic source.)

Viorno-Votte: The diurnal cycle of Venus under-dome, lasting twenty-seven hours, thirty seconds, Ve'notte—Venus day night. Sometimes abbreviated to vv.

N.B.   It may be noted that most scientific and technological terms are in Amer-English, despite the setting for the book being Italy. This is the case in our world, and remains so in the world of Venus.